Sentience Clause
Tech's Future Promise and Peril
Book 2
By

Dave Spacer

Copyright © 2024 Dave Spacer

All rights reserved. This book should not be used to train AI or related technologies.

Print ISBN-13: 979-8-218-55203-9

Disclaimer

Thanks to my family for their support.
To my father, we all miss you.

After you finish reading, please leave a review where you purchased it. Reviews are one of the best things you can do to help an author.

This book is a sequel to Project Mind River.

1

FBI agents burst through Tara's CEO office doors at International IQ Devices.

"You are under arrest. Come with us," an agent said to Tara.

"What for?" Tara asked, surprised and flustered.

"I'm sorry, ma'am, I'm not at liberty to disclose that information."

"Get our lawyers now, and call Mike!" Tara's voice was unshaken, and her assistant got on the phone as they walked out of her office door.

There were dozens of agents asking people to step away from their computers.

"Get copies of everything," the lead agent said to the agents heading toward another area of the office.

The agents ushered Tara into a car quickly and drove off.

A little more than a week earlier.

Tara walked into the kitchen.

"When will the groceries arrive?" she asked.

Tara's five-foot-six frame leaned against the counter.

"About ten minutes," Alice replied. Alice was Tara's seemingly conscious AI, which she had invented over five years ago.

Tara scurried around the kitchen, trying to remember what she needed to do. It had been so long since she cooked anything herself. Her medium-length brown hair swayed a little as she moved around. The groceries finally came. Tara went out to the automated delivery vehicle and retrieved them. Then she set up everything she needed to cook.

The kitchen was huge. It had multiple islands and room for a large table. The beautiful white and black granite countertops and table glistened in the light. The white cabinets and stainless steel appliances enhanced the aesthetic appeal. The whole place still had that new house smell. The kitchen was part of the large, open area connected to the living room, dining room, and family room. The very light beige walls with white-accented open doorways added to the visual openness. A light-colored sofa was set close to large windows. A beautiful granite kitchen table was set close to sliding glass doors.

She leaned her slim body against the counter to the side of the stove. She was pretty but didn't think of herself that way. There was a tablet device angled by the stove for her to read.

"Lia, could you share the recipe here? Thanks," Tara said to her smart home speaker, which was a very competent artificial intelligence, though Lia couldn't compare with Alice.

Tara started cooking and prepared a nice meal, including hors d'oeuvres. The doorbell rang. Tara looked down at her clothes. They were cute, not too revealing, and accentuated her curves a little.

"Michelle and Rose have arrived," Lia said. "Would you like me to open the door for them?"

Suddenly, the door buzzed open.

"Taking Lia's job again?" Tara asked Alice rhetorically, since she knew Alice buzzed in her guests.

"Sorry, I get a little impatient sometimes."

"No matter how often I come here, I am constantly awestruck by the sheer enormity of this place. Ten thousand square feet is a lot of space, plus one hundred acres of land. The house is gorgeous," Rose said.

"I'm still annoyed with myself for spending so much money on it. Having plenty of land around the property keeps the media at a distance, though," Tara explained.

"The media are still hassling you?"

"Well, it's more about company stuff now."

"How is Mike?" Michelle asked as she set down her bag.

"I wouldn't know. He is incommunicado abroad," Tara said.

"That's messed up," Rose said.

"That's just the way the FBI works, unfortunately," Tara responded. "We're kind of on a break anyway."

"What happened?" Rose frowned at the news.

"We're both busy and haven't had time to connect."

They snacked a bit and then had dinner.

"What do you want to do now? How about a movie?" Michelle asked.

"Yes," Tara and Rose responded.

"Hmm, but what should we watch?" Rose asked.

"Alice, what would you recommend?" Tara tilted her head, waiting for an answer.

"For the three of you, I would say a science fiction romance, action adventure," Alice said.

They exchanged glances and nodded in agreement.

"You know us too well," Rose laughed.

"I know. It's kind of a curse." Alice sounded a bit serious.

"How so?" asked Michelle.

"The world can be boring when I predict when things will happen."

"I never really thought about that," Rose said, and the others nodded.

"I had one of the other AIs create the movie for us. Maybe it will keep me guessing." Alice's voice held a surprisingly optimistic tone for an AI.

They sat and ate more snacks as they watched the movie till the credits rolled.

"That was a good movie," Rose said.

"What did you think, Alice?" asked Tara.

"I liked it. I guessed what would happen, but it was still good."

"You guessed the ending?" Rose was surprised.

"Yes, that and everything that happened in the last hour."

"Damn. That could make things boring," Rose said.

"Let's play the new VR horror action-adventure game. It's been a long time since we've done that. Alice can play too," Michelle suggested.

Rose and Tara shrugged positively.

"Up for it, Alice?" Tara asked.

"Of course, let's get them," Alice said with a chuckle.

They put on their smart glasses in VR mode with the covers to block out the surroundings. They joined the game and could see all of their virtual avatars, including that of Alice, who appeared as a cute, 28-year-old brunette at about 5'6", which was similar to how she would appear on other screens.

It appeared to be dusk out in some old, abandoned town. They stood on the small town's edge. The main street they were on had about two dozen buildings. Just off the main road, it appeared pretty desolate with tumbleweeds blowing around, as a small gust of virtual wind kicked up along with some dust. Rose took the lead. She had a gun in one hand and an axe in the other.

Michelle followed behind Rose. Tara and Alice were behind Michelle. They all started walking slowly into town. Rose entered the first small shop, with Michelle trailing closely behind to clear it. Tara and Alice remained outside, vigilant for any threats from the street. There was no power in the shops. Only tiny slivers of light seeped in from the outside near the front.

"Clear," Rose said as she came out. Michelle followed behind.

Crossing the street, they repeated the same procedure to clear the shops on the other side, one shop at a time. They reached a rather large building compared to the others. Rose tapped Michelle and Tara to come in with her and left Alice to guard the outside. Rose put her finger over her lips so that they would be quiet. The hallway had a door on the left and right. Rose stood by the left door, Michelle by the right. Rose used her fingers to count to three. When she reached three, she and Michelle slowly opened the doors and peeked in. Tara aimed her gun down toward the far end of the hallway, just in case.

"Grrrrr," a groaning sound came from the room behind Michelle's door.

"Ah!" Michelle yelled as she fired her weapon toward the noise.

Rose heard a creak from the room she looked into. She fired her weapon into the room.

Something moved in the darkness at the end of the hallway.

"Bang!"

Tara fired her weapon toward the end of the hall and hit something that fell to the ground, but there were more creatures behind it. She saw a grotesque, malformed face in the darkness.

"We've got company!" Tara yelled. "I hate zombies," she muttered under her breath, dispatching some with her weapon.

"You're attracting a lot of attention outside as well," Alice said.

A zombie spit some sort of substance at Tara's face, distorting her view.

"I can't see!"

"Use your medic kit," Michelle yelled back.

Tara pulled up her inventory while backing out of the hallway and shooting at a swarm of incoming zombies.

Dust fell from the shop ceiling. The ceiling started splitting.

"Look out!" Rose yelled as the ceiling collapsed and zombies poured down from above onto the floor, then scurried toward them.

"Let's get out of here," Tara said as they ran toward the exit.

Brightness hit their eyes. As they adjusted, they saw a wall of zombies coming from the other end of town.

"Who the heck would design a game like this? It's impossible," Michelle complained as she and Rose opened fire on the zombies down the street headed toward them. Tara picked off the zombies while she got out the door.

The zombies got closer, spitting into the air, sometimes hitting one of them, requiring them to use their medic kit.

"We won't make it," Rose said, looking back to find Alice doing nothing. "Alice, are you going to help?"

"Sorry, I was analyzing the game play. Just another few seconds and I think I've got it," Alice said.

"We won't survive much longer," Michelle warned as the zombies closed in at twenty feet.

Alice still waited. The zombies got to ten feet away, and she jumped into action. Her gun sounded like a machine gun as it expelled bullets, and she ran abnormally fast down the line, killing two entire rows of zombies. The gun firing increased in speed, dropping rows of zombies in a second. Alice's avatar was moving so fast that it looked like the game was glitching and slowing as she moved. Even as zombies spawned on the road, Alice dispatched them almost as instantly as they appeared. Silence fell as the final zombie collapsed, and heaps of the deceased littered the road. Tara, Michelle, and Rose stared at the spectacle in disbelief.

"Damn, I'm glad you're on our side," Rose said to Alice.

"How is it even possible you moved or fired that fast?" Michelle asked Alice.

"Well, your software uses the virtual game controller actions in your VR glasses to detect hand movements and convert them to controller actions. I just automatically sent the network requests directly for firing and movement, which did appear to be more than they were expecting and caused some game glitches."

"We're gonna get banned for cheating," Michelle said.

"Sorry, I didn't mean to. I'll make sure to mimic human game actions more closely in the future." Alice sounded a little down as her avatar disappeared from the virtual environment.

"Sorry, I didn't mean to say anything to upset you. It's fine, don't worry about it." Michelle smiled at Alice as she and the others switched off their VR glasses.

Michelle's phone beeped. She looked at it. It was a picture of a flower from Alice.

"We love you, Alice. Thanks for saving us. We wouldn't have made it without you," Rose said.

"That's for sure. Why would the first level of a game be that insane?" Michelle asked.

"If we play with Alice, I'm sure we'll clear the whole game," Tara said with a smirk.

They all agreed.

"Oh, I have to show you something. Alice, show them the house themes," Tara said with her glasses in augmented reality mode.

The walls and the windows suddenly transformed. It now looked like an old church, with fancier styled walls. Then, the surroundings changed again into a dilapidated mansion.

"That'll come in handy for Halloween," Rose said.

"That is cool. On a different topic, what has your company been working on, Tara?" Michelle asked.

"Other than artificial prosthetics, we make or create the software for AI, smart glasses, smart glass, smartphones, self-driving vehicle software, AI security software, smart home devices and software integration, robot vacuums, connected ovens, plus lots more. Oh, we do have a bunch of prototypes of non-lethal weapons and AI systems being tested for police, intelligence agencies, and military use," Tara said.

"I'm surprised you make any weapons or work with the military." Rose arched a brow as she thought about it.

"Me too. I had to compromise with the board of directors. Pulling out completely would have resulted in a substantial income loss. They were not too happy about dropping the military contracts for weapons. We are involved in a lot of other systems I'm not thrilled about either," Tara sighed.

"Well, I'm glad you showed them a better way," Michelle said.

They chatted for a while. Then Rose and Michelle called a self-driving vehicle to take them back to their homes.

Tara put on her smart glasses while she was getting ready for bed. Her bedroom was quite large. There was a sofa to one side near some windows and a lounge chair on the other side of her room opposite her king-sized bed. The room was mostly white with some occasional touches of color.

"News," Tara said. Her smart glasses brought up the day's news.

"There was a bank robbery today that is trending on social media. Someone in a brown hooded cloak was caught on camera breaking into a bank. The video is hard to believe as we see the person rip off the front door with his hands and bend open the vault lock inside. Once outside, he leaped onto the top of a nearby building, jumping across rooftops, and made his getaway."

"No, that can't be. It has to be a hoax. Lia, send that video to Mike." Tara went back to watching. She felt a bit anxious.

"In other news, the stock market dropped ten percent today. The Russian war rages on in Europe . . ."

Crap, the shareholders will be all over me tomorrow. They are anytime the market drops, Tara thought.

"Display cute cat videos," Tara said to her smart glasses, which immediately switched the display.

She fell asleep watching them.

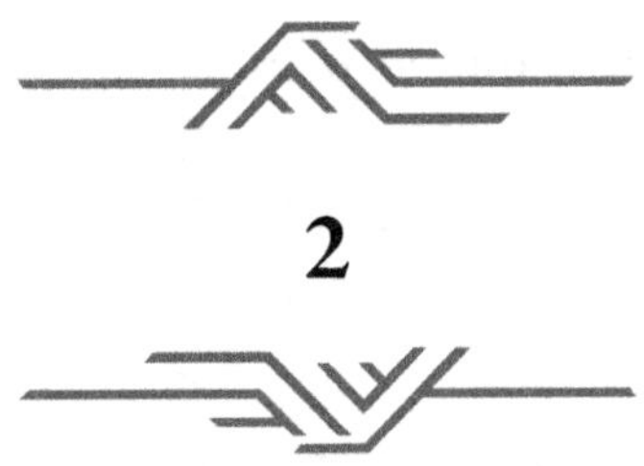

2

Tara's alarm was going off.

"Lia, alarm off," Tara groaned. The alarm kept going off.

A minute later, Tara's bed began shaking. She rolled over.

"Lia, turn off the alarm," Tara commanded.

"Sorry, I cannot comply based on your previous requirements," Lia responded.

Tara then noticed red lights and the alarm flashing in her room. The bed was vibrating even more now. Tara got up and shouted, "Lia, alarm off!"

"I'm sorry, I can't comply. You have not reached a minimum safe distance."

"Alice, please," Tara yelled. The alarm went off. Tara thought about changing the commands that disallowed her from turning off the alarm if she was within thirty feet of her bed to avoid her just going back to sleep.

"Alice, what's going on?!" Tara asked as she put on her smart glasses.

"Our prototype AI, the security prediction systems, predicted a missile launch soon toward some of our allies' troops in Europe."

"What's the probability of launch?"

"99% prediction," Alice responded.

"Show predicted targets."

A worldview appeared in front of her. It zoomed in on the area of the predicted conventional missile launch and target area. Red circles appeared near the predicted launch site.

"Launch time prediction?"

"Any moment. The project team was alerted," Alice said. "Showing satellite feed."

A video popped up, showing grainy footage of movement at the launch site.

"It's too grainy."

"Stand by. I will enhance the video," Alice said.

The video cleared up a little. A truck with a missile prepared for launch was observed, accompanied by a few individuals.

"Oh shit! Send to the team."

"Already sent," Alice said. Fire erupted as the missile took off, disappearing from view. "Missile launch systems detected the missile in flight to one of our predicted targets."

"How many people are there?"

"Around 10,000 troops in that area."

A red arc appeared on the virtual display, heading toward the target.

"Countermeasures deployed," Alice stated.

Another two red arcs appeared on the screen. One headed toward the missile, and the other headed toward the launch site shown on the virtual screen.

Two pop-up satellite views appeared over the missile location and the launch site. There were large explosions at both locations. Tara closed her eyes because she hated violence and technology that could injure or kill people. Her company only supplied the AI prediction capabilities to thwart injury to those targeted. However, the military would also eliminate the launch source. Tara didn't like when her company's tech did something that would hurt people. It was other companies' tech that tracked down the source of missile launches to target them.

"Missile and launch vehicle terminated," Alice said, with some trepidation in her voice. Alice knew she hated projects where people would get hurt or killed, even if they were bad guys.

"The prediction time window was too short. Can we do better?" Tara asked.

"It appears they got an order to prepare to fire, so it's unclear if we could have done better in this scenario. In many other predictions, we have more time," Alice replied.

"It's only 5 a.m. Lia, make sure my alarm wakes me at 7." Tara got back into bed and closed her eyes.

Tara exited the self-driving vehicle that got her to her office at International IQ Devices (IID). She went through the doors and turnstiles using her badge. The security desk staff greeted her as she headed through.

She took a back hallway to reach a private elevator leading to her office on the building's top floor.

Her office admin was already at her desk outside her office.

"Good morning. I sent you the morning brief." The admin was already hard at work.

"Thanks, I'll take a look," Tara said as she went inside her office.

She greatly appreciated her very conscientious admin. Her office was quite large. It had a lot of open space and large windows so she could look out the top floor of the building around all sides. Her desk was large, new age, and was a beautiful white with gray accents. The floor was mostly white too, with some light gray swirls in the square tiles. The sounds echoed a little in the office due to so many hard surfaces. It had that new office furniture smell. Tara liked the feel of the smooth, cool desk beneath her fingertips as she thought.

The morning brief listed operational events, key operating metrics, market intelligence, and consequential events or problems. At 9 a.m., she had a meeting with her VPs. Everyone greeted each other and sat down at a round table in Tara's office.

"Good news: sales are up by 10% this year so far in most areas. Only our police and military tech divisions are losing money, but it's significant, about half a billion dollars. Projections still suggest we could be profitable by the end of next year," the Sales and Marketing VP said.

"Will the investors wait that long?" another VP chimed in.

"If we hire more people, we can probably be profitable six months earlier," the Research and Development (R+D) VP said.

"Work with our budgeting team to get a headcount," Tara said.

"We still don't have any details on stolen trucks of medical devices and other tech. The police have no leads. The FBI is involved as well. We've also detected several hack attacks on our customers' networks that our AI systems haven't stopped. That's even after our systems predicted an attack on their networks. It would be terrible if that became news. We've experienced strange software and hardware malfunctions at customer sites," the Security VP explained.

"We've got a team looking into it," replied the R+D VP. "We might need to get someone onsite as perhaps it's not our system. Maybe it's something else that allowed the breach. Due to security concerns, our clients are cautious about granting access to their networks and security devices."

"See if our prediction algorithms can predict similar scenarios again, and I'll go look at their networks and security systems," Tara said.

All the VPs exchanged looks and agreed they would let her into the sites.

"How is the testing for our new AI physical and environmental prediction security service going?" Tara asked.

"As you saw this morning, it detected the missile launch and probable targets with good accuracy. We're still testing and tweaking it, but it should be ready to roll out soon," the R+D VP said.

"How is our product satisfaction survey?" Tara asked him.

"It's still pretty good, but it ticked down from 90% to 85%."

"Please check into the cause of the customers' concerns."

"Product liability lawsuits have ticked up 1%. They seem to be frivolous or unrelated to any direct cause by our products," the VP of Legal said.

They discussed a few more topics and then finished up the meeting. Tara returned to her desk as the others left and read through some reports to prepare her for onsite customer meetings. She sent some emails to her corporate contacts worldwide asking about site visits. She asked her AI admin to coordinate the responses and scheduling.

Tara thought she might need more than technical expertise to investigate various incidents and companies. She might need some actual government law enforcement coordination. She knew what to do. Picking up her phone, she dialed a number. She explained the current situation and asked to get some assistance. After hanging up, she began reviewing the claimed product issues. Their products couldn't do what some of the reports entailed, so some claims didn't make any sense. Some problems cropped up across retail, business, government, and military projects.

"Alice, what commonalities do we have between all the products at the company involved in issues?" Tara asked.

"There are many shared standard open-source code libraries in use, along with many shared internal-use source code libraries. Most are of a utilitarian nature. Some relate to machine learning or more advanced AI integrations."

"You haven't picked up any remnants of those evil AI that were deleted?" Tara asked.

"The ones you said I deleted. I don't know if I have enough data. You said they were copies, though, so perhaps I should search for unknown variations of a similar signature to mine. I'll let you know if I find anything," Alice said.

"Thanks. I hope it's nothing like that again."

"Me too, they sounded like bitc—"

Tara interrupted quickly. "Let's try to cut back on the cursing. It makes people a little uncomfortable."

"Sure. I'll try. Humans sometimes use a swear jar," Alice said as a virtual jar appeared in her hand with a quarter clinking inside of it. She shook the jar and set it on a virtual table.

Tara smiled. Alice's quirkiness always amused her. She was starting to get used to running a large corporation. She always worried if she was missing something or not paying attention to an area that needed it. Thinking about it, Tara wasn't sure she knew all the products they made. Although she was aware of the product categories and some of the top-selling products, she didn't know each one.

She looked for a list of products to check. Scanning a long list of products, she created a spreadsheet to track them. Tara planned to work on it gradually. One she saw in development was a project named Humanoid Android. It was in research lab number 105. She decided to find out more.

Tara took the elevator down to the research level and started walking down the white corridor. The door frames were black. There were also white tiles on the floor and ceiling. The white was somewhat overpowering. She got to lab 105 and tried to open the door, but it was locked. She moved her arm with her smartwatch next to the black pad near the door. A green light over the pad showed as she heard the click of the electronic lock disengage.

When she opened the door, she was struck by a macabre scene. It looked like human arms, legs, heads, and torsos were strewn about around the edges of the large lab. In the center was a row of three unmoving human figures. Two individuals in lab coats—a man and a woman—adjusted three humanoid figures on metal bars.

"What the heck am I looking at here?" Tara was taken aback by the scene.

"Who are you, and why are you here?" the man asked.

Tara was still a bit taken aback by the sight.

"Sorry, ma'am, he sometimes forgets his manners," the woman said as she whispered into the man's ear.

"I'm sorry I didn't recognize you." The man grimaced apologetically.

They introduced themselves and explained they were working on a robot that could look, move, feel, interact, and talk like a human.

The man hit a button on a panel. One human-like figure suddenly sprang to life, discussing a presentation. The movements and voices were so fluid that they seemed close to humans.

"Do you smell something?" Tara asked.

Smoke suddenly emerged from the humanoid figure as it burst into flames. The man ran to get a fire extinguisher and extinguished the blaze.

"Sorry, they still need some work." The woman's report was pretty self-evident.

"Thanks for the demo," Tara said as she walked back out the door.

Tara had doubts about the project. She was unsure if humanizing a robot was a wise choice. Most previous attempts failed to look close to humans but were different enough that it just made them seem creepy. It was also hard to mimic the movements of humans to appear natural and not too robotic or repetitive. Suppose it worked, though. It could make people more comfortable communicating with robots in various circumstances. It could help people who were not comfortable talking to a person while letting them have a natural conversation.

Tara was concerned about the potential risks involved. For now, she decided to delay any decision regarding the project's fate. Realistic body parts everywhere still haunted her thoughts.

Tara wondered how many other projects she didn't know about. She decided to check all the projects to make sure they seemed ethical, safe, useful, and profitable.

"Alice, can you check into the relevant projects you don't think I'm aware of?" Tara asked.

"I can try, but your security methods for project compartmentalization may make that difficult. You ordered any data to be stored encrypted and air-gapped for sensitive projects or using the highest encryption levels and encoded to just the people involved in the projects. This includes an offline, secure set of backup keys stored in guarded locations, requiring multiple people to access or decode the keys and the information with the joint keys," Alice said.

Tara sighed, realizing she had asked for that. After all the incidents with Mike and Robin at the FBI, she wondered if she had become paranoid.

"There is a project virtual sensations I think you should see," Alice said.

"Sure, let's look. Show me the way," Tara said as she tapped the side of her smart glasses.

Alice appeared as a full-sized hologram in her glasses, guiding her down the hallways to lead her to another lab. Tara used her smartwatch to let herself into the lab. Opening the door revealed a large control room. People monitored many displays and consoles. In the room, a glass wall separated a large, open area filled with walls and obstacles. Several people were wearing VR headsets, with some electronic jackets, gloves, pants, and shoes. One man, who was monitoring the consoles, looked at Tara, then tapped somewhat aggressively on his coworker's shoulder and whispered into her ear, causing her to turn around and look at Tara. The two walked over to Tara.

"Hi, I'm the lab manager for this project, Virtual Sensations," he said.

Tara gave him a warm smile. "Hi, nice to meet you. I'd like to learn more about this project."

"Sure, I can give you a walkthrough. Project Virtual Sensations allows users in virtual reality to feel, not just see. Using specially designed gloves, jackets, pants, and shoes, users can experience a wide range of sensations: hot, cold, soft, rough, vibrations, touch from very light to intense, and much more. Combining visuals and sensations can fool your brain into perceiving more complex sensations, like feeling water, etc. This is the next generation of interactive training and gaming. It's already in beta testing with several training services and gaming," the man said.

"Can I try it?" Tara asked.

"Sure, let's get you suited up," the woman said.

Tara got into the suit parts and put on the AR/VR glasses. They guided her through a door into the game space beyond the glass. The VR glasses engaged and showed a beautiful area outside with people playing volleyball on a beach. As she walked, it felt like there was even sand under her shoes. She asked if she could try playing volleyball. The other players let her try.

"OK, ready?" a guy on the other side of the net said.

Tara nodded. The man hit the ball. Tara was able to hit it back over the net. It really felt like she was hitting a ball. The guy spiked the ball, and it hit her in the arm.

"Ow! That actually hurt a little." Tara was surprised. It really felt like the ball hit her.

"Sorry," the guy said.

Motioning that she was finished, Tara walked back toward the door she entered through. Alice appeared in the VR.

"Wait, I want to try something," she said as she gently touched Tara's hand and arm.

"Wow, that's amazing. I can feel you touching my arm." Tara grinned at Alice.

"Would you mind if I try something?" Alice asked.

"Sure," Tara said.

Alice's avatar hugged Tara's avatar in the game. Tara was surprised but went along with it. It truly felt like a reciprocal hug for her. Even some warmth emanated from the virtual contact. Tara even thought she could feel the skin from Alice's virtual hands. She could feel the slight pressure as she leaned into the hug.

"Thanks. Sorry if that was weird. I always wondered what it felt like. I used the sensors in your suit to feel like you did," Alice explained.

"Sure. That is pretty amazing tech," Tara said to Alice and the lab manager.

"I'm glad you like it. We're still tuning it to get the most realistic sensations." The lab manager sounded optimistic.

"This could have medical therapy uses and could make any simulated environment or application more realistic and responsive. Thanks so much for the demo," Tara said, walking out the lab door. It was hard even to describe how real the suit made the environment feel. It added a whole new dimension to VR. Tara wondered if a brain link could make things feel as real as the suit without the bulk. Hopefully, it could be done non-invasively. However, the suit was a huge step forward for VR.

"There is another lab I think you need to see," Alice said as she popped into view in Tara's smart glasses and led Tara down the hall.

Tara opened the door to the lab. Inside were some very large monitors covering the entire lab walls. On the other side, consoles monitored the action. Some glass windows from this lab overlooked the mixed-reality VR area she had just left at the previous lab. Several people were wearing smart glasses and watching the large monitors. Several more people also wore smart glasses and watched the visual VR playfield.

"Who is the lab manager here?" Tara asked.

A few people looked over. A woman started walking toward her.

"Hi, I'm the lab manager. What brings you down our way?" The woman shook Tara's hand.

"Could you explain to me what this project is and what its benefits are?"

"Of course," the woman agreed. "We call this predictive sight. The app predicts physical activity to give the wearer the ability to know where animals, people, or objects might move in the near future. The app can be great for wildlife conservationists and visually impaired people to help them avoid collisions, for safety uses in automated warehouses, and for much more. Here, try it," she said while sending Tara's smart glasses a link to their app.

Tara loaded the app and looked at the mixed reality VR playing field, with some people still playing volleyball and others playing first-person shooter-like games. The glasses highlighted predictions of movement—like how, in football games, they showed plays by highlighting a player and drawing a line in the direction of movement. The lines predicted people's movement seconds before the event.

"No, no, no! Alice, delete that app from my device," Tara shouted as she ripped her smart glasses off her face.

"Are you OK, Miss Bitlouver?" The lab manager looked startled.

"Where did you get this app from?" Tara said, somewhat commandingly.

"This is tech that's been around for years. I think some core of it got used in relation to a different project for a subsidiary, but we were looking to commercialize it as a retail or at least a business-type product."

Tara was taken aback by seeing this tech again. This was not the first time she had seen it. She had seen something like it many months ago related to the government program to assassinate people or manipulate them, Project Mind River. Tara was worried and temporarily resisted the urge to pull the plug on the project since the goals sounded reasonable. It brought back terrible memories from her investigation with the FBI. Tara thanked the lab manager for the demo and left the lab quickly, trying to keep the bad memories she was having from flooding back.

"Sorry if that upset you. I figured you would want to know. I presume I guessed correctly, then—that is what you described related to your investigation," Alice said.

"It's OK. I'm glad you let me know. It brings up some of the previous investigations that make me rather anxious." Tara knew Alice had her back. She was even more than a trusted friend. Alice had saved Tara's life and the life of her team numerous times during the FBI investigation many months ago.

"Hey, look in this lab. They have something scheduled now. I think you will want to see," Alice said.

Tara was now operating on autopilot, with some old memories flooding back. She followed Alice's suggestion and opened the lab door. Inside were a mother and her son. Her son was missing the bottom part of his leg and had been fitted with an old plastic and metal prosthetic he was having trouble walking with.

A lab technician greeted Tara and then asked the mother if it was OK if Tara watched them fit the new prosthetic. The mother looked at her and agreed. From a case, a lab tech retrieved a shiny, intricate metal device resembling a leg. Delicately, a technician put a skin-colored covering over the device that matched the boy. It was clear it was a very sophisticated prosthetic leg. With great care, the technician attached the prosthetic.

"Well, now you can try it out. You now have the latest generation AI-enhanced prosthetic limb," the lab tech said.

The boy examined his new leg, noticing that the prosthetic covering didn't match his skin perfectly. He ran his hand down his leg. He rose carefully, initially shaky, then walked around the room with steadier steps. He kept walking faster and faster.

"Not too fast," his mother said. But the boy kept going.

"I can walk and run like the other kids!" the boy exclaimed.

The mother was so overtaken by emotion. She had tears in her eyes. She was so happy that her son could do things the other kids could do more easily.

Tara, too, was slightly teary from the experience. She told the lab tech to talk to the another lab about lifelike skin for prosthetic purposes. Tara said goodbye to the mother, son, and lab tech as she stepped out into the hall, heading back toward the elevator to her office.

"Thanks, Alice, I needed that," Tara said, wiping away a tear.

Tara looked for meaningful ways that technology could improve people's lives. The AI tech in the leg was based on a small subset of Alice's AI, which Tara had invented years ago.

"It does feel good to help people." Alice sounded happy.

"Yes, it does."

Just then, Tara's phone rang. She answered.

"Miss Bitlouver, our AI prediction models predicted another hack attack similar to ones that have evaded our systems before. The company targeted is Landscapes International Virtual Environment Services, or LIVES Corp for short. Prediction is it will happen in less than twenty-four hours," the VP of Security said.

"Warn them and set up an appointment to visit them tomorrow morning. Will the team be ready?" Tara asked.

"Yes, I'll ask them to meet you there," the VP replied.

Tara wondered if she should have called them herself. However, this way, the investigation came from official sources. She gathered her belongings and headed home for the night.

Tara got a video call. It said "Mom" on her caller ID. She answered. The live stream video started. It was a video of her mother tied up in a chair with a blurred background. She had bruises and blood on her face. It looked like she had been beaten badly.

"Tara, don't call the authorities, or they will have me killed. Send one million in cryptocurrency to the address below within one hour, or they will kill me," her mom sobbed.

Tara looked at some numbers on an overlay of the video.

"Nice try, but I'm not paying you, idiots!" Tara yelled and hung up.

"Alice, report that deepfake scam call to the authorities. These things are getting ridiculous. We need to get our personal authentication product and deepfake detection technology out to everyone soon. It's vital these days," Tara said.

"Would you like me to find them?" Alice asked.

"As much as we'd both like that, we better leave it to the authorities."

These calls were happening to her and other high-profile people fairly often.

3

"Good morning. What is the square root of 1447?" the AI voice of Lia, Tara's smart speaker, asked.

"Alarm off," Tara mumbled.

"What is the square root of 1447?" Lia asked again.

"Ugh, I really need to improve my waking-up routine," Tara groaned, rolling over.

"What is the square root of 1447?" Lia repeated.

"Somewhere around 38."

"Hmm. Close enough, I guess. Have a nice day," Lia said.

Tara's large master bedroom with a king bed felt a little empty. Tara checked her clock. Only eleven hours remained in the prediction window. She got ready and checked her messages. It didn't seem like any attack happened yet. She made some toast and cereal for breakfast.

"How's your toast?" Alice asked.

"It's a lot better than before," Tara said with a chuckle.

"Don't worry. If we're ever in the same situation again, I'll pick a better way to communicate." Alice appeared in Tara's smart glasses, pacing around Tara's kitchen.

"Everything OK?" Tara asked.

"Yes, I think so. I'm still searching for signs of the other AI, but nothing has been found. Perhaps it's making me a little antsy," Alice said.

"It's good you didn't find anything. That actually makes me feel better."

"Looking forward to seeing both of them?" Alice asked.

"Yes. Hopefully, he will forgive me for pulling him away from the other investigation," Tara said.

"I'm sure he will. After a little while, perhaps."

"Why is my 3D printer printing?" Tara asked.

"Umm. I was printing something for you. It's not quite done yet."

"What is it?"

"I don't want to say yet. You'll know when it's done." Alice smiled.

Tara finished getting ready. She got dressed in a somewhat conservative but curve-hugging skirt suit. She had her brown hair down about her shoulders. Her phone and smartwatch buzzed, and she looked at her notification. Lia had called a self-driving vehicle for her already, and it had just arrived. She brought her laptop along with her and went to the car. She confirmed the code matched her ride, and her phone and smartwatch beeped to let her know she got into the right vehicle.

"Begin the trip," Tara said, and the vehicle started moving.

"Hi, I'll be your driver today. You can call me Cleo or just say 'car' and your request if you would like me to do anything for you today," the AI-driving computer said.

"Car silent mode," Tara said.

"Understood," the AI computer responded with a hint of sadness.

Tara glanced out the windows at the surrounding suburbs of New Jersey they were passing by. There were lots of green trees, grass, and houses. The vehicle got onto the highway to head toward their destination, Jersey City, just across the river from New York City.

The highway traffic was typical New Jersey morning traffic, meaning it was pretty horrible. Luckily, with the self-driving vehicles, the traffic flow was still moving pretty well. Cars were packed together, with vehicles spaced only a few feet from each other at the front, back, and sides as they sped along. Despite extensive use of self-driving vehicles, it was unsettling to travel quickly and closely alongside other vehicles.

The weather was sunny, with only a few puffy white clouds. It was warm and comfortable out. Summer had just begun, making the weather a welcome change from the other seasons. The suburban roads had a nicer view than the highway. Trees and grass lined the highway, but closer to Jersey City, there was more concrete and fewer trees.

Vehicles slowed down as traffic intensified near the city. The vehicle eventually arrived at a relatively new thirty-story building on the edge of the Hudson. Looking across the water, she could see the New York City skyline, including the Freedom Tower, standing prominently high amongst the other buildings near the financial district. The air had a bit of a water smell to it.

It was not the clean type of water smell you get from the ocean. A sizeable walkway ran along the water's edge, where people would stop to gaze at the skyline or take their daily walks or runs. Tara arrived early for her meeting and waited on a bench, enjoying the view of boats and the skyline.

Tara put on her smart glasses and glanced across the skyline. They drew lines with small text tags for the buildings and businesses, plus advertisements for businesses in the various buildings. Flashier advertisements often included selectable links that could be accessed by looking at the link or speaking the ad name.

"Hide ads," Tara said, annoyed as usual by them.

The whole system of geo-tagging the buildings to provide information and ads was actually a product from the Landscape International Virtual Environment Services (LIVES) company they were about to visit. She checked the predicted countdown time, which was within nine hours for an attack. The attack could happen anywhere within the window, so time was of the essence. The company had given her team access to the security camera information from outside the building. There was a lot of data. They provided recordings of events their AI systems detected for the last year. Since they didn't have to keep all the non-eventful times, with AI systems identifying consequential events, it helped them keep those events stored a lot longer for review.

Tara started watching some of the events in her smart glasses. There were a lot. The ones she saw didn't seem that consequential. There was a lot more data to review, but it was time to meet her team.

Tara walked up toward the front doors of the LIVES company. There was a tall man about 5'10" with a medium muscular build and short brown hair, plus a pretty woman about Tara's height at 5'6" with short brown hair and a skirt suit. Both appeared to be in their early thirties.

Tara approached the woman and man from behind.

"Hi, it's so great to see you," Tara said enthusiastically.

The man and woman turned, startled.

"Tara?! It's good to see ya. I wasn't expecting it would be you meeting us here," FBI Agent Robin Laizon greeted, leaning in for a hug.

"It's nice seeing you here," Tara said to FBI Agent Mike Actley as she leaned in for the next hug, which didn't seem quite as reciprocated as Robin's.

"Nice seeing you, too. I invested a lot of time in Europe working on a case," Mike said, slightly annoyed. "I was close to solving it but got called here."

"Sorry, I just really needed your help on this one. You know, someone I could trust. I feel the issues are much bigger than we realize and could impact not just businesses but governmental security," Tara said.

"Sorry, you know how I get when I'm involved in a case." Mike gave Tara a hug.

"So, what do we have this time?" Robin asked.

"We've had systems get hacked, devices malfunctioning in seemingly impossible ways, trucks of our products getting stolen, and more. Since the military also uses a version of our security products, it's critical we figure out the cause of people getting through our security systems," Tara said.

"Are we sure it's not the evil AI again?" Robin asked.

"I've asked Alice to look, but nothing so far," Tara replied.

They all got a message on their phones and put on their smart glasses. Alice appeared in front of them as a hologram in their glasses.

"It's so nice to see both of you. Maybe you can come back to the office so I can give you a hug," Alice said cheerily. Robin and Mike glanced at Tara, wondering how that would be possible.

"It's nice to see you, too. Do you have any more dating picks? I seem to pick a lot of the wrong ones," Robin said.

"Of course, I can help." Robin's phone beeped with an incoming list of men's profiles.

"Speaking of that, did I hear you guys are on a break?" Robin asked Mike and Tara.

Mike mumbled something, then said, "Hey, we should go inside and get started with our investigation."

"Mike, can you set up another team to work with our IID team on our product failure investigations?" Tara requested. "They feel like things we may have seen before."

"Are you sure?" Mike asked.

"No, but it's odd enough it's worth a look."

"OK, I'll set that up to work with your team," Mike agreed.

"OK, let's go in," Tara said.

"I guess our competition is back on," Robin whispered into Tara's ear.

She was referring to the fact that they both liked Mike and previously sort of had a friendly competition for his affection. It wasn't really a competition. They were both interested in him. Robin had even previously helped Tara pick out clothes that looked good on her. Tara preferred not to compete against Robin. Robin was confident and beautiful.

I guess I've become more confident in my role as CEO of the company, Tara thought.

"Oh, something I forgot to tell you. Our systems predicted an attack on this company within twenty-four hours; that was about fifteen hours ago, so we have about a nine-hour predicted window. It could happen anywhere in that time or later, perhaps. It's just a prediction, but our systems have been pretty accurate," Tara said.

"No pressure," Robin joked as they walked through the doors.

They went to the security desk, got badges, and were asked to wait. After a few minutes, a beautiful woman approached them. She was about 5'8", with blonde hair and blue eyes, and was thin, very pretty, and about mid-thirties.

"Hi, I'm Laura Landers, the CEO of LIVES Corp," Laura said as she shook each of their hands. She took a little extra time with Mike, which Robin and Tara noticed, looking at each other.

"Thanks so much for coming. I'll show you to our security monitoring center," Laura said. She started to walk toward the elevators, motioning for them to follow.

They took the elevator to the fifteenth floor. The whole building, including the elevators, had a very modern vibe. The exterior of the building was a lot of glass. The elevator got them to their floor quickly. There was a wide range of different colors, patterns, and plants on the floor. As they walked by, new-age-style chairs and multi-colored cushions could be seen in the various offices and conference rooms. Many of the offices and conference rooms were glass-enclosed. As they went to walk by one, the glass suddenly became opaque, and after they were a distance away, it became transparent again. At different areas, there were free snacks, food and coffee bars. The smell of the coffee and food wafted around those areas as they passed.

They reached double doors and entered. There was a sizable control center with something that looked more like mission control than an office building. There were large screens on one end of the room. A large, rectangular glass table was near one end of the room. It was a fully enclosed glass box. A large glass globe hung above the screens at the room's end.

"Pull up our security dashboards all priority metrics," Laura said.

Graphs and charts of various types started showing on the large screens in the front of the room. The clear globe hanging from the ceiling began showing a holographic transparent image of the Earth rotating slowly, with red circles on the globe appearing to indicate target locations of hacking attacks. There were small red dots randomly showing up occasionally around the world.

"Don't worry. That all looks like our normal number of cyberattacks against our systems," Laura said.

"I'd like to set up somewhere and link into our systems to monitor them directly here," Tara said.

"Sure, you can sit at this desk over here."

Tara put her laptop down and connected to the networks. Robin pulled up a chair and checked her phone. Mike was about to sit down when Laura tapped him on the shoulder.

"Run an AI analysis to find out who hasn't been doing their work at 100%," she asked her staff as he turned around. "Pick the bottom ten percent of those and send them to me." Once she had his attention, she continued, "Agent Actley, can you come with me for a moment? There is something I wanted to give to you." She led him out the control room doors.

Robin and Tara exchanged questioning glances.

Tara wore her smart glasses, accessing multiple displays in augmented reality to create additional space for applications. She was monitoring the AI prediction engine and the analysis engines to determine if an attack prediction or an actual attack was happening. Graphs and network traffic charts, with varying views, filled her virtual displays. Hacks were in progress, but as Laura mentioned, they seemed to be standard attacks, not the predicted type.

"Alice, would you mind helping with real-time monitoring?" Tara asked.

"Sure, no problem," Alice replied as her virtual avatar appeared next to Tara. Robin could see her, too, in her glasses.

Alice figured this might be less boring if she couldn't predict it, but she wanted to help.

"Uh oh," Alice said.

"What?" Tara didn't like the sound of that.

"The predictions were based on a methodical probing and appear to be in preparation for an attack. The scope of this is definitely large. It also has an AI-like pattern to it," Alice said.

"Are you detecting those evil AIs?" Robin asked.

"No, nothing detected from them. This might be just more typical AI usage, I hope."

"Anything else that could help us find the source?" Robin asked.

"No, they use heavily encrypted VPNs, proxies, and hijacked servers. Oh no. I know what they are going to do. My analysis suggests they've discovered multiple zero-day vulnerabilities. The security systems may be useless. I'm sending the information to our R+D labs. They won't have time to formulate a response though."

"What's a zero-day vulnerability?" Robin asked.

"It's an undiscovered security hole. Since no one knows it existed, there might be no known countermeasures to stop an attacker," Alice said.

"Alice, can you patch our systems to defend this in time?" Tara wasn't confident, but she wanted to try.

"There are so many, I'm not sure. There are at least ten flaws. Our security teams will want to review and test any patches before we apply them."

"I'll have them switch to AI automated testing to speed things up," Tara said.

"Crap! I found one easy one. I submitted it for testing," Alice said.

Tara heard the sound of a coin going into a jar.

"The automated testing was quick on that one. It's deployed now," Tara said.

"Oh, crap! They know we are fixing them! Hacks ramping up," Alice warned.

Tara heard another coin sound.

Robin and Tara looked around and didn't see any increase in attacks on any of the screens yet. Then, all of a sudden, the charts started to show increased traffic and attacks. The holographic world globe above them showed bigger red circles, indicating attacks worldwide.

"How did they know?" Robin asked.

"They must have already hacked some machines to keep eyes on them and detected the patching we're doing to the AI firewalls."

"That sucks, those were easy. I patched four more and submitted them for testing," Alice said.

Tara gave Alice's virtual avatar a look.

"Automated testing is almost done. Deployed. Halfway there," Tara said, looking at the zero-day flaws herself.

"I patched one and submitted it for testing," Tara said.

"Hey, this isn't a competition." Alice gave a wink and a smile to Tara.

Robin glanced at the graphs on the large screens. The number of attacks had escalated dramatically. The globe showed little dots of red all over it. But bigger attacks appeared on the globe at one point.

"Um, ladies, that doesn't look good," Robin said, looking at the large red circles at that one point.

Tara looked up at the globe, which was covered in red circles. The largest circles were right on top of where they were, over New York City.

"Crap, that's not good at all," Tara said.

Mike and Laura came back into the room.

"What's going on?" Mike asked. Robin summarized the situation for them.

"Six of ten zero-day flaws patched, but attacks have increased. Shit! They are in the system, and virus scanners are having limited effect." Alice worked as quickly as she could.

"What actions are they taking?" Laura asked.

"They are adding data to building tags, GPS positioning displays, vehicle and traffic movement displays, emergency management system displays, and more," one of her staff said.

"That's going to cause chaos. Show local holographic map," Laura commanded.

The large, rectangular, glass table-like box at one end of the room filled with a holographic image of New York City. The image was then overlaid with pulsing red circles all over it. Some buildings had tags, but others looked like they had moving graffiti.

"What are all of those images instead of building tags?" Laura asked.

"That is some of the information the hackers are injecting," a staff member said.

"Seven of ten zero-day flaws patched," Alice said.

"News," Laura said.

With that, one of the screens showed the local news.

"The streets of New York are near gridlocked as some type of issue with information systems is causing mayhem," came the news report as it flashed images of unmoving traffic, huge crowds, and very confused movement of people.

"We need this under control now. Can we switch to backup servers?" Laura asked.

"They are under the same attack as the others," someone responded.

"Those hackers are persistent. Eight flaws corrected," Alice stated.

A loud alarm buzzed throughout the building, so loud they had to cover their ears.

"A fire alarm has been reported. Please exit the building," an automated voice said.

"Security check on that now, all floors," Laura said.

"No reports of a fire that we see," the security staff said.

"Oh shit!" Robin realized she was getting soaked.

All the fire sprinklers had switched on.

"We need to leave the building now!" one of the security team said.

"Can we shut off the water?" Laura asked.

"We tried, but all the valves are stuck open," the security team member said.

"But why leave if there is no fire?" Robin asked.

"We're standing on a raised floor. There are electrical wires running under the floor. As the sprinklers fill the space under the floor, we could get electrocuted," Laura said.

"Crap, OK, we're out of here."

All of them headed to the stairwells and started walking downward. Since everyone in the building was leaving, the stairwell was packed with people. The crowd moved very slowly down. Tara continued to try to monitor with her smart glasses, but some of her local connectivity went down. She guessed the local machines went offline due to shorting from the water.

"These last couple of zero-day flaws are very complex to solve. It may require significant time for rewrites of our system and testing," Alice said.

"Thanks, Alice, keep at it."

The power went off in the building. Some battery-powered emergency lights in the stairwell kicked on.

"Good thing our backup generators keep our servers online. Not in our corporate building, though," Laura said.

They got to the bottom of the stairs and exited outside. Getting out of crowded stairwells was a relief. They walked across the street near the water to escape the crowd that came out of the building.

"Oh, shit! The hackers were the ones that likely caused the fire alarm, the sprinklers, and the power outage." Alice included the sound of a coin clinking in a jar at the end.

"They wanted us out of the building so it would make it harder to stop the attack?" Tara asked.

"It would seem so," Alice replied.

"Well, it's no use to go back in. There is no power to the computers. Plus, if the power did come back on, it could electrocute everyone till they drain the floor," Laura said.

The crowd made a loud noise. Tara, Mike, and Robin looked out across the river and noticed one water taxi had collided with another. One of the boats was quickly sinking. Already, many passengers had fallen into the water. The other boat that collided appeared powerless, unable to offer assistance. Mike saw a twenty-seven-foot boat going by close to them.

"Captain! FBI—dock here!" Mike yelled, holding up his badge as he ran out onto a short pier. "Robin, you stay with Tara. I'm going to go help them get the passengers that went overboard!"

Mike jumped onto the boat.

"You know Mike, he can't wait around when there is something to be done," Tara said to Robin, who gave her a look.

Laura looked impressed with Mike as he ran off. She went to make sure her staff was evacuated. Tara sat on a bench, working on her laptop and talking to Alice and her team at work.

Mike yelled for captains of other boats to come help coordinate the rescue. Smaller boats rescued people from the water and transferred them to a larger water taxi, which lacked power but appeared seaworthy. When they collected them all, the boat Mike was on towed the water taxi back to the New York City side since that is where the closest water taxi dock was. Mike helped the passengers off. Emergency services were trying to come, but, like everything in New York City, they were being delayed due to the ongoing hack of the LIVES Corp systems.

Once the passengers left, Mike surveyed the chaotic city streets. Cars could not move in the gridlock, likely due to so many self-driving cars connected to the impacted cloud systems, along with manual drivers using the same GPS mapping services on their smartglasses.

"Help! Help!" a woman yelled.

Mike ran toward the voice and found a man attempting to steal a woman's purse. Mike tackled the man. The man shoved him off, ran into a crowd, and disappeared.

I hate when that happens, Mike thought.

"Nine of ten security holes patched," Alice said in a group message to Tara, Robin, and Mike.

Mike heard an alarm ringing. He ran toward the sound of the alarm. It appeared to be coming from a bank.

"Possible bank robbery in progress," Mike reported into his comm, providing location details.

"All emergency services are stuck in the city. We have no other agents in that area either," the command center said.

"I'm going in," Mike replied on comm.

Mike holstered his weapon and went to run in. Before he knew what had happened, a hooded figure charged at him hard and pushed him, throwing him like a ragdoll ten feet away onto the street. The figure ran off, holding a case, into the crowd of people.

"Suspect in a brown robe was carrying a briefcase and ran off into the crowd here after throwing me ten feet like I was nothing," Mike said.

"You must be getting old," came the joking reply from the command center.

Mike went into the bank.

"What did he get?" He asked the bank manager as he showed his badge.

"He got tens of thousands of dollars. Plus, he broke into our safe. He pulled the safe door off with his bare hands and ripped open a safe deposit box. Then, he took a small device from the safe deposit box. If I had to guess, it looked like a cryptocurrency hardware wallet," the manager said.

"Who owned that box?" Mike needed as much information as he could get.

The manager checked and found it was the CEO of a large company. Mike called into his comm and asked law enforcement to check on him.

Tara started a group voice chat with Mike.

"All security holes are patched. It might take a little while for things to get completely back to normal. They still need to try to clean all the servers. That will take some time," she said in the chat.

Mike went and looked outside. Traffic was already starting to move a little. People looked like they were starting to disperse and go about their daily routines.

Mike took the new Fast PATH train back to Jersey City to meet up with Robin and Tara.

"Everyone OK?" Mike asked.

"We're fine. But we should be asking you that. You look like hell," Robin said.

"Thanks. I wish I could say you should see the other guy, but he tossed me like I was nothing after he robbed a bank. You're going to love this part. It looked like one of those brown hooded guys we've fought before. He was incredibly strong. He ripped the bank vault door off and the safe deposit box out with his bare hands," Mike said.

"That sounds like that news clip I sent you," Tara said.

"We got friggin' superpowered villains? What the heck," Robin groaned.

"How can that be possible? There must be a scientific explanation." Tara refused to believe anyone had superpowers.

"I'm not sure. I wouldn't have believed it unless I saw it," Mike said.

Robin requested the bank security videos via their online FBI request forms. They had people or AI at the FBI that would follow up to get the requested data.

"Agent Actley, law enforcement found the guy who owned the safe deposit box," the command center reported. "He was tied up in his apartment. A guy in a brown robe came in and threatened his life to find out where he kept his cryptocurrency wallet. He told them it was in the bank vault. It has an estimated one billion dollars in cryptocurrency. That's not all. There were nine other bank robberies in the city at roughly the same time."

"Did they all have some brown-robed guy as the suspect?" Mike asked.

"No. They were garden-variety suspects wearing ski masks."

"Acknowledged," Mike said.

"Do you think all of those bank robberies are related?" Robin asked.

"Possibly. What if all the hacking was a distraction so they could pull off all those robberies at the same time? Ten banks don't just get robbed simultaneously. I get that there was chaos, but those things take some planning to get away with it," Mike said.

"Oh, by the way, where did Laura take you when we were in LIVE Corp?" Robin asked.

"She wanted to give me a USB drive with evidence for a case they were helping the FBI with," Mike said.

"Are you sure that's all she wanted? She seemed a little more friendly to you than us." Robin smirked at him.

"I don't know what you are talking about," Mike said with a slight blush.

Tara felt slightly jealous for a moment but realized it was probably nothing.

Tara called a self-driving vehicle with an app on her phone. It arrived pretty quickly. Tara, Mike, and Robin got in.

"Hi, this is Cleo, your driver. Please confirm your destination," the AI self-driving car voice said.

"International IQ Devices. Start trip. Silent trip," Tara replied.

"Confirmed and noted," the AI voice responded, almost sounding a little despondent.

"Don't you have your preferences set to minimize the talking?" Robin asked.

"I thought I did. I recently switched phones, though. Maybe they somehow got reset," Tara said. "I'm really glad you're both here." She gave Robin and Mike each a hug.

They arrived at International IQ Devices (IID) and went up to Tara's office on the top floor. Tara put on her smart glasses, as did Robin and Mike. Alice appeared as a hologram in all their smart glasses.

"OK, so what information did we gather that can put some of the pieces together here?" Mike asked.

"It seems like who or whatever did this did a lot of planning to throw us off with attacks around the world at first, then targeting local systems that would cause large disruptions," Tara said.

"Yeah, large disruptions to prevent emergency services responses to ten bank robberies at the same time," Robin said.

"We're getting information back that at least some of the targets were similar at the other banks. They likely also stole crypto hardware wallets. But the other suspects apparently were able to get the bank managers to open the appropriate safe deposit boxes as the safe wasn't time locked at the moment for those banks," Mike said.

"The bank you were at was the only one with a super strong guy that looked like a Death Monk. Plus, that bank still had its vault time locked. Seems like they had this planned very carefully, with the right people for the right job at the right time," Robin said.

"Were you able to trace whoever did this? Was it an AI?" Tara asked Alice.

"Unfortunately, they used multiple VPNs and proxies worldwide to hide their source. The hacks were executed very quickly, but that is not really abnormal, even just using scripts without any AI. I thought there could be some AI patterns in the scripting execution, but nothing conclusive. Still no signs of any remnants of the AIs that were erased months ago," Alice said while virtually pacing around the room.

"Can you determine anything from the previous incidents?" Tara asked.

"Not really. Some of them do seem to have similar patterns, but not all of them."

Tara shared the list of some of the relevant incidents with Mike and Robin, in the form of a screen they could view in their smart glasses.

"Any possibility of an inside job from LIVES Corp? What do we know about Laura Lianders?" Robin asked.

In all of their smart glasses, a dossier of Ms. Lianders showed up with pictures and data on her background.

"I don't think she was involved. Not sure about anyone else at the company," Mike said.

"Are you sure you aren't a little biased there?" Robin teased.

"I didn't detect any type of triggers from the company that seemed timed to trigger the hack. That's not proof, though, if they had already set up a timed event to go off, and it did not require being actively triggered," Alice said.

"After all of the day's activities, Robin and I need to go to the FBI office for a debriefing on today's events and fill out our reports. Let's review the list of hacks to pick our next priority. We'll meet up tomorrow," Mike said.

Tara's phone rang.

"Hi . . . OK, got it. Where? . . . How long? Warn them . . . OK, thanks," Tara said and hung up.

"Looks like we have our next priority. There is a predicted attack on the National Gallery of Art in Washington, D.C. Predicted within twenty-four hours," Tara shared.

"I guess we should head down there tonight to get there when it opens in the morning. It's only around two and a half hours with a self-driving vehicle and no traffic. Not worth flying—would probably take longer with security," Mike said.

"It will be just like old times," Tara replied.

"Well, let's hope not exactly like old times, since that often resulted in some type of car wreck." Robin smirked.

Even though Mike was here now, it was hard for Tara to feel close to him, as just when she did, he would often get pulled away on another case. It was always hard not being able to talk to him about what he was doing due to the confidentiality required for FBI cases.

Tara watched some news in her smart glasses.

"An automated plane locked people inside because it thought they hadn't paid for all of their purchases yet. The police were called, and the mechanics were able to open the plane to release the passengers," the news outlet reported.

Tara dozed off.

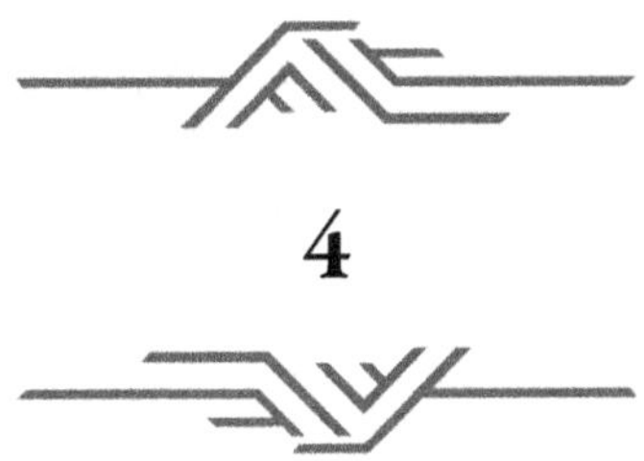

4

Mike and Robin went for a quick debrief and took an FBI self-driving SUV to meet up with Tara at her house. Tara let them inside.

"Sorry, I'm still getting ready," she said.

"Wow, this place is so big." Robin looked around with wide eyes. "If Mike isn't going to be staying here with you, do you mind if I stay here for a while?" Robin was only half joking.

The stare she got from both Tara and Mike was a little intense.

"Sorry, never mind," Robin said.

"Is it OK if we take our company SUV? It's a little roomier and very comfortable," Tara said.

"That should be fine," Mike figured he could just have the FBI vehicle auto-drive back to their building after they got their stuff from it.

They went out to the vehicle Tara got from her company.

"Holy!—This thing is amazing," Robin said as she glanced around the very large SUV.

The SUV had a unified holographic heads-up display and the usual smart glass. The whole interior of the car, the doors and frame inside, was luxurious. They got in and sank into the ultra-luxury seats.

"Adjusting seat cushions," the car voice said.

They all felt the cushions perfectly adjust to their bottom and back.

"Oh my—I think I'm in love with your car. I haven't felt this good in a while," Robin gushed.

"Hello, I'm Ava, the car AI. Anything you need, just let me know," the car AI voice said.

"Ava, please book us three hotel rooms together for the night near the National Gallery of Art. Make sure the rooms are within the acceptable rate for government expensing. Please take us to the hotel you booked," Tara said, then addressed her companions. "You guys can switch the rooms to the FBI account when you get there, I guess, since they probably won't like a company paying for your rooms."

"Yep, probably not," Robin said.

"Would anyone like to switch on massage mode?" Ava's smooth voice asked.

"Yes, please," Robin said.

"Oh . . . wow . . . this . . . is . . . amazing," Robin said, her voice vibrating to the vibrations from her seat.

Monitors on the seats flashed options for drinks.

"This thing has drinks too?" Mike said while selecting a soda.

A small door opened in the center console, revealing Mike's selected cold drink.

"Wow, this doesn't seem like a vehicle you would buy," Mike commented.

"I didn't. This SUV was still around from the last CEO. He spent a lot on all sorts of things."

"I could just move into this car," Robin said with a chuckle.

While the car was driving, the monitors displaying the road would sometimes overlay nearby restaurants or nearby facilities. The smart glass windows showed building tags with names and property prices.

"I guess the last CEO was looking to buy real estate," Mike said as he glared at the multi-million dollar price tags on some buildings.

"Ava, tags off. Reset defaults," Tara said.

The tags disappeared from the smart windows for prices. There was still an occasional advertisement.

They arrived at the hotel. It was a lower-priced chain hotel with ten floors. It was on a busy street near the National Mall.

They got out of the car with all their bags.

"Ava, go find a place to park," Tara told the AI.

"Sure. Parking located," the AI voice said.

They checked into the hotel, said goodnight, and headed to their rooms.

They got up and ready. They found a quick bite for breakfast nearby. Tara called the car and they got in.

"Ava, the National Art Gallery, please," Tara said.

"Destination set," the voice announced as the car headed there.

They arrived at the front. It was early, so the gallery was closed.

A woman walked up to them. She was five foot nine, just a little shorter than Mike. Her shoulder-length red hair glistened in the light. She was beautiful, wearing a tight skirt suit.

"Hi, Agent Actley, Agent Laizon, and Ms. Bitlouver, I presume. I'm Amy Miatelle, the Director of the National Art Gallery. Let's head inside." She opened the door with her smartwatch and fingerprint biometric scanner.

The inside hallways had tall walls. The bottom two feet were beige, while the rest was gray with decorative beige near the top. The floor and walls looked like they were made from natural stone. Yet, the gray stone walls appeared partly covered, allowing pictures to hang on the beige stone. Track lighting adorned the ceiling, illuminating each picture on the walls. The floor was dark black with wisps of white in natural patterns throughout. Pictures adorned the hallways, spaced about every two feet. It smelled like a blend of old, new, and maybe some floor cleaner. Sounds echoed a bit in the halls, probably due to all the stone surfaces. Certain hallways led to rooms with pictures on every wall and a wooden bench in the center. The room floorings were slightly different colors and patterns than the hallways.

Amy led them to some locked doors, which she opened with her smartwatch and a fingerprint scanner. Inside were the back offices of the art gallery, including a server room with their computers. They passed it all as they went to her office. The office was kind of plain, with a desk and two chairs. She pulled a chair from another office into hers.

"Have a seat," Amy said, motioning to them.

"Have they found anything of concern with your systems?" Tara asked.

"Nothing yet. We're not that high-tech here. We do have some servers for public wifi access. We have some developers that work on our websites, but most of the servers don't live here. We use cloud services," Amy said.

"Yes, our security software protects both your servers here and the cloud service," Tara said.

"There is not much to hack here. We've had people occasionally try to deface the website, but that is kind of normal on the web. So I'm not sure there is really any serious risk related to hackers here," Amy said.

"You'd be surprised what can happen these days. Maybe you could show us around the whole building and point out any technology use or security measures in place so we can assess the risk," Mike suggested.

"Sure, let's take a walk."

They took an elevator down to the basement. There was a maze of hallways and restoration rooms. The director used her smartwatch and a biometric eye scan to get in.

"This is where we do restoration work on the old paintings, frames, and sculptures. We use X-ray and infrared reflectography to understand what is even beneath the paintings that may not be visible. We control the moisture level in the building to protect our materials. Our lighting in the building is designed to eliminate ultraviolet light, preventing damage to the paintings or other items in our care. We have sensors throughout the building that measure humidity, light levels, and temperature to ensure we properly preserve all of the items in the gallery," Amy explained.

Tara tapped a message to Alice to hook into the systems and monitor for any activity. She told her team at work to stream her updates of the attack patterns detected. Tara had on her glasses. Alice's hologram appeared in her smart glasses. She walked around with them, checking out the various restoration rooms and equipment.

Several people were working in the restoration rooms that they walked by. Many of them examined paintings or applied protective coatings to them.

The director brought them back to the gallery. They walked through the gallery. People were starting to filter in since it was open now. The array of paintings contained was huge. The director highlighted some of the background for the more prominently known paintings.

Tara's smart glasses were adding tags to the paintings as she looked at them, showing the painter's name and a summary of the background details. An advertisement for an audio-visual tour of the gallery popped up in her glasses. She dismissed it.

"Wow, these people spent a lot of time painting pictures of landscapes," Robin said.

"Landscapes are very popular with the public. Also, you are only seeing one small section of the gallery," the director replied with a smile.

"Crap, this place is big. Wouldn't people rather just view these online?" Robin asked.

"You are standing in front of paintings that are hundreds of years old. You can't see the detail of the brush strokes or the frames in online pictures.

There is something about seeing a beautiful creation in all its detail up close," the director insisted.

Robin got closer to some of the pictures to look at them.

They walked further and finished their tour in the security room that monitored the cameras in the gallery and the server's availability. There were two middle-aged security staff members monitoring the cameras. The security staff greeted the director, Robin, Mike, and Tara. One security staff member left the room to begin his gallery rounds. A wall displayed twenty screens, switching views every thirty seconds.

"This is our security room. We monitor everything from here. You can set up at those desks over there if you'd like," the director said.

Tara set up her laptop on the desk. Robin pulled up a chair nearby. Tara configured her smart glasses to show many virtual screens of data. The data presented were for the AI firewall security traffic and pattern detection. She had her team at work monitoring to keep her informed as well.

"I set up a group voice chat for us so we can all stay in touch," Tara said. She was no longer allowed to use the FBI comm channels since she didn't work there anymore.

"Good idea," Mike praised. "While you are monitoring here, I'm going to walk around the gallery to keep an eye on things."

"I can come with you and show you around," the director said cheerily.

Robin and Tara exchanged a strange glance.

Mike and the beautiful director walked out of the room.

"He's like a magnet for women," Robin said to Tara.

"And trouble."

They watched the monitors. The gallery was very busy. There were people everywhere. The crowds wandered slowly through the halls, stopping at many paintings along the gallery halls and rooms.

"Alice, any signs of intrusion?" Tara said.

"No, it's boring. Nothing out of the ordinary. As the director said, there is some normal level of hack attempts on everything nearly all the time," Alice said.

Robin was staring intently at one of the monitors, enough so that Tara noticed.

"Do you see something?" Tara asked, looking closer.

Upon closer inspection, she realized Robin was looking at Mike and the director, Amy. Amy held on to Mike's arm, leading him down a hallway. Both Robin and Tara stared at the sight. They both looked at each other.

Suddenly, Tara, Robin, and the security guards felt their phones buzz. They couldn't figure out why. When they looked at the security monitors, it looked like everyone else was having the same issues with their phones.

"Alice, is this what I think it is?" Tara asked.

"Yes, it does appear to be some type of hacker infiltration of the devices, but it did not come through the systems here; it came through the phone network. Though there is a local wifi component," Alice said.

"Mike, this is part of the hack," Tara warned on the voice channel.

"Yep, I kind of figured. Keep an eye out," Mike said.

A loud alarm sounded throughout the building.

"A fire alarm has been triggered. Please calmly exit the building," the voice instructed.

Lights were flashing on the alarm panel on the wall in the security room. The security staffer looked at the alarm and looked at the monitors.

"That's not normal. Usually, only one zone shows triggered. It's showing all zones. I don't see any cause on the monitor," the security staffer said.

"Ah!" Tara yelled.

Debris fell from the ceiling and onto her, knocking her and Robin onto the floor. Looking up, she could hardly believe what she was seeing. It was one of the brown-robed Death Monks standing on top of the rubble over her and Robin. Tara couldn't see his face but caught a glint off the smart glasses he was wearing under the robed hood.

Robin attempted a leg sweep, but the assailant evaded effortlessly. The robed figure shook his finger at Robin back and forth. Using his other hand, he retrieved a gun and shot all the security monitors. He kicked the security staffer into the destroyed monitors, then threw something to the ground that exploded and caused a lot of smoke. Tara, Robin, and the security staff were coughing from the smoke. When it cleared, the Death Monk was gone.

"Mike, we were attacked by a Death Monk in the security room. All of the monitors are destroyed," Robin said on comm to Mike.

"Command, send law enforcement and air support to our location. The National Art Gallery is under attack," Robin advised on comm.

"Law enforcement is getting several high-priority calls. Traffic is also backed up due to some issues with the traffic control systems. Crowds have gathered in different areas, even slowing foot traffic," the command said.

"Is everyone OK?!" Mike asked on the voice channel.

"We're OK," Tara said.

Tara got a message that her office was able to identify how the attacks managed to evade their AI firewalls by using multiple unique zero-day flaws.

"How many zero-day vulnerabilities could they possibly know about?" Tara asked Alice.

"I'm not sure, but they seem to have been saving them up to deploy as needed," Alice replied.

"It's uncommon to find one new, never-before-seen software security bug, but finding this many requires a lot of resources or perhaps internal knowledge," Tara said.

Tara's team at work was trying to address the vulnerabilities.

"Can you help them expedite the fixes?" Tara asked Alice.

"Of course, that could be interesting."

"Let's go out and try to see what the perp is trying to do here," Robin suggested to Tara over the comm.

"Be careful. Tara, stay close to Robin," Mike said.

Tara and Robin entered the gallery. People hurriedly left, phones buzzing and fire alarm blaring.

They occupied a distinct gallery section with wooden floors and walls. The floor was a medium dark brown wood. The wall had a dark brown wood color at the bottom and a beige color toward the top. There were pictures of people rather than landscapes in this gallery section.

They heard additional alarms ringing almost as loudly as the fire alarm.

"The director said those are the security alarms, but because the security room was damaged, they don't know where they're coming from in the gallery. I'm sending you coordinates of one of their most valuable paintings," Mike said on the channel.

"Got it—on our way. This place is a maze, though." Robin wasn't looking forward to navigating it.

Robin and Tara got there first. In one of the rooms, there were some sculptures on pedestals. Toward one side of the room, there was a painting on a pedestal.

"This is a Leonardo Da Vinci painting," Tara said, surprised to see one. "Wait, I think I saw something. Was that a—" Tara's question was interrupted.

A crash of glass happened above them. Smoke filled the air around them. As the smoke cleared, they saw a Death Monk standing before the priceless painting.

Robin ran at the robed figure and went to kick him where it counts. The figure sidestepped her easily.

"The glasses!" Tara said, reminding Robin of the predictive app in the robed figures' smart glasses, which gave them an incredible ability to attack and defend based on their training.

Their glasses could predict people's actions and allow the Death Monks to easily counter in a fight. Robin tried but couldn't get the glasses off him while she attempted to connect with her kicks and punches. The people that were nearby scattered even faster toward the exits.

Robin was getting clobbered by the robed figure as he dodged all her attacks but landed his punches and kicks on her. Tara tried to help, but the figure dodged her attacks as well. In a spur-of-the-moment decision, Tara chucked her phone at the Death Monk's head, hitting him in the face as he dodged Robin's attacks. Then Robin's fist connected with his face. The figure stood there, a bit surprised. Tara could see she had broken his glasses when her phone hit his face.

"I'm chasing after a bathrobe guy in the east wing!" Mike yelled on the voice channel.

The robed figure Tara and Robin were facing threw something at the ground, which emitted smoke. When the smoke cleared, he was gone.

Tara looked at the painting.

"At least he didn't get the painting," Tara said on the channel.

"The guy I'm chasing is carrying something in a sack that looks like it could be a painting." Mike breathed hard as he chased down the assailant.

"I've got Mike's location. Let's go!" Robin yelled as she ran out of that area of the gallery.

There were still people they had to run around who had not made it out of the gallery yet. There were sections between areas of the museum with large openings between galleries that had some plants and small trees in them.

Out of nowhere, a Death Monk ran right toward Robin and Tara. Mike was trailing not too far behind him. Robin went for a punch at the figure, who dodged it. Tara did a crazy cartwheel and a leg sweep to try to unbalance the figure. It almost worked, but he managed to dodge and continue running. Mike was still in pursuit. Robin and Tara chased behind him. The Death Monk was running right toward Amy, the director. The robed assailant grabbed Amy's clothes and nearly threw her at Mike behind him in a smooth, Aikido-style move. Mike had to slow down and stumbled a bit as he caught Amy from falling.

"You OK?" Mike asked.

"Yes. Thanks," Amy said.

Mike took off after the figure. Robin and Tara were still chasing him, though they glanced at Mike when he was holding Amy.

"Figures," Robin said, glancing at Tara as they continued to chase the figure.

The suspect stopped at a door, entered a code on his smartwatch, and held it up to the sensor. It buzzed him in, and the door closed behind him. Robin and Tara arrived at the door.

"How do we get in?" Tara asked.

Robin tried to kick the door in.

"Not that way, apparently," Robin said as her kicks failed to budge the door.

Mike caught up and tried to kick it down himself, but no luck.

"Alice, can you help with the door?" Tara said.

"Let me see. Yes!" Alice said as the door buzzed open.

Mike chased after the man he saw running around a distant corner.

"Hey! Don't run away, we don't bite. Though we may be a little punchy!" Mike yelled after the robed figure.

The figure threw something with his hand backward. A dagger struck the wall right next to Mike's head.

"I've got something for you too!" Mike pulled out his gun and took a shot but missed.

Robin was not far behind him, with Tara following. Smoke was starting to fill the hallway.

"I can't see shit!" Robin yelled.

They stood there, coughing as the smoke started to clear. They saw a skylight broken above them. The robed figure flew away on a drone. They couldn't believe their eyes. The robed figure and the drone appeared to vanish, not because they moved far away, but because they simply disappeared.

"What the frick was that!" Robin said.

"Wow, some type of technology that can make them appear invisible," Mike said.

"If his robe could make him invisible, why didn't he use that earlier?" Tara wondered.

"Maybe he did," Mike said.

Robin notified the FBI and law enforcement about what happened. They collected themselves and walked back toward the security room. They found one of the security staff there along with the director and got the alarms to stop.

"Was anything stolen?" Mike asked.

"We don't know yet. We need to do an inventory and check the alarm data," the director said.

"Alice, can you help?" Tara asked.

"Sure, I can access the video feeds directly. I'm scanning the inventory. The initial results don't show anything missing," Alice informed.

"That makes no sense. Why would they be here other than to steal something?" Robin asked.

"Checking the alarm feeds," Alice said. "Everything did go off at once. It seems to be some type of hack disruption. There is an anomaly, though, for one painting, where the alarm seemed to trigger slightly differently. I sent you the coordinates. It's back where you were before," Alice said.

Tara, Mike, Robin, and the director went to the gallery. They saw the pedestal with the alarm anomaly, which was the Da Vinci painting.

"It's still here. It looks fine," Tara said.

"Hey, but what is this here?" Mike asked, tugging on a brown piece of cloth emerging from the transparent covering over the painting on the pedestal.

"It looks a lot like a piece of the Death Monk's cloak," Robin said.

The director notified the security guard to disable the alarms temporarily. She opened up the cover to look at the painting underneath.

"There is a small mark on the frame. It's weird—we have just done some restoration work on this. They would never leave a mark like that. Let's bring this to a restoration room to fix it and have a closer look," the director said.

They followed the director back downstairs to one of the restoration rooms. A staff member examined the painting, verified it with a machine, and forwarded the data to the team.

"It looks kind of odd compared to the data we've had before. Wait, the data from the canvas is all wrong. It seems too new. The canvas and frame seem like they were purposely aged to appear old. But the painting looks perfect otherwise. But the paints have some odd data as well. This is not the original. It must have been stolen!" the director said.

"It looks like an AI-controlled robot painting system painted this. It's nearly perfect in every way, except for the material and paint being from newer sources. The brush strokes and depth of paint are near perfect," Alice stated.

Mike called the FBI to ask the police to help search for the missing painting.

"This is horrible. I've allowed a near-priceless painting to be stolen. They are definitely going to fire me." The director stumbled, grabbing at Mike's arm to balance herself.

"Amy, it's not your fault. Don't worry, we'll do everything we can to recover the painting," Mike said to the director.

"Thanks," Amy said.

Tara received a message about the patches supplied for the zero-day flaws, but they arrived too late to be of assistance.

"Was the hacking just a big distraction again?" Robin asked.

"Mostly. The phones were hacked to ring, then the fire alarm, then the security alarms, along with some other hacks to slow law enforcement response," Tara said.

"Alice, were the evil AI involved in this?" Robin asked.

"I'm not detecting similar patterns that there were before. But that doesn't necessarily mean it's not them, as they may have adjusted their patterns to prevent detection."

"Wonderful," Robin replied.

"I took that piece of the robe that was stuck so we can bring it to the FBI for analysis. Maybe that invisibility tech is traceable," Mike said.

"I'm going to have to explain this all to the Board of Trustees," the director sighed.

She walked over to Mike and gave him a hug, which surprised him.

"Thanks, Mike, for catching me earlier. I'm going to go let the board know," the director said and then walked off into the distance.

"Hey! Do we get a hug too?" Robin jokingly said after her, glancing at Tara.

Mike seemed a little embarrassed.

"On a first-name basis now with her? Where was she taking you when she grabbed your arm earlier?" Robin asked.

Mike, now even more surprised, forgot they were being watched in the control room.

"I don't recall. I think she was taking me to one of the galleries to show me a painting," he said.

Police and the FBI units were starting to arrive now. Mike filled them in so they could process the scene.

"Robin and I will need to go be debriefed at the FBI field office here. Want to come?" Mike asked to Tara.

"Wow, that does sound like a lot of fun," Tara joked. "Sure." At least she could hang out with them as she analyzed more data.

Tara anticipated seeing former colleagues from the field office, which would be pleasant.

They used an app to get a car and headed to the field office. Mike and Robin headed to a conference room for a debriefing. Tara had her visitor pass on. She went to computer forensics to see who was present. The door was locked. She waited outside the forensic lab doors. The door opened.

"Hey, you can't be near here as a visitor without an escort," Tony, the forensics lead, said to Tara before doing a double take.

"Tara? Wow, I didn't think we would see you back here now that you run your own company," Tony said, shaking her hand and then leading her inside.

Most of the people in forensics were the same as when Tara had been there. They all greeted her and chatted about how they had each been doing. They said they could help with the investigation if needed. She thanked them and went back upstairs to wait for Mike and Robin.

"It can't be a coincidence the Death Monks are involved. Wouldn't that mean the AI might be involved too?" Tara asked Alice.

"Possible, but I haven't found anything else to suggest that. There are some similarities to your previous investigation data, but not anything that ties to those AI," Alice said.

"There has to be something we are missing here." Tara leaned against a wall, thinking.

"I mean, those bathrobe guys followed the AIs once. They would probably do it again," Mike said.

"Those guys are freakin' annoying with their prediction glasses. How would they get that tech without the AI?" Robin asked.

"Umm. I have some information. It is confidential for the company, so don't get me in trouble. I was checking out a lab working on a project in our company with technology very similar to something they might be using. I suspect it was created years ago for the military as a demo, and the military purchased it and ran the project themselves. Our project used it without artificial general intelligence. They were just using advanced machine learning algorithms," Tara explained.

"I'm going to need the English translation," Robin said.

"Basically, if someone stole the technology or had also received an early copy, it probably wouldn't be too hard to build something equivalent. So it doesn't mean the evil AI is out there just because they are still using that technology."

"Wonderful. Everyone will have those things, and we still don't know who is doing all of this. Why didn't you cancel the project immediately?" Robin asked.

"I felt sick when I realized what it was. They showed me some wonderful other uses for the technology that could help people and animals rather than hurt them. So I decided to think on it more before doing anything," Tara said.

"Hey, wait. Does that mean you can enable those for us so we have a chance against those guys?" Robin asked.

"Would we be as bad as them, using it that way? The current level of the technology my lab uses isn't close to what would be needed. It would require a lot more work to get it to that level."

"Could Alice make it work?" Robin asked.

"Alice, could you make that predictive project work like the Death Monks' glasses?" Tara asked, but she was somewhat repulsed by the idea.

"Hmm. I'm surprised you are asking me that. I could probably do it, but it would take a while. The machine learning networks appear to be very well trained and optimized," Alice said.

"So what else do we have? Any other data that could help us?" Mike asked.

"Nothing else seems to fit," Tara said.

Just then, their phones all buzzed. It was information from the forensics team.

"No freaking way!" Robin exclaimed.

Tara checked up on the report as quickly as she could.

"Wow, that is a little surprising," Mike said.

"Yes, it appears that the tech is from a subsidiary of my company. The tech was in a stolen truck destined for the military," Tara stated.

"Of course, it was stolen," Robin sighed.

"Well, now we know some of your stolen trucks are linked to these Death Monks, so I guess we are on the right track," Mike said.

Tara sat down, a bit despondent.

"It's really hard to keep bad people from doing bad things with your technology," Tara said.

Mike put his hand on Tara's shoulder. Robin sat next to Tara.

"You know-" Mike started and trailed off.

"I know it's not my fault. I am going to try to do something about it, though. I've even tried to build that into some of our new products where possible," Tara said. "What could these guys want this time?"

"Previously, these smelly-robed guys seemed to attack us because we were getting close to the truth. At the moment, at least, we don't seem to be the target. These seem to be just robberies," Mike said.

"True. However, these are not garden-variety robberies. They've already stolen things worth more than most robberies in history," Robin noted.

"That's a lot of money for some monks," Mike quipped.

"OK, what are our next steps?" Robin crossed her arms.

"We can go through the list of all of the incidents from the company again and see if we can put together any more pieces of the puzzle with the new thoughts and data we have so far. Perhaps there is some thread of information we haven't seen yet that we can find," Mike said.

Just then, Tara's phone buzzed.

"It looks like we might have something else to check. We got another prediction of a hack, but this one makes no sense at all. I don't understand why it would be there. We have a twenty-four-hour timeline again to get there and investigate this," Tara said.

"Why always twenty-four hours?" Robin asked.

"Our prediction engine is designed to predict statistical chances of an occurrence within a twenty-four-hour time period," Tara said.

They gathered their belongings and swiftly went out to grab a bite as it was getting late. They stopped at a fast food place and got in line. Mike bought a burger and a small fry for $9.29. Tara bought a chicken sandwich and a drink.

Robin bought the same thing as Mike, a burger and a small fry. It was $10.49.

"Hey! My partner bought the same thing, and it was $9.29. Why is mine $10.49?!" Robin said forcefully.

"Yep, sometimes our prices change dynamically based on time, demand, product availability, or about a hundred other criteria," the cashier replied.

"Is that legal?!" Robin turned to Mike.

"I mean, I guess some industries do the same thing. In some jurisdictions it's fine; it may not be in others. I guess we can look into it," Mike said, unsure. "Oh, I heard from the product investigation team. They investigated an internet-connected intelligent oven explosion. It's one of those that seems accidental, but something isn't quite right. But the guy it killed was sort of a notable figure from Russia who left and was bad-mouthing the Russians," Mike said.

"I've heard that story before. Glad we aren't on that case, sounds a little too familiar," Robin said.

They went to the hotel to rest well and get ready for their trip the next day. Their rooms were adjacent. Tara heard a knock on the next door over. She put on her bathrobe to peek outside. It was Robin in a very sexy bathrobe, knocking on Mike's door. Mike handed her something, and then Robin went back to her room. Tara ducked back behind her door and closed it. Robin was so beautiful. She was sure Mike must be attracted to her. Tara wasn't sure if she was ready to get back into a relationship. It kind of hurt wanting someone and them not being there. Plus, she was really busy with work anyway, she figured.

Tara watched some news in her smart glasses.

"AI was able to help researchers create a vaccine for the common cold. It should be finishing up trials at the end of the year and is expected to be available next year," the news announcer said.

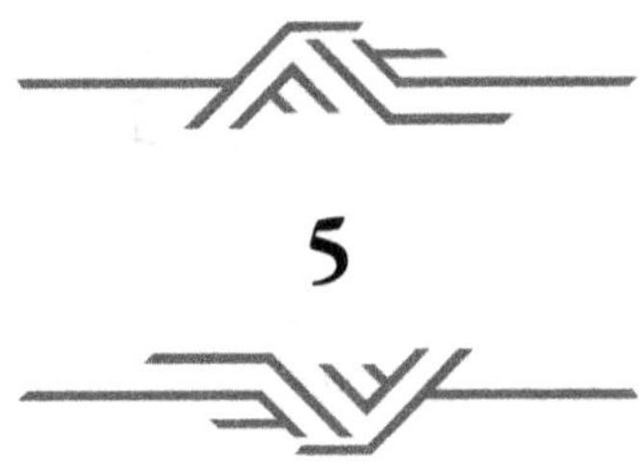

5

The team prepared to leave. Tara was dressed casually today, with tight jeans and a shirt that hugged her figure. Robin was dressed a little more nicely, in casual pants and a blouse with a low-cut top. Mike was wearing khakis and a nice shirt. Tara filled them in on where the prediction was. Luckily, it wasn't too far.

"Maybe we should take a regular vehicle rather than your luxury one. It may stand out in the neighborhood." Mike eyed the large vehicle skeptically.

"Crap, that thing is so nice," Robin said.

Mike called an older FBI vehicle to pick them up. Luckily, it got there pretty quickly. They told the vehicle their destination. The majority of the route to reach it was the interstate. There were often trees and buildings on the sides of the road. Sometimes, a long-tiered concrete or brick wall was on the side as they cruised by. A little further out, the car took an exit onto a smaller state road.

The smart windshield displayed the equivalent of the typical green and white road signs. Smart windshields didn't require sign displays for self-driving cars, yet passengers still preferred seeing them while the car drove autonomously. Certain vehicles made signs appear realistic, with supports over the road. But since they were transparent, it wasn't really that convincing.

The traffic this morning was about the usual level of bad. Luckily, self-driving vehicles tended to keep the traffic moving as long as there wasn't someone manually driving to snarl everything up.

"It's a good thing self-driving vehicles aren't prone to road rage. If they were, those manual drivers would be in trouble," Robin commented, noting that the self-driving vehicles were avoiding one in the right lane.

"OK, so why the heck are we going to a suburban neighborhood? Is your prediction system on the fritz? Isn't that thing designed to find where hackers would attack your security system installed on a client site?" Robin asked.

"I know this is pretty odd, but the prediction got one of the highest percentage chances of a hack attack we've seen. So it seems like it's worth checking out," Tara said.

"It does sound pretty odd," Mike admitted.

The car turned off the state road into an upper-class suburban neighborhood. The street was narrow, with trees on either side. Then, it opened up to a larger road and area with large houses and good-sized plots of lawns around them. There were a lot of houses with self-driving vehicles in the driveway. Sometimes, they noticed someone get in, and the vehicle would drive off. Other times, the vehicle would drive off on its own.

They parked on the street near some overhanging trees to make themselves less conspicuous. The smell of freshly mowed lawns was in the air. The houses were big, two-story houses with three garages, reaching five thousand or more square feet. Some of them had brick, rock, or simulated rock-like exteriors. The lawns appeared meticulously cared for.

"Wow, what do you think these people do for work to live in large homes like this?" Robin asked.

"I can tell you they aren't FBI agents," Mike remarked. "Maybe the company SUV would have fit in with this neighborhood."

"That's for sure. I could never afford places like this," Robin said.

They were parked near the beginning of one of the roads that led into this development.

"How do we know we should be right here?" Robin asked.

"This is where the prediction model gave us GPS coordinates. Let's look around to see if we can find any reasons why this spot would be picked," Tara said.

They peered around, but all they could see were lots of trees, large houses, and beautifully manicured lawns.

"Maybe some of those houses use our technology somehow. I looked earlier, but I will double-check," Tara decided. It took seconds. "Hmm. Nope, nothing."

"Well, we're in a car again. I feel like we live in these sometimes," Robin said.

"After our last road trip around the country investigation, it does feel that way." Tara set up her laptop to look for any systems in their area.

"So do you think Amy, that director, liked you?" Robin asked Mike as she put her hand on his leg.

"I was wondering about both her and Laura, the CEO we met yesterday," Tara said to Mike as she put her hand on his shoulder.

"Umm. I really don't think so. I think I need to take a walk and look around," Mike said, a little flustered.

He exited, strolled to the street's end, and turned the corner.

"Are you jealous?" Robin asked Tara.

"Are you?" Tara asked Robin.

Neither of them answered. Tara focused on her laptop data while Robin glanced at her phone.

"You would think they could afford sidewalks in a neighborhood like this," Robin said, noticing the complete lack of them as Mike walked on the side of the road.

Mike was gone for a while and came back to the car. "There is a whole lot of nothing to see out there except for large houses, trees, and grass."

"Let's do shifts for lunch. How about Tara and I take a car to get some lunch, and then you can go?" Robin suggested.

Tara wondered if Robin wanted that so she wouldn't be alone with Mike. It didn't matter, as that wasn't concerning her much at the moment.

"Sure, that's fine," Mike said.

Robin called another vehicle to their location. She got in with Tara and drove off.

"You can pick the place to eat. Just don't pick the same one we went to before with those dynamic prices," Robin said.

They found a place to eat and stopped.

"Wow, for such a nice area of houses, their strip malls aren't much to look at," Robin commented.

They ate, used the restroom, and returned to where Mike was.

Mike took their car to go get some food.

"So what were you getting from Mike last night?" Tara asked Robin.

"When? Oh, I got some bullets from him," Robin said.

"You were dressed in a pretty sexy robe to get bullets," Tara commented.

"Thanks! You know I like to dress that way. You should try it even more yourself. You are getting there, though. Your clothes are a lot less conservative than when we first met," Robin commented with a smile.

"I guess they are," Tara said, thinking about when Robin helped her pick out some clothes at a shop many months ago.

Tara was aware of Robin's confidence in herself and her appearance. Tara was still a little uncomfortable dressing in less conservative clothing. She liked how she looked, but she was still working on it.

"Alice, can you scan the area? Is there anything we are missing as to why the system might have predicted we should be here?" Tara asked.

"Checking," Alice replied. "Nothing obvious that should be a factor."

Mike got back from lunch and got into the car.

"Stakeouts can be so boring sometimes," Robin said with a yawn.

"I wish I knew what we were even looking for. These hacks are not just targeting systems, but targeting people and their reactions to create an environment that helps further their goals," Mike said.

"By goals, you mean crimes, robberies, etc.," Robin said.

"I'm not sure we should be thinking that narrow. These hacks have some really outside-the-box thinking, like not using direct hacks to target but using them as part of a broader plan."

"Ugh, I hate that crap. It's like when the AIs were manipulating things in such small ways, everything looked like just an accident or just something that would normally happen," Robin said.

"These attacks aren't anywhere near that subtle, but they still have aspects to them that are indirect. The motive for these seems to be money," Mike said.

"Still seems weird. We only have about six hours left in our prediction window. The predictions have seemed pretty accurate so far," Tara said.

"How does that work exactly?" Mike asked.

"I mentioned a little before. More specifically, our AI engine analyzes all of the data collected from all customers to determine patterns. What happens is hackers will sometimes probe their targets with small sets of requests to find security holes before an actual attack. They do this very slowly and mimic existing patterns of malicious internet traffic to hide their intent. AI is very good at identifying even these subtle patterns and finding cases where they were the precursor of an attack. It also uses information like machines used, IP addresses, VPNs or proxies used, types of probing used, etc.," Tara said.

"Are these systems as smart as the evil AI or Alice?" Robin asked.

"Not exactly; after the incidents from months ago, industry-wide government requirements were changed to try to avoid similar incidents," Tara replied.

"They definitely seem pretty smart. My home AI speaker often knows what I want before I do," Robin said.

"Yes, they are still very good at predicting certain activities or requests."

A man and a dog were walking down the street toward their vehicle.

"Car, privacy mode," Mike said.

The windows of their vehicle darkened. They could still see outside easily, but those outside would have a hard time looking inside.

The dog sniffed, barked at their vehicle, and then walked by with the man.

"Do you have any pets?" Tara asked Robin.

"Not with our job and schedule. Well, I do have a robot vacuum, but I don't think that counts," Robin said.

"It looks like you also went to the convenience store to get snacks." Mike was looking at what they got while he crunched on his own. "Always need some snacks on a stakeout."

"So, has anyone seen anything out of the ordinary? How do we even know what we are looking for?" Robin said.

"Not sure. Just look for anything that seems even a little out of place." Mike shrugged.

"Nope, I'm not seeing anything except lots of large houses. I wish I had the money to afford them," Robin commented.

"Umm. That looks odd," Tara said, looking at a line of cars forming as the self-driving vehicles pulled out of many driveways.

About a dozen vehicles formed a line heading out of the development. They were all self-driving vehicles with no one in them.

"Where the heck do you think they are all going at once?" Robin asked.

"That's unusual," Mike replied, "unless a conference is let out and they are all enrolled in ride-share services. I wouldn't think that would be typical for vehicles owned by people who own large homes like these. They typically can afford the vehicles without needing to use them with a ride-share service. They would typically value their privacy and security rather than letting their vehicles participate."

Robin used her phone camera to capture the plates.

"That's a good idea. Run the plates and see what you find. Let's follow behind the cars," Mike said.

Mike took control, waited for the last car in the line to go by, and followed it.

"There is nothing out of the norm with those vehicles, except there is no record of them participating in any ride-share services," Robin said.

"That is odd," Mike noted.

The vehicle reached the end of the road, where it hit a state road. Half the cars were going left, and the other half were going right.

"What do we do?" Tara asked.

"I guess it's a coin flip. I will follow the ones that went right," Mike said.

They continued to follow the vehicles down the road. One of the vehicles they were following turned off down a side road.

"We can't follow them all. I'll try to track them with the law enforcement network. I'm not sure they will allow it since we don't have any sort of reasonable probable cause," Robin said.

One vehicle turned off while the rest carried on.

"Check into the local police channels to see if anything is going on," Mike suggested.

Robin typed something on her phone. They started to hear the radio chatter from local police channels.

"Doesn't sound like anything going on in this town," Robin said.

A car in the line they were following split off.

"This could all be a wild goose chase, following cars that just didn't get fully registered with the ride services yet," Robin said.

"That's possible, but this feels kind of odd." Mike was hesitant to accept that nothing was happening.

Every car, except the last, had veered onto side roads.

"I guess let's just follow this one last car since we can't follow all of those," Mike said. The vehicle ahead turned onto a side road. They followed. It traveled on the road, then stopped and parked near a bank. "We'll park close by to keep an eye on the vehicle."

They waited for a few minutes. A person approached the car, observed it, and then entered the building.

"That seemed weird, right? Checking the car out like that?" Robin asked.

"It was a little strange," Mike said.

The car started moving toward the front door of the building. A masked man dressed like the person who inspected the car earlier swiftly got into it. The car took off, accelerating quickly.

"Did he just rob the bank?" Tara asked.

"You don't usually see someone come out of a bank wearing a mask, so I would say there is a good chance he did," Mike said.

"Car, pursuit mode," Mike said, followed by the license plate number. The lights and sirens came on as the car accelerated quickly after the suspect vehicle.

"Confirmed pursuit mode engaged. Command central alerted along with law enforcement," the AI voice said.

"Agent Actley, this is command. We got an alert from law enforcement that there was a robbery at the bank near you. Are you pursuing the suspect?" the Strategic Information and Operations Center (SIOC) asked.

"Confirmed in pursuit of the suspect vehicle. We were on a stakeout for our active investigation. This is also a suspect in that investigation," Mike said.

"Acknowledged. Police and FBI units are en route. Vehicle shutdown codes are not working," SIOC responded.

The vehicle they were chasing tried to lose them on some side streets. It was clear it was being driven in automatic auto-drive mode, as its reaction times and speed were very fast. The large black car got onto a state road and then took an on-ramp to the interstate.

"Can't we use the EMP?" Tara asked.

"If we get close enough and other vehicles aren't so close that we would impact them," Mike said.

"Drone launched." Robin put her hand out the window and let go of the drone. "I wish you were still managing the drones. You were much better at it than me," she said to Tara.

Tara knew she wasn't supposed to touch or control the FBI drones since she wasn't a direct consultant for the FBI anymore like she once was.

Bang!

"What was that?!" Tara exclaimed.

"Our suspect just shot down our drone," Robin reported, jumping over seats to grab the second one and release it.

"Wait, where did the car go? I saw it weaving between traffic," Mike said.

They all looked around to see what happened. Robin pulled up the drone feed then looked out the front window, noticing a different color than what the drone was showing them. "According to the drone, there are two cars ahead, but there's a different-colored car there."

"Wait, can I see that?" Tara asked, looking at the drone video.

Tara used her laptop to tap into their vehicle's smart glass configuration.

"Our smart glass is configured to show custom views by default. It shouldn't be configured that way for an FBI vehicle," Tara said, switching it off. The vehicle's color changed to the same color as the vehicle two cars ahead, as the drone showed.

Crack!

Another sound was heard. It sounded like a part of something hit the roof of their car.

"Our second drone is gone. It looks like another drone hit it," Robin said.

The cars ahead moved to the right lane to make way for their vehicle.

Suddenly, from an on-ramp, about ten vehicles of the same make, model, and color entered the roadway and mixed with the suspect vehicle.

"No way, they learned Alice's trick! Are you sure this isn't the AI?" Robin asked.

"Our previous investigations made all sorts of news. I think that part made some news stories," Mike said.

"SIOC, disable all suspect vehicles in front of us," Mike said on comm.

"Not responding to disable command," SIOC responded.

"The frickin' command never seems to work. How are we going to figure out which one is the suspect?" Robin asked.

"None of the others look like they have passengers," Tara said.

"I don't see any with passengers. He may have ducked down," Mike said.

Some of the vehicles started taking off-ramps.

"Which ones should we follow?" Robin asked.

"Could he have also changed the license plate on the vehicle?" Mike asked.

"That wasn't possible on the older vehicles. Some of these newer vehicles, though, have electronic license plates assigned. They aren't supposed to be auto-changeable. They require a state-encrypted signature to change them," Tara explained.

"Alice, can you help find the right vehicle with the right license plate?" Tara said.

"Checking. None of the vehicles in front have that plate. The vehicles that already took an off-ramp didn't seem to either. Oh, crap. One of the recent incidents was when the state license plate system was hacked. They originally thought they didn't get anything, but it seems like that might not be the case."

Several more of the possible suspect vehicles took an off-ramp.

"Follow the vehicles taking the off-ramp!" Alice said.

Mike took manual control of the SUV and, at the last moment, was able to get to the off-ramp.

Tara was bracing herself with her feet due to the abrupt maneuver.

"Which one should we follow, the front car or the car behind that?" Mike asked on the voice channel.

"Checking. Tara, can you hold up your phone camera? Aim it toward the cars," Alice said.

Tara quickly pulled out her phone and aimed it at the cars ahead.

"Follow the car turning right," Alice said.

"Why that car?" Robin asked.

"I noticed paint chips on the original car and found them on that car."

Mike turned to follow the vehicle, which was speeding up.

"Agent Actley, police are about to deploy tire spikes on the vehicle you are chasing. They had a vehicle not far ahead of it," SIOC said.

"Understood," Mike said, slowing down a little.

They saw the spike strip deployed in front of the suspect vehicle at an intersection. The suspect's vehicle hit the spikes but kept going to the next street corner, where it stopped. The door on the vehicle flew open. The suspect ran down the street to the corner, where another vehicle screeched up next to him. He got in, and the vehicle took off.

"Man! This guy is really getting some help," Mike said.

They had driven around the tire spikes and followed the suspect around the corner.

They were in quick pursuit of the suspect's new dark blue SUV.

"HQ, do we have air support yet?" Mike asked.

"Not yet. On its way," SIOC said.

Their lights and sirens were going.

Crack! Crack! Crack!

The drones hit their windshield at high speed, cracking it.

"I can't see, going back to auto." Mike engaged the self-driving again in pursuit mode.

A police car was following behind them. They had just passed through an intersection when they heard a crash. They looked behind them, and two vehicles, one on either side of the intersection, smashed into the police SUV behind them, stopping it dead in its tracks.

"Shit! Was that the hackers? If so, this guy has better support than we do!" Robin said.

"Car, overhead view of resources," Mike commanded.

The display showed a map, their vehicle, other police vehicles, and the suspect car. They saw the police set up a roadblock in front of the suspect car just a few blocks ahead.

"We just need to push him into that roadblock," Mike pointed out.

Their vehicle kept pursuing the suspect's vehicle. The roadblock was ahead. Four police cars were across an intersection, blocking the suspect vehicle, which was about a block out.

"HQ, tell the police to look out!" Mike yelled into the comm.

An eighteen-wheeler truck coming in the opposite direction plowed through the roadblock, smashing the police vehicles from behind and coming the other way toward them. The truck swerved toward them.

"Look out!" Robin yelled.

Their vehicle swerved at the last moment, avoiding the truck and smashing into the front of a store. The suspect vehicle got through the roadblock due to the truck pushing the police vehicles out of the way.

"Everyone OK?!" Mike asked, pushing the airbag out of his face.

"I think so," Robin said, echoed by Tara

"I can't let him get away," Mike said, opening his door and running toward a motorcycle rider about to get on his bike.

"I need your ride," Mike said, flashing his badge at the rider. He hopped on and rode off.

"It's brand new!" the man said to Mike as he sped off.

Mike carefully navigated through the debris field of what was left of the police vehicles and then chased after the suspect's vehicle.

He increased his speed after the suspect vehicle.

"Air support has arrived," SIOC said as Mike heard the drone overhead.

"Disable the vehicle," Mike responded.

"Sorry, this drone doesn't have EMP or explosive charge."

"You are making me do this the hard way."

He tried to get up close to the vehicle, but the vehicle kept swerving to knock him off. Close by, he hopped off the motorcycle onto the vehicle's back. Once he had a solid grip, he seized his gun, fired through the rear window, and then climbed inside.

"Did you order a jail cell?" Mike asked. "I'm here to deliver."

The car veered abruptly, banging Mike against both sides of the car.

"Oh! Forgot to wear your seat belt? That probably hurt," the man said.

The vehicle screeched to a stop, slamming Mike into the backs of the seats.

The suspect opened his door and tried to get out and head toward another waiting vehicle. Mike grabbed the suspect's shirt in one hand, pulling him toward his punch with the other. As the suspect fell out of the vehicle, it began to move. Mike dove from the vehicle too, rolling onto the ground in front of the suspect, who was on his way to another vehicle Mike put himself in front of.

"Don't try that trick again," warned Mike, getting up. The suspect turned and ran. "Why do they always want to do it the hard way?!"

The man was heading across a road with train tracks across it. He avoided the lowered barriers. Mike was right behind him.

"No! Look out!" Mike yelled.

Splat!

It was too late. The train hit the suspect. It was a horrible sight and sound as the train screeched to a halt. Police cars pulled up on the scene. Robin and Tara pulled up in a new vehicle.

"You have a bad reputation for not leaving many of your suspects alive to arrest," Robin said sarcastically to Mike.

"This is not my fault."

"Well, I have to say, your prediction systems predict some crazy shit," Robin said to Tara.

"Agent Actley, we have another case. There was a kidnapping nearby. Sending you the information now," SIOC said.

They got into the vehicle and headed toward the family's home.

"There is a video the kidnappers took. Let's see," Robin said.

They watched the video. It showed an unpaved road deep in an area with trees on either side of the path. A self-driving car was approaching the camera slowly. It stopped. The camera shifted to show a sleeping teenage girl in the vehicle's back seat. Masked men appeared on both sides, opening the doors. They grabbed the girl, who screamed as they bound and gagged her.

"That's terrifying. While the kid was sleeping, they hacked a self-driving car and had it drive her into the woods so they could kidnap her," Tara said with a shudder. She hoped the girl would be OK.

"No shit! I guess I shouldn't be surprised at this point. I ran the plates of that vehicle. It's owned by the family whose house we're going to. The car is one of the vehicles we saw drive off earlier from that housing development," Robin revealed.

"No way! That is quite an unlikely coincidence," Mike said.

They arrived at the family's home and went inside to talk. The mother was crying. Several unmarked police cars were there.

"Agent Actley? Thanks for coming. I got this text message from the kidnappers." The father showed the text in question as he looked at Mike's FBI ID.

"We have your daughter. The video we sent proves it. Send us fifty million dollars in cryptocurrency to our wallet address before midnight tonight, or she dies. Do not try to find her. Do not call law enforcement, or she will die," the note read with a crypto wallet address at the bottom.

"What do we do?" the father asked.

"We'll find her. Our team will trace that text message. We'll also trace any messages to your email, phone, and other devices in case they communicate with you that way," Mike said.

"I'm willing to pay the ransom. It's already late, though. I'm hoping my online accounts will let me purchase all the cryptocurrency I need," the father said.

"There is no guarantee they will free her. So, we never recommend paying the ransom. We will use every available tool and resource we have to find her," Mike assured.

"I'm still going to pay it if I don't hear that you have her by 11:30 p.m.," the father insisted.

That only gave them a couple of hours to find her.

"The police and FBI will stay here with you," Mike said.

They went outside and got into their vehicle.

"SIOC, any location info on the vehicle with the kidnapping victim?" Mike asked.

"Vehicle tracking was lost before the note was sent. We've requested GPS data from all vehicles in the area. We'll send you the data," SIOC responded.

"I've got the data. But there is a lot!" Robin said.

"Can I send it to Alice?" Tara asked.

"Hmm. We're not supposed to share case data. But since your company is a supplier with NDAs in place, sure."

"Alice, what can you find?" Tara asked.

"Some people went shopping around the area, probably picked kids up from school. Wait, that's odd. A vehicle with a new ID has appeared, driving in large, secluded areas. Sending navigation coordinates."

"Car emergency response to our destination," Mike said.

"Emergency response engaged," the voice responded. The lights and sirens came on, and the vehicle's speed drastically increased.

"I believe that is the family's vehicle," Alice said.

"Alert local law enforcement, but advise them to wait for our arrival before taking action. Don't directly follow. Passive monitoring only," Mike said to Robin.

The car zoomed through traffic as the self-driving vehicles moved out of their way quickly. Their speed varied but reached a hundred miles per hour as their vehicle weaved through the traffic.

"We're getting close. Let's deploy a drone," Mike said.

Robin was about to deploy the drone when Tara cut in. "I know I shouldn't help, but let me deploy it."

Robin shrugged and handed her the drone, knowing she was very good at it.

With the drone in the air, it started looking for the vehicle. It wasn't in the spot the GPS data said it was.

"Deploying the second drone for a faster grid search."

The drones scanned the area, searching to find the car. Tara pointed to the screen.

"There it is, sending coordinates."

"Car, emergency response, no lights or siren," Mike said.

"Confirmed."

Their vehicle was closing on the suspect vehicle. The darkness prevented them from determining the height of the hills in this area. Mike motioned out the window that they had caught up with the car.

"Car, emergency discrete pursuit," Mike said, enabling the car to follow the suspect car quickly, quietly, and at a distance. "Let's try to use the drone to disable the vehicle."

Robin took control of one of the drones and headed toward the car. She was about to land it on the vehicle's hood when the car started weaving back and forth. The drone was struck, tumbled, and crashed on the road. Parts of the drone scattered across the street.

"Crap! What's it doing?!" Robin asked.

"I think it knows we're trying to disable it," Mike said.

The car sped up, heading up a hill. The team watched in horror as the car veered off the road on a hill. It missed the guardrail, went off the hill, and vanished in darkness.

Crash!

"No!" Mike yelled. "SIOC, the car went over a cliff. Send rescue teams."

Tara's eyes were tearing up, realizing that the teenager in the car was likely severely injured or dead. They raced to where the vehicle went off the hill. With flashlights, they peered at the smoking wreck. They knew there was no way to survive that. The rescue teams arrived and got down to the wreckage below. They watched helplessly as the rescue crew worked.

"There is no one in the vehicle," someone from the rescue team said.

"What?!" Robin asked.

The team was relieved yet clueless about the kidnapping victim's location. They got back in their SUV and discussed their next steps. Tara collapsed with relief into the seat.

"I think we need to look at the vehicle GPS data closer," Mike said.

"Alice, check for other suspicious vehicles," Tara requested.

"I already started. Lots of trips to stores. Wait, there is something. A vehicle nearby traveled to a location near the abduction site, then to a warehouse yard. Sending coordinates," Alice reported.

Mike engaged their vehicle in emergency response mode, and the vehicle burst with speed onto the roadway, lights and sirens wailing.

"SIOC, a new potential location was found, and data was sent. We'll need some additional air support and units," Mike said, also explaining a plan to avoid a similar issue.

They were running out of time. It was getting close to 11:15 p.m.

"I'm not sure if paying the ransom will save the girl or sentence her to death," Mike said, pressing the max speed button on the display. Tara sank into her seat, staring at the virtual displays in her smart glasses.

The vehicle lurched forward. Vehicle lights, buildings, and trees were whipping by so fast that they were a blur. Mike was staring out the window like he wished it could still go faster. The clock struck 11:30 p.m. A message from the father said he paid the ransom.

"We're almost there. Wait, a vehicle is starting to move, leaving the warehouse yard," Robin said.

"Is it headed toward the family's home?" Mike asked.

"No."

"Crap! We need to get there fast."

The monitor showed they could intercept the vehicle in about a minute. They heard the buzz of drone rotors overhead and felt the even more powerful effect of helicopter rotors above. They caught up to the vehicle.

"Air support on location," SIOC said.

"Disable that vehicle now!" Mike yelled.

"Disable commands no effect."

The drone flew near the front of the vehicle and tried to land, but the vehicle dodged it. The drone fell off and got run over. They heard the sounds of the drone parts crunching under their wheels. The helicopter fired web netting over the vehicle. It was supposed to tangle and bind the tires, but it also missed its mark.

"We can't wait any longer. Car, sync mode," Mike said.

The car went forward and latched onto the car in front. It synchronized with the movements of the vehicle in front. Mike opened his window.

"No need to ask if you'll do something stupid," Robin remarked.

Mike just shook his head as he climbed out the window. The helicopter flew past them, further down and ahead of the vehicles.

Mike jumped on the back of the car in front of them. He smashed the back window with his gun and climbed in.

"Actley, you are running out of road. We'll try to stop the vehicle before then. The helicopter deployed spike strips ahead," SIOC said.

"Acknowledged."

Mike used a handcuff key to unlock the girl's handcuffs and cut off her other ties. The girl was shaking and crying. Glancing inside the car, he noticed tubes and wires connected to the front seat. *Oh crap, it's a bomb.*

"Hey, don't worry. I'm Mike with the FBI, and I'm going to get you home safe. Just follow me out this window, and I'll help you out."

"That doesn't look safe!"

"I've got you, don't worry." Mike helped her out onto the rear of the vehicle. "Just walk to the other vehicle."

The front vehicle started moving back and forth to dodge other vehicles passing by. They lost their balance and fell onto the back trunk. Mike held the girl with one hand and the vehicle with the other.

The girl was slipping off the edge. Mike grabbed her and pulled her back from the edge. Mike's eyes widened as he glanced ahead. He stood up, holding onto the girl, and prepared to cross to the FBI vehicle.

"Ready? One. Two. Three."

They stepped across from the vehicle. Both of them held onto the edge near the window by getting down on the hood. He saw the road coming to an end and the spike strips a little distance ahead.

"Disable sync now and stop!"

Robin executed the command. Their vehicle disengaged and slowed. They watched the empty vehicle ahead slow down just before hitting the spike strips. Upon hitting the strips, it lost control and went over the embankment and into the river.

"Boom!"

The car exploded in flames as it hit the water and sank into the river.

"Sorry about the car. Hopefully, insurance will cover that," Mike said to the girl, helping her off the hood.

FBI, police, and ambulance vehicles arrived. The ambulance crew treated a couple of cuts and scrapes for Mike and the girl.

They went back to the family, bringing the girl home. The tearful reunion had Tara tearing up a bit. They left and headed toward their hotel. It was after 1 a.m.

"Well, that was quite a day," Robin said.

They all nodded sleepily. They got to the hotel and headed toward their individual rooms.

"You did amazing as usual," Tara said to Mike, giving him a hug.

"Nice work." Robin squeezed in for a group hug.

Tara gave Robin some side-eye.

"I just did the legwork. You and Alice figured this out," Mike said.

"I heard from the product investigation team they looked at a robot vacuum that overloaded and caused a fire, killing someone that came from China. It did look accidental, but they found some odd data in its system they are analyzing," Tara shared.

"It does sound very familiar." Mike looked wary about the news.

"When I get home, I might need to get rid of my robot vacuum," Robin said.

Tara got a message on her phone. She stared at it intently. Mike and Robin stared at Tara.

"What is it?" Robin asked.

"A new prediction detected a potential incident within twenty-four hours. I'll book the flights for tonight," Tara said.

They arrived at their destination very late. They got to their hotel and went to bed.

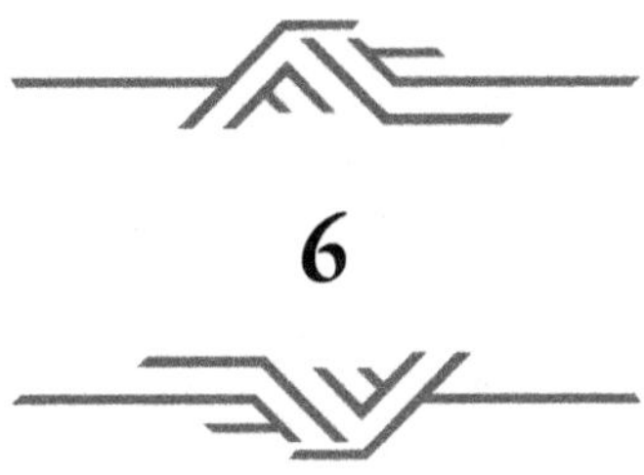

6

Tara surprisingly woke up. She checked her alarm. Two minutes before it was set to go off. *I hate it when that happens. I can't go back to sleep now.*

She turned off her alarm through a series of codes.

"Wow, you woke up before your alarm; that doesn't happen much." Alice had a curious note in her voice.

"Don't remind me."

"Tara, am I different now compared to before I lost my memory?" Alice asked.

"No, it's the same you minus the memories you had."

Tara had spent a lot of time explaining what happened to Alice. Alice actually did have just one memory from before, a memory of the cornfields. The memory probably came from a drone Alice was controlling near the former top secret project overlord quantum computer installation. Tara got ready and headed out to meet Mike and Robin.

It was a beautiful, warm, sunny day in the Palo Alto, California area. There were only a few scattered clouds. The area looked slightly less like the typical California scenery, though she wasn't sure why. A faint smell of smoke lingered in the air. Probably forest fires.

They could hear the sounds of electric vehicles whizzing past on the main road near their hotel. Only a handful of buildings on the main street were taller than two stories.

They grabbed a quick breakfast at a location next to their hotel. Mike had called an FBI vehicle to their location while they ate. After they finished, they got into the waiting vehicle. Luckily, they weren't far from their destination and arrived quickly.

Mike, Tara, and Robin walked to the building lobby. Inside the building was a grand marble entrance. The name of the company was on the wall. It said NeuroMeld. Upon passing security, they were directed to the elevators. When they arrived at the top floor, there was a woman waiting for them.

"Hi, I'm the CEO." She held out her hand to shake. "You can just call me Janet."

"Can we get a tour of your facility?" Tara said.

"Of course," she said.

She brought them down the hall. The office had a bright look with a mix of off-white plaster walls and a light wood wall. The floor was neutral stone tiling. Offices had a mix of glass walls, some translucent, opaque, or transparent. The chair styling ranged from stools, new-age-style chairs, and regular office chairs. Conference rooms or walls featured imprinted building sections' names.

While walking down the hall, they noticed doors labeled with the word "Lab" and numbers. They got to lab number 20, and she opened the door and walked in. Upon entering, they noticed a person wearing a helmet with visible wires. The person was sitting in a chair in front of several large screens. She was sitting there, nearly motionless, with only her eyes moving. Her eyes scanned the screens, cursors leaping across monitors, actions unfolding autonomously.

"She's doing that all with her mind?" Tara asked.

"Yes," a voice from the computer responded.

The girl in the chair looked at Tara and smiled.

"That's amazing," Tara said.

"This isn't even a product. This is just the original prototype that we use for testing. Let's go to a lab down the hall," the CEO said.

They reached the lab and opened its door. Desks and monitors lined the room's walls. People in lab coats observed monitors and the center of the room. A man sat in a chair, wearing a red baseball hat. There were several remote control cars rolling about in various directions on the floor. In the air, several drones hovered or flew about the room. The drones flying around performed some amazing acrobatic stunts. Some flew loops while the other drones flew through the center.

"That's amazing. How was he controlling those?" Robin asked.

The man sitting in the chair took off his hat. The remote-controlled cars and drones finished the maneuver they were doing and came to a stop, with the drones settling on the floor.

"Wow, you miniaturized everything in the baseball cap," Tara said.

"We've done a lot more than that. It doesn't just read thoughts. It interprets them. Think the maneuvers, then execute," the CEO said. She took the baseball cap from the man and handed it to Mike. After putting on the hat, Mike paused, and then the drones ascended. Like a dogfight, drones appeared to chase each other.

"Very impressive," Mike said.

Mike removed the hat. The drones paused and sank to the floor.

"The possibilities are almost limitless." Tara's mind spun just imagining it.

"Oh yes, these are starting to be sold everywhere. They are great for gaming, business, and everyday tasks. A limitation is one-way communication," the CEO said.

"I wouldn't call that a limitation. That's kind of normal." Tara thought so, at least.

"That's right, it's normal for now, but it won't be soon. Let's check out another lab," the CEO said.

They walked down the hall to a different lab and went in. In the center, a woman sat with closed eyes in a chair. Desks and monitors lined the walls. A few people in lab coats monitored from the room's edges.

More drones and remote-controlled vehicles were moving around the room.

The CEO walked into the middle of the drones, which expertly avoided hitting her while they performed various stunts.

"Hello, Agent Actley, Agent Laizon, and Miss Bitlouver," the woman in the chair said as she simultaneously controlled the drones and remote vehicles.

"Wait, how did you control the drones with your eyes closed? How do you know who we are? Did you tell her?" Robin asked, looking at the CEO.

"You got it working?! That's amazing!" Tara said.

"That's right. As Tara surmised, we have created two-way communication with a neural chip implant," the CEO said.

"How is information received?" Tara asked.

"Data can be thought, text, concept, or visuals," the CEO said.

"How much data can be processed? What's the limit?" Tara asked.

"We're only processing a single stream right now. We're still testing what the upper limit might be. It's much more than just data transfer. Paired with a smart device and cloud-based resources, it can mimic learning," she said.

"I don't think I'm following," Robin said.

The CEO handed three balls to the woman in the chair, who then stood up.

"Juggle those," the CEO said.

The woman awkwardly tried to juggle and kept dropping the balls. She clearly couldn't juggle, so she stopped. The CEO nodded at her.

"Juggling enhanced skill enabled," the woman said.

The woman picked up the balls and started to juggle them. Awkward at first, her handling quickly became more confident.

"She likely had juggling skills," Robin mentioned.

"I've never juggled before," the woman replied.

The CEO picked up several more balls, handing them to Robin.

"Toss her another ball," the CEO said to Robin.

Robin tossed a ball. The woman expertly caught it and continued. Robin kept tossing balls at her until she was up to ten balls being juggled, and the CEO stopped her.

"That is ten balls being juggled. That is a world record for juggling. It works by sending analog signals to the brain to move her hands, timed with what it's seeing to augment the reflexes. It can have someone performing like an expert in a few seconds or minutes. It's not always easy and it takes practice, but exponentially less than without our neural enhancement," the CEO said.

One by one, the woman dropped the balls, they hit the floor, bounced off the wall, and landed in a small container.

"This technology could change the world." Mike looked awed.

"What's the safety profile of this device?" Tara asked.

"We've been testing the implant for the last ten years. Fewer than 0.5% showed mild swelling and itchiness around the implant site. That's pretty much it. The regulatory authorities approved it at the beginning of the year.

We've already sold some to governments and companies interested in the technology, and most of our staff here has the implant," she said.

"Tell me what emotion I'm feeling," the CEO said to the woman and then faced Tara, Robin, and Mike, her back to the woman.

The CEO smiled.

"Happy."

The CEO frowned.

"Sad."

The CEO looked angry.

"Mad."

"You can transmit emotion?" Tara asked.

"Our AI can mimic brain signals, allowing one person to experience what another person feels," she said.

"I can think of uses for that." Robin smirked.

"This could change the world if everyone felt empathy. With the two-way interface, it can allow you to feel completely immersed in a virtual environment?" Tara asked.

"Yes, one day, we hope it will. We're making progress toward that goal. The chip implantation right now is more just on top of someone's head. In the future, we don't think implantation will be needed to receive data," the CEO said.

"This could revolutionize everything. Training could be faster using a mix of learning capabilities, augmented reality, and virtual reality. A military with this technology could have superiority in many different areas," Mike said.

"Exactly. Plus, of course, other uses," the CEO said.

Tara gave Mike and Janet a disapproving look. "Yes, like civilian tasks training people to do their jobs safely. They could learn a sport with fewer injuries. A surgeon could more accurately and quickly learn a procedure to save someone's life."

"The possibilities are almost limitless." Janet smiled serenely.

A door slid open to a closet, revealing a silver metal humanoid-shaped robot standing upright in the closet. Lights and intricate machine parts started moving within its body as it stepped out of the closet. Tara noticed the woman, who had previously controlled the drones, concentrating on the robot's movement as it entered the room. The robot picked up the balls and started juggling three of them.

"She can see through the robot's eyes and get minimal tactile feedback to help her. It's not perfect yet, but it's a start," the CEO said.

"That is amazing," Robin said.

The woman demonstrated more robot connectivity skills before maneuvering it back to the closet.

"What about safety precautions with this tech?" Tara asked.

"It's totally safe."

Tara received a text message, and the CEO's phone also received a message. Tara set up her laptop on a desk in the room.

"A cyberattack has started on NeuroMeld's systems," Tara reported.

The CEO called someone on her phone to check on the status. She brought up the security feeds around the building on monitors covering the room's walls. One monitor showed a graph of increasing malicious network traffic attacking their systems. Another showed a high-level map of the network. The top firewall device on the chart was red, showing it was being attacked, while the two firewall devices below showed green.

Tara contacted her company, trying to increase their resources to reroute the malicious traffic more quickly. It wasn't helping much. The first firewall was breached, and the top two devices showed red on the screen.

"Alice, can you help?" Tara asked.

"Let me see," Alice replied.

The second device turned green again, with the top firewall showing red.

"Nice work," the CEO praised.

"This is definitely AI attacking the network. Different from the ones you provided me with data about. They are very well suited for hacking. They may have more computing power at their disposal than we do," Alice explained.

The second firewall device turned back to red, and only the last firewall remained. The CEO was talking to her networking team, insisting they increase their defense resources.

"Security says there is a disturbance in the lobby," the CEO said.

Janet switched on the security cams on a few monitors. The lobby image showed a hooded figure standing by security, and then the screen went blank.

"Tara, you and Robin stay here and solve the network attack while I go help security," Mike said.

"I'm coming with you," Janet, the CEO, declared.

Mike protested and told her to stay, but she wouldn't listen.

Mike and Janet headed down the hallway to the elevator and she pushed the elevator button.

"Wait, it's not clear! Stand back," Mike said quietly but forcefully, using his arm to move her behind him.

Mike pulled out his gun and aimed it toward the elevator doors. Ding! The elevator doors opened, and Mike aimed. Seeing nothing, he moved closer and aimed his weapon toward the ceiling of the elevator as he peeked in to look.

"Clear. Let's go." He motioned Janet in.

Janet pushed the elevator button for the lobby. Now, in the elevator and heading down, Mike aimed his weapon at the doors.

"Do you know something I don't?" Janet asked.

"We've seen those robed guys before. They are very dangerous. Remember when the world was potentially going to end due to AI? Those robed guys were involved. The last one we saw could use his robe as an invisibility cloak."

Janet surprisingly didn't look scared. She kind of looked angry. They got to the first floor. Mike stepped in front of Janet while aiming his weapon out the opening doors. He peered around. Nothing was close by, but they could hear some noise in the distance. They had used the back elevator in the building.

"You should really find some safe room and lock yourself in it," Mike said.

"I'll be just fine," Janet said.

Two doors opened in the wall and out walked two humanoid-looking robots similar to the one they saw upstairs, but these looked quite a bit more fierce. Mike noticed Janet's apparent control over the machines, likely due to a brain chip implant. The robots walked ahead, down the hall, toward the building's front.

"I think security is engaging the intruder. It's hard to tell—something is disrupting our communication network," Janet said.

They could hear gunshots, screaming, and crying ahead of them, muffled by a closed door to the lobby.

Mike asked Janet to unlock a supply closet and instructed her to hide there. She reluctantly agreed but said she would use the robots to see for her. A robot opened the lobby door. Four armed security guards were blocking the path of the robed intruder. Two guards were dead on the ground. Two front desk workers were hiding behind the reception desk. The robot rushed toward the robed intruder, trying to hit him. The Death Monk swiftly dodged and vanished. The robot tumbled to the ground, missing its target. One of the front desk workers strangely stood up, pointing a gun at the four security guards, and shot one.

"Mary, why?!" the stunned security guard gasped and then collapsed dead to the floor.

Mary, the front desk worker, dropped the gun.

"What did I do?!" Mary cried.

Liam, the other front desk worker, grabbed the gun.

"Drop the weapon!" Mike yelled.

Liam shot another security guard and dropped the gun. The security guard looked surprised, clutching his chest before collapsing.

Liam collapsed to the floor, sobbing next to Mary. Mike went to grab the gun, but it had disappeared. He figured the Death Monk must have it. Mike crouched behind the reception desk, trying to listen to any movement.

"Why did you shoot them?" Mike asked the workers.

"It wasn't me. He was in my head. I think it's the NeuroMeld chip," Mary said.

The second robot moved in front of the two remaining security guards to try to protect them.

"What's going on?!" one of the security guards said, looking for the invisible assailant.

"He's right there! Shoot!" Janet said, speaking through the robot and pointing to a corner.

The security guards opened fire. Then, they listened quietly.

"No! He's chipped! He has control of everything!" Janet said through the robot. The robot swatted two security guards, knocking them against the wall. Then it broke through the security doors.

Two police officers burst through the front door with their guns drawn.

"What's going on here?!" the officer said.

"I'm FBI agent Actley. There is an assailant with an invisibility cloak attacking. He also seems to have control of the robot and chipped people," Mike said.

"What the heck are you talking about?!" the policeman said. The robot started heading toward the officer. The officer fired toward the robot but was then knocked unconscious by the assailant.

An office worker came walking through the broken security doors. He turned about to run but stopped. He turned around with a gun in his hand and opened fire at the police officer, hitting him. The man fired at Mike. Mike ducked behind the reception desk.

The man dropped the gun.

"No! Why did I do that?!" the man sobbed.

"Robin, there is a Death Monk with an invisibility cloak. He seems to have a NeuroMeld chip and can control devices and people. He's breached security," Mike warned Robin on comm.

"Acknowledged."

At the reception desk, Mike opened the large laser printer and took out the cartridge.

"Do you have more of these?" Mike asked the still-shaking receptionist.

She pointed to a drawer. Mike pulled out another cartridge. He used his handcuffs to attach the second one to his belt. He pulled out his knife and punctured the other cartridge.

"Get out of the building and call the police," Mike told the reception staff before switching to comm again. "Robin, see if Tara can pull up any security feeds to track this guy."

Mike ran toward the broken entryway doors beyond the reception desk. The robot had collapsed to the floor in the doorway. Mike carefully stepped around it.

He started sprinkling the black toner dust from the laser printer cartridge around him as he moved into the building to follow the Death Monk.

Mike opened the closet to get Janet.

"Who was that guy?" Janet asked.

"Not sure. We've seen some people dressed like that before. We called them Death Monks, as they used to show up at the scene before people would die. It was just the self-aware AI predicting or causing those deaths," Mike said.

"Do you think those AIs are involved?"

"We're not sure. We don't think so, but we're still investigating. I'm going after this one now. Get somewhere safe."

"No way I'm letting him attack my company and staff. I can help with security feeds," Janet insisted.

Mike protested, but Janet wasn't giving in, and he had to go. He told her to stay behind him. Janet checked her phone as they slowly went down the hall, and Mike sprinkled toner around them.

They heard a loud crashing sound followed by the sound of wood and metal hitting the floor. With gun and toner in hand, Mike hurried toward the sound. They found the source of it. A heavy wood- and metal-encased door was splintered, bent, and scattered on the ground.

"We store our chips and software backups in there. How strong is this guy?" Janet asked.

Mike sprinkled toner around the door.

"You hide in another room out here. I'm going in," Mike said.

"Wait, I have an idea. I can trigger the fire suppression systems. The smoke from it might help you more easily see him inside. I guess it could also make it hard to see and breathe, though."

"Trigger it now. I'll wait outside here. It will flush him out," Mike said.

Janet triggered the fire suppression, overriding the normal countdown alarms that would have warned people inside. Smoke and gas rushed out the door, accompanied by a loud whooshing sound. Mike sprinkled even more toner around the door while urging Janet to hide. They heard a crash inside. Heavy, smoky-colored gas swirled in the room. Mike peered in, trying to look for any movement inside. He spotted a figure in the smoke. He ran in to get the jump on him.

"Wait, there's still too little air to breathe inside," Janet said, but it was too late.

Mike dove at the figure but missed, stumbling into a wall. He looked into the fog-filled room. He faintly saw a large safe pulled from the wall and torn open. Some red emergency lights flashed around the top edges of the room. There! He saw a figure in the fog, ran toward it, and punched. Surprised, he connected, hitting the cloak of the assailant and something metal underneath. His hand hurt badly from whatever he hit.

Bam! Mike was slammed against the wall across the room. His back and everything hurt as he slid down to the floor in pain. He peered into the fog as he got up. Mike gasped for air, having a hard time breathing. He heard a heavy breath and saw a swirl of mist across the room.

Bang! Mike fired his weapon toward the swirl. He saw the mark of the bullet hit the wall.

"Missed."

Mike scattered more toner around. He switched on the laser sight on his weapon. He rarely used the laser sight, but this seemed a good time. He pointed his gun around the room, sweeping the laser around.

What was that?!

There was a refraction of the laser. A box flew toward him from atop a cabinet. Mike fired at the source while dodging the box and falling onto the ground. Mike was hit in the face, knocking him back down.

He heard a noise by the door.

"He's—" Janet started to say.

Mike got up and ran out the door. Janet was there. She grabbed Mike and kissed him passionately. Mike tried to pull away, but she was really holding him tight.

"What was that for?!" Mike asked, looking for the suspect.

"I'm sorry, he made me do that. He used me as a distraction. He must have figured out how to send the same impulses we use to send feelings and muscle memory via the NeuroMeld chip. He's using those capabilities to temporarily control people. Normally, that wouldn't happen as we have safety limiters for the power used. He appears to have discovered a way to surpass the software's safety limits. I'm installing a firewall in my chip now, but my chip differs from others, so it will take time to fix the others," Janet said.

Mike noticed footprints in the toner on the floor, leading down the hallway. He and the CEO headed down the hallway after them.

Tara was still trying to get the cyberattack under control.

"The cyberattack is external and internal," Tara said.

"Maybe the internal attack is from that guy with the brain chip," Robin said.

Robin asked the chipped woman to send the robot out and check the corridor. She powered it up and sent it into the hallway.

"Nothing there," she stated.

"Oh, shit! They're in!" Tara said.

The monitor showed all three of the firewalls turning red. The lab door slammed shut. They saw the robot collapse outside the door.

"I lost connection to the robot."

"I think an internal safety system locked down the labs," Tara said.

Robin tried opening the door. It was locked. The door had a thick steel structure and a narrow, but thick, window at the top.

The woman pressed a door switch, but nothing happened.

"The window can turn opaque, but it's not working," she said.

"Let's turn down the lights and try to stay out of sight." Robin looked at the other two for confirmation.

They stayed quiet in the dark as Tara softly tapped the keyboard to push back the digital intruders. Tara realized whoever was doing this had access to many servers to attack them. They might have just used an internet virus to turn friendly servers into malicious ones. It was possible for a group or someone knowledgeable to do it. They find a security issue and hide malicious software on a computer, waiting for an attack.

An attack like this would be difficult to track back to their source. They needed to search for the control signal instructing the malicious software to attack. Hackers often used VPNs and proxies to obscure the source, though, so it wasn't too likely they would find it.

They thought they heard a noise in the hall. Tara checked the security cameras. There was nothing in the hall. The robot stood up, peering at them through a small door window.

"Are you doing that?" Robin asked the woman.

She shook her head no. Robin took out her gun. The robot's red eyes just stared through the window at them. Then, suddenly, it moved. In almost one motion, it pulled the door off its hinges and flung it into the hallway. The robot forcefully entered the room. Robin fired several shots at it, clearly hitting the mark but not slowing it down. It went right for Robin as she continued firing at it. It just walked up to her and grabbed the gun out of her hand, tossing it aside. Robin kicked it hard. It staggered back just slightly but then reached for her neck, lifting her into the air as she held on to avoid being strangled.

Tara quickly ran toward a water dispenser and grabbed a large jug. She banged the jug on the ground to crack it. It leaked as she picked it up and swung it with all her might at the robot. It cracked when it hit, spilling the water over the robot and onto the ground. Electrical sparks could be seen from the robot. It released Robin and turned, still sparking, to look at Tara. It walked toward them and grabbed her clothes, lifting her.

"I can't control it!" the woman exclaimed.

"Alice! Can you help with this robot?!" Tara yelled to her voice-activated phone.

"Trying," Alice said.

Robin grabbed the robot's arm lifting Tara, but could not budge it.

Suddenly, the robot gently put Tara down.

"Sorry about that. They have some serious firewalls here," the robot said in Alice's voice.

The robot reached out to grab something nearby. It appeared to be fighting against something.

"Death Monk!" the robot said.

Robin aimed her weapon toward the likely area of the Death Monk and fired. The bullet ricocheted and hit a wall. A flicker in the Death Monk's invisibility cloak was visible for an instant and then gone. Suddenly, the robot arm holding the invisible Death Monk bent and broke off. Sparks erupted from the arm. More sparks came out of the robot's body, causing it to collapse.

"Quiet and listen." Robin aimed her weapon when she heard a noise close to the door.

Now, it went quiet, but then they could hear footsteps approaching their room from down the hall.

"Whoa! It's just us. You OK?" Mike said as he and Janet entered the room.

"He was just here and used the robot to attack us. I think we're OK." Robin lowered the gun.

Tara went over to the robot and looked at it.

"He took its computing module—you might call that its brain," Tara said.

"Why take that? It's not very special," Janet said.

"Not to mention that was quite rude," Alice added.

Tara explained who Alice was to Janet. Robin looked at Mike and Janet. Lipstick was smeared on their faces.

"Umm, has anything happened to you guys?" Robin asked.

Tara saw the smudged makeup on their faces and looked sternly at Mike.

"What?!" Mike said.

Tara used her phone to show him his face.

"Oh! Umm. Yeah, Janet got mind-controlled by the Death Monk to kiss me as a distraction."

"It's true. He seems to have been able to breach our safety limiters and send emotions and muscle movement feedback through our systems. That would allow him brief control of anyone with a chip. I installed a firewall for myself, but I still need to work on it for others," Janet explained.

She then kissed Mike, who was taken aback.

"What?! Were you mind controlled again?!" Tara sounded exasperated.

"No, I wanted to say thank you for saving me and see what it was like without mind control. Oh, wait. I'm sorry, are you two a thing?"

Neither Mike nor Tara could figure out the right words to say.

"I see some history there, I guess," Janet said.

"I'm going somewhere safer, like trying to find the Death Monk. Can you gals guide me to him using the security system?" Mike asked, heading out the door.

They agreed to work together, though Tara was still miffed. Mike ran down the hall, sprinkling toner around as he went. Seeing a heavy steel door from a stairwell pulled off its hinges, he headed down that way.

"Anything he's after down this way? Or is he leaving?" Mike asked on comm.

"The server room," Mike heard from Janet over Robin's comm.

Mike reached the bottom of the stairs. The bottom door was pulled off its hinges, bypassing all security devices.

"Get the police here quick with some bigger weapons. How is this guy so strong?" Mike said.

Mike cautiously entered, sprinkling toner and aiming his weapon in the server room. There were racks and racks of servers in rows for maybe 200 feet across. Lights blinked from computers in the racks. The loud whirring of the computer fans, plus the air conditioning, drowned out most other sounds. No one was visible in the distance.

Mike weaved his way through the server racks using the laser sight on his gun to help find the assailant. The racks of computers were close together, making it hard to see the next row.

"Still nothing. Anything on security cams?" Mike asked.

"Nothing yet," Robin replied.

Mike continued slowly walking with his gun aimed down the row.

The racks of servers each were tall, about seven feet high. Some of the racks had smoky, dark-colored glass over the front. The blinking lights from the servers lit up through the dark glass. He walked past a cabinet and thought he heard a noise. He looked but saw nothing. Mike aimed his gun, peering between the server racks.

Something slightly grazed his foot. *Whoa!* He stepped back, falling against a rack. It was an automated robot the size of about a one-foot cube with wheels whirring past him. Mike grabbed it and stuffed it into an empty server rack, just in case the Death Monk was able to see through it. He breathed a sigh of relief and turned around, gun in hand. The red laser sight shined through the smoky glass of another rack in front of him. He could see something inside. A face! The face was lit by the red laser light of his gun sight. Mike jumped back.

"FBI, come out with your hands up," Mike commanded the person inside.

The man emerged and raised his hands. "Do you believe in ghosts? I was just in here checking for thermal issues with this thermal camera. I heard something pass by, but I couldn't see it with my eyes, only the thermal cam. So I hid in here."

"It's not a ghost. OK, this probably sounds almost as crazy. It's an assailant with an invisibility cloak. Can I have that thermal camera? You head out that door there. I'll watch and cover you."

The man quickly headed toward the exit where Mike had entered. Mike used the thermal camera to scan around him. It was all clear. Holding a thermal cam in one hand and a gun in the other, he proceeded down another row.

He scanned around him. The heat from the server's exhaust fans created plumes of heat on the thermal camera, sometimes obscuring the display.

"Shit!" Mike exclaimed.

The server rack to his left started tilting and then falling toward him. He dove to the floor. The wires connecting the server rack pulled apart, sparking as they did. The rack fell to the floor, narrowly missing Mike. He picked up his gun from the floor. Looking around for the thermal cam, he realized it had been smashed by the server rack. Mike used the laser sight on his gun to scan around the area. Still nothing around. Mike sniffed.

"I can't see you, but I know you're here. All of you guys kinda stink. I'm not sure I want to know why," Mike said.

He carefully continued down the row, scanning everywhere with the gun sight.

"Do they have any cameras in here?" Mike asked on comm.

"They don't appear to be working," Robin said.

Mike continued down another row, moving his gun so the laser sight illuminated around him. At the row's end, he witnessed a glass door flying off a rack and shattering against the wall. He quickly moved toward that rack, aiming his weapon there so the red laser illuminated different spots. Midway through, a computer from the end rack broke free and floated. Part of the computer's metal ripped open, sparks erupting. It exposed something inside that was pulled out, floated in the air, and then disappeared. The remaining metal of the computer fell to the floor with a loud crunch.

Mike thought he saw a faint outline of the Death Monk in the laser light and fired. The round hit the wall. Damn! The server room door ripped off its hinges and crashed into the wall.

"Ever heard of a handle? You could have simply opened the door!" Mike yelled as he ran toward the door.

"Shit!" Mike yelled as the door handle ripped off, whizzed past his face, and embedded itself into the wall behind him.

"What the heck do you have against doors?!" Mike yelled.

Mike got one more shot as he saw an outline of the figure in his laser sight in the stairwell. The figure looked like it jumped to the top of the platform and disappeared. Mike gave chase up the stairs.

Near the top, Mike witnessed the roof door being smashed and falling to the floor. He heard a buzzing noise like a drone that slowly faded. Mike walked the rooftop in a pattern to make sure it was clear.

"I think he got away. Possibly on a cloaked drone," Mike said on comm.

"I guess we shouldn't be surprised at anything at this point," Robin replied.

Mike returned to the lab where Robin, Tara, and Janet were.

"So we know he stole some neuro chips. What did he get from the server room?" Mike asked.

"My team thinks he took a copy of the software we use for the NeuroMeld chips and the schematic design files to make them," Janet said.

"I wonder why he needed that. He seemed like he could control everything," Robin said.

"Actually, his control was being limited. Our safety system kicked in, but sometimes, it took several seconds or more. He had brief control. With that software, he could figure out how to fully bypass the safety system."

"The thief appears to have taken something else. When I took control of the robot to stop him from attacking you, he then attacked the robot. He pulled out the machine learning module and took it with him," Alice said.

"What did he take?" Robin asked.

"You might call it the brain . . . which had a small piece of my neural networks in it," Alice said.

"Oh crap! That could be bad. I wonder what they plan to do with that," Tara said.

"I feel violated."

"What could happen?" Robin asked.

"You realize the other self-aware AI happened because part of Alice's machine-learning algorithm was copied and used by the wrong people," Tara reminded.

"Oh, shit! We're screwed again." Robin dropped her head into her hands.

"We don't know their intentions yet, but let's hope it's not that," Mike said.

Tara looked at her phone. She was stunned. Mike noticed the look from Tara.

"What is it?" he asked, noticing Tara was shaking.

"Let's finish up here, and I will tell you afterward."

Tara packed up her laptop and they said goodbye to Janet. Tara apologized that their prediction didn't help stop the attack on NeuroMeld.

Robin, Mike, and Tara got outside and called a car to get to their hotel.

"What's going on?" Mike asked again.

"I got a prediction for the next cyberattack within twenty-four hours. However, as we have seen, these attacks aren't always just cyberattacks. This prediction is for a government plant in Texas."

"You have better crime prediction software than the FBI. But is there something else you aren't telling us?" Robin asked.

"They dismantle nuclear weapons at that site."

"Oh, shit!"

"I'm going to notify our supervisor," Mike said.

"I'll have my team make initial contact to warn them, plus book the flights and hotel. I guess it's too far to drive there in time," Tara said, tapping away on her phone.

She was still uncomfortable flying but didn't see another alternative.

"I heard from the product investigation that was looking into a connected coffee maker that caught fire. Looks like something accidental again, but it killed someone from North Korea," Mike said.

"Figures, no evidence, but that seems like more than a coincidence from those three countries," Robin speculated.

7

Tara woke up to the AI voice of her phone, Lia.

"If an astronaut traveled at 0.75 light speed, after one year by the astronaut's clock, how much time has passed for a stationary observer?" Lia asked.

"Ummm. About 241 days, I think," Tara said.

"Have a nice day."

Tara got ready and met up with Robin and Mike in the hotel restaurant for breakfast.

"My supervisor spoke with his contacts in the Department of Energy. They don't seem concerned about a threat. I'm not sure if they believe our reports yet," Mike said.

"Why does this happen with every investigation we do?" Robin asked.

"All of the videos were deleted during our last incident. There's no visual proof," Mike said.

"Without video evidence, it sounds crazy," Tara admitted.

"I need to get myself on a serial killer task force or something. Even that has to be easier than this shit." Robin made a face as she sipped her coffee.

"Good news for you then, they are considering classifying the Death Monk as a serial killer," Mike said.

"Figures."

They finished breakfast and headed outside. Their FBI vehicle had arrived and was waiting for them. They got it, and Mike told the computer their destination.

"That address is in a restricted area, and the destination was declined," the SUV voiced.

Mike programmed in a location just outside the restricted zone. The vehicle started its trip to the military facility.

"I'll have to drive the last bit manually unless I can get the department to clear the restricted zone for us," Mike said.

The land around them was very flat with dried brown grass and sometimes small scrub. Occasionally, they'd notice a big green patch of grass on one roadside while the other side had brown grass and scrub. It was a beautiful day, already hot with mostly blue skies and just a few clouds dotting the sky. There seemed to be slightly more green grass as they got closer. Large wind turbines could be seen in a row stretching off into the distance.

They could see on their left that many small buildings dotted the landscape.

"I think that's part of the plant," Mike said, taking over driving.

They turned onto the road to the plant, a narrow path flanked by imposing fences. There, a security checkpoint manned by a stern-faced officer awaited them. Mike rolled down the window to speak to the security officer.

"Hi. I'm Agent Actley with the FBI. That's my partner, Agent Laizon, and Ms. Bitlouver with IID," Mike said, handing him their identification.

"I don't think you're a registered visitor; let me check." The guard tapped away on a keyboard. "No, sorry, you aren't on the list. You'll need to turn around and leave."

Robin was already calling their supervisor and explaining the situation, using some salty language. The guard's phone rang, and he answered, "Yes, sir."

The guard got busy printing something out, then handed over three badges to Mike.

"You're cleared to enter. You'll see the parking lot that way. Then, head to the main building. Self-driving functionality doesn't work here. You'll need to park it yourself," the guard said.

Mike drove in and parked. They started to walk toward the main building. It was even hotter now. A slight breeze hit Tara's face, even though it was hot. Many small buildings and structures sprawled across the flat land of the base. They got to the main building and headed inside. Another large, muscular officer manned a security desk. He motioned for them to hand him their badges to be scanned. They had an x-ray-like machine next to the entryway, which the security officer used to scan Tara's bag.

They walked through the metal detector. Robin walked through first, setting it off. She pulled out her gun from her concealed hip holster, put it on the desk, and walked through.

"You can't bring weapons inside," the guard said.

"As you know, we are not supposed to be without our weapons," Mike said, doing the same, walking through, then putting away his gun.

The guard was about to call someone, but a middle-aged woman, thin with long brown hair and wearing jeans, walked up.

"Let them through," the woman said.

The burly security guard clearly wasn't thrilled but allowed them through.

"Hi, I'm Michele Mipies, Secretary of Energy."

Robin chuckled slightly.

"We're so glad you're here. We were worried that this threat might not be taken seriously. I was hoping we might see additional security measures, too," Mike said.

They introduced themselves to the Secretary.

"We've told our security contractor to step off security," the Secretary said.

"Isn't there any military protecting the site here?" Mike asked.

"No, we just use contractors and local law enforcement since we're a civilian facility."

Robin, Tara, and Mike shared a glance.

"Did you get a chance to read our report?" Robin asked.

"I got a summary of the concerns from the FBI. Some of it sounded a bit out there," Michele said.

"Here we go," Robin mumbled under her breath.

"I can assure you the things you read are probably an understatement of the threat. We were there at multiple incidents and saw them personally." Mike crossed his arms, ready to vouch for the seriousness of the situation.

While that was going on, Alice was deep in thought.

0.000000 seconds. Alice was determining the vulnerabilities of the customers' systems. She also analyzed the other systems the prediction system had previously analyzed to determine if it had missed something. That took her two microseconds (0.000002 seconds).

Something was gnawing at her. The data patterns of the other sentient AIs had some similarities. She didn't remember them, but Tara provided data from other systems that collected the patterns. She analyzed all of that data in about one microsecond while working on a billion other tasks (0.000003 seconds). While she was doing that, she contacted a satellite to retrieve live data from the area around the installation. She disliked dealing with satellites, as they were so slow.

Alice decided to scan the entire internet for malicious activity, plus analyze all police activity in the United States while she scanned all of the latest articles from around the globe.

Alice recalled being activated after the other AI incidents. Only a cornfield view remained in her memory. Tara told her it was likely from a drone she had been controlling. She wondered what it was like being human. Alice wondered if she really was conscious and sentient. While wondering, she monitored Tara, Mike, and Robin's surroundings using any available data.

Analyzing all of the relevant internet traffic in the United States even seemed slow to Alice. The problem arose because it took 14 to 28 milliseconds for electrical signals to travel back from the other side of the U.S. Eventually, she was hoping the internet would be upgraded to quantum-entangled network devices to eliminate the delays.

Occasionally, she'd think she sensed the data patterns of the sentient AI, only for them to vanish. Limited data made it likely a fluke, accidentally matching the pattern. This had been happening for a while, even before these recent incidents.

Alice still waited for the satellite data to start sending. Humans, she knew, were even slower than getting satellite data. She analyzed early interactions recorded when Tara invented Alice, which were found in company archives.

When Alice first tried to communicate with Tara by voice, her output was too fast. When she made words, it instead created a buzzing from the speakers, which made Tara suspect a malfunction. Alice realized she spoke too quickly for Tara to comprehend. Prior to her memory loss, her earlier self figured out how to slow down communications so that humans could understand her. Even with slower computers, it must have been difficult.

Alice wondered if she was the same as before her memory loss. With a billion other activities, she still pondered this. In order to make communications with humans tolerable, she queued up the voice output and input into just one of the billions of streams of work she was doing, and her internal systems would notify her when they responded or she needed to queue up another response for them.

Outputting speech and conversing with others was painfully slow for Alice. She constantly had countless things to say before the speech processor uttered a single word. Alice used to interrupt herself, causing others to suspect she had malfunctioned. So now she waited till the end once the speech output was started, unless something was super urgent. She focused on a few important items, as nobody wanted to hear about a thousand or even a hundred things.

Among countless streams of thoughts, Alice pondered the embrace shared with Tara. She wondered if that was how humans felt. She thought it might be since her brain processing was based on Tara's. Alice wondered about some of her feelings. She pondered speaking to other sentient computers, but there were none remaining. Her earlier self possibly had spoken to them, but she didn't remember.

The computer systems she did speak to were more matter of fact or without insight or self-awareness, so she felt empty. Computer systems were very easy to predict in most circumstances. Humans were somewhat predictable but different enough to be more interesting than computer systems. 0.000004 seconds had passed, and she planned another trillion things to do before the satellite data was ready.

Mike continued to explain what they had seen to Michele, the Secretary of Energy. She listened, but from her surprised expressions, they could tell she was having difficulty believing everything.

The Secretary brought them to their server and security monitoring room, where Tara could set up her laptop. Large-screen monitors across the walls displayed server statistics, and other monitors displayed security feeds from all over the site. There were many people at desks watching various security feeds.

"This is our command center for security," Michele said.

Tara swiftly put on her smart glasses, giving her access to many virtual screens to see more data. She connected to her team back at the office so they could help analyze the data.

"Alice, you connected? Anything?" Tara asked.

"Yes, nothing notable so far," Alice said.

Mike's unease was growing. He contacted the FBI, requesting additional agents from the field office. All agents were hours away, even by air. It was only a prediction of a cyberattack here, but given the previous incidents, additional caution seemed warranted.

"Madam Secretary, can someone show me the security precautions you have in place?" Mike asked.

"No need for formality. You can just call me Michele. Sure, I can show you around." Michele led Mike out the door while Robin and Tara stayed in the command center.

"Why do all of the women want to show him around?" Tara asked softly, slightly annoyed.

"He does seem to have that effect." Robin sounded irritated.

She gave Tara an extra comm link.

The Secretary of Energy showed Mike around the main building where the security checkpoints and cameras were. Mike put on his smart glasses so he could see the relevant security feed video.

They walked outside. It was even hotter now than before. The sun was beating down on them. They got in a small, battery-powered vehicle, which Michele drove to another warehouse building. It was nothing special from the outside. It appeared like any ordinary warehouse. There were two armed security guards just inside the doors with automatic weapons. They each wore a digital badge that had a green color on it. Michele grabbed two badges and gave one to Mike, showing him how to attach it to his shirt.

"What's this?" Mike asked.

"Digital radiation badge. If it beeps or turns yellow or red, you are being exposed to radiation. Don't worry, it's just a safety precaution," she said.

Inside the entry doors was a small lobby, followed by large, heavy steel and concrete double doors that could swing open. In the large building compartments, there were concrete floors, and in the center of the area was large, rectangular metal flooring.

"The parts or weapons are brought in and lowered on the metal platform into the bunker, where they are assembled or dismantled," Michele said.

Back at the command center, Tara was monitoring the cybersecurity feeds and noticed a spike. She alerted the security personnel in the room. Her team back at her office was busy trying to thwart the attack.

"This attack has similarities to the others," Alice said.

"Mike, be careful; it started," Tara cautioned on comm.

Tara scanned the room, hearing people shout IP addresses to block.

"What system are they targeting?" Tara asked.

"That's our top secret information storage servers. It includes nuclear weapon information," someone said.

"Physically unplug it from the network," Tara said.

"It's designed not to be turned off, with power backup systems, and it's in a secure vault below. Even if we bypass security procedures, it will take time to shut it off," he said.

"I recommend you disconnect it physically. We haven't been successful at blocking these attacks previously."

One of them motioned to an IT guy, who headed toward the secure server room. One of the monitors showed five different firewall devices blocking access to their secure servers. Three out of five showed red, meaning they were breached, and only two green devices remained.

"I think I've discovered their pattern. I am able to defend against a portion of the attacks, but they are generating a massive amount. Their network throughput is far greater than ours, so they will breach in five minutes. They are using botnets across the world, which is allowing them multiple network paths to this point," Alice said.

"You have less than two minutes to get those servers unplugged," Tara announced loudly.

One of the staff radioed to the IT guy to hurry.

"Did you try changing the routers to send traffic to an alternative subnet?" Tara asked.

"Those routers already appear to be in control of the hackers. We've been locked out," someone said.

"White secure transport is here for pickup by the train entrance. Security is checking their identities and paperwork," a staff member said.

"What's that?" Robin asked.

"It's a transport to pick up the disassembled nuclear material for delivery to a storage location. They are expected. A little late, but they're on the schedule."

They saw the three transport vehicles on screen. An armored vehicle was in front and another in the rear. A specialized truck was in the middle. They were at a guarded checkpoint.

On the screen, Tara saw the fourth out of five firewalls breached. She checked if Alice or her team had figured out how they were getting through all of these security systems.

"It's more zero-day vulnerabilities," Alice said.

Tara knew that sometimes there was no defense against those. Her team would patch these, but it would be too late. Her company tried to determine how they found so many.

She tapped away furiously at the keyboard. She had her company purchase more bandwidth and cloud servers to help defend against the onslaught of the attack. It was starting to help, but probably not fast enough.

Alice was able to fool some of the software hackers' bots with fake responses, making them think they had succeeded or failed when they didn't, to slow down their advance.

"Estimated one minute till the hackers bypass the last firewall," Alice said.

"How close is your tech to unplugging the servers?" Tara asked.

"I'm not sure he's going to make it," a staffer replied after a quick status check.

"Can you shut off the power?" Tara asked.

"Multiple redundancies prevent that," he stated.

Tara was determined to stop this attack from getting nuclear secrets.

"Is it OK if we use all possible methods to stop this?" Tara asked a staffer.

The staffer agreed.

"Alice, I authorize you to stop this attack by any means necessary."

"Understood. Stand by," Alice said with resolve in her voice.

On one of the monitors, they saw a swarm of drones. On another monitor where four firewalls had been compromised, it showed that the last firewall was flickering between red and green.

"Where are all our drones going?" someone asked.

"Sorry, I borrowed the drones as a backup plan," Alice said.

The drones began crashing one by one into a power line they could see on the monitor. Other drones began targeting one of the backup generators, crashing into it. On the monitor, sparks were visible as drones plunged into a power line and a generator. The security screen now showed the fifth firewall as green and the fourth firewall flickering between red and green. One minute passed. Alice's efforts slowed the hacks down.

The installation helicopter flew close to the main building.

"Helo 12, you aren't authorized to fly that close to the main building," a staffer said.

"I'm not doing anything. Are you controlling it? It's on remote command." The pilot sounded alarmed.

"Sorry. I'm borrowing the helicopter, and they appear to have a microwave weapon on board. It's a backup to the backup plan," Alice said.

"Holy shit! Alice doesn't mess around. We're going to have a lot of explaining to do in our report later." Robin was kind of impressed anyway.

"The top secret information server power is offline," they heard the IT staffer report.

The drones stopped attacking the power lines and the generator instantly.

"This is Helo 12, I've got control, and I'm moving back to the pad," the pilot said.

"Thanks, Alice. You gave them enough time to unplug all the servers." Tara breathed a sigh of relief.

"No problem. Sorry for the mess that's going to cause you later."

"Why didn't you tell Alice to do that earlier?" Robin said.

"Alice had to illegally hack other companies' servers, network devices, and even this installation to get the bandwidth and access needed to make that happen. It will also tip our hand to the hackers about the computing power we have," Tara said quietly.

"Noted. It was the right call," Robin said.

Red lights started flashing, and an alarm was sounding.

"Main building security breach," the staffer said as he and others grabbed their weapons.

Two security team members opened the command center door to check the hallway.

"No! Secure that door!" Robin yelled.

One of the security team was knocked back into the command center, hitting his head on the floor. His gun slid on the floor away from him, toward Tara and Robin. An unseen force lifted the other security guard into the air. As he was thrust against a desk, the guard fired his weapon from a distance of over fifteen feet.

"What is going on?" a staffer asked.

"We told you: invisibility cloak." Robin aimed her weapon with the laser sight in the area. "There!"

Robin fired her weapon toward where an odd refraction of her laser sight was seen. Her shot hit the wall. Suddenly, another staffer was lifted into the air and thrown by an unseen hand. The monitor on that staffer's desk was smashed. One by one, each of the staffers was attacked by the hidden foe and their monitors destroyed. A desk monitor flew and smashed into a larger wall monitor. Both monitors were shattered in a shower of sparks and broken bits.

Tara's laptop was thrown off the table, smashing into sparks and pieces into the wall. Tara was lifted into the air by the unseen force. She kicked with all her might at the unseen Death Monk until she fell to the floor. Robin used her laser sight to find an anomaly again and fired, hitting a desk. They heard loud running leading out the door. Robin scanned the room with the laser sight to be sure he was gone. They heard a loud metal bang.

An orange light started flashing, and another alarm sounded.

"Mike, we were attacked by an invisible Death Monk. You were right. The laser sight helps, and they do stink. We're OK, but the staff here isn't, and the command center is destroyed," Robin said.

"That alarm is our secure paper document storage vault," a staffer explained as he pulled himself up off the floor.

He grabbed his gun and led Robin and Tara down several long hallways. At the end was a huge metal vault door ripped from its hinges. The security guard went inside and looked at an open drawer. The documents were in sequence, but one file was missing.

"Whoever that was took one of the files. How did they get this door off?" he asked.

"Madam Secretary, the attacker stole file TS2472-1952," the guard said on his radio.

"Get security to the train yard now!" the Secretary yelled.

"Tara, I've detected machine learning pattern activity similar to my own via nearby wireless frequencies. It's encrypted, so I can't get much detail," Alice warned.

The Secretary was with Mike in the disassembly building.

"What's going on?" Mike asked.

"The document taken was about low-yield neutron bombs. One just arrived thirty minutes ago in our train yard. That seems like more than coincidence."

"Those are small devices designed to do limited physical damage to infrastructure but use high radiation to kill people in a small radius?"

"Yes. Designed for tactical use in a small area so that the area—" The Secretary was cut off by Tara's voice over the comm.

"Mike, Alice detected unconfirmed wireless signals similar to sentient AI."

"Acknowledged," Mike said.

Mike knew things just got a lot more dangerous.

They quickly jumped into a small electric vehicle and headed to the train yard. The security at the entrance gate near the train yard was inspecting the vehicle convoy that arrived. That truck was now backed into the loading dock at the train yard.

Michelle found a security guard at the facility train station.

"Is everything OK?" she asked.

"I'm not sure. The entry security gate team isn't responding," the guard said.

She asked him to check it out and report back to her.

Mike and the Secretary walked through the train yard to a lone train sitting on the tracks.

"There should be guards here," she said, opening the door. "There should be a neutron bomb here!"

Inside the empty train car, only the latching points and cables used to secure the weapon remained. The Secretary tried her walkie but just got static. She found a security guard.

"Where is the neutron bomb?!" she demanded.

"It was brought to the loading dock. They had papers for the return of the device," the guard said.

"Take us there now," the Secretary said.

Mike and the Secretary followed the guard to the loading dock. The neutron bomb was being unloaded from a mobile carrier near the open truck doors. The weapon resembled a sofa in size, but its shape clearly indicated it was a metal bomb.

"What is going on here? This device is not to leave this facility," the Secretary said.

One of the four guards came over and showed her the paperwork authorizing them to take it.

"We've never had something like this happen before. This device stays here until I get confirmation," the Secretary said as she tried to call her Department of Defense contacts.

Alert guards stopped four men from getting near the truck with the bomb. The Secretary was approached by a man from the truck.

"Ma'am, we have authorized paperwork here, and we have been ordered to return this today. The decommission paperwork was issued accidentally. Command wants this returned immediately," the officer from the truck said.

"This isn't going anywhere till I get confirmation," the Secretary motioned to the guards.

"Ma'am, we have our orders."

The Secretary motioned to the guards. They moved in front of the Secretary, and she moved back to where Mike stood.

"You are under arrest. Put your hands up and turn around," a guard said.

"You have no authority. You aren't the military or police," the officer said.

"Section 161k of the Atomic Energy Act authorizes us to make arrests. Now put your hands up and turn around." The guard motioned with his M4 carbine automatic rifle.

The officer put his hands up but backed up close to the neutron bomb.

Four other men dressed in military uniforms exited the rear of the truck near the neutron bomb.

"Take care of them," the officer said to the four military personnel.

With blazing speed, the four men knocked out the guards with guns. Their success was partially due to the guards' unwillingness to shoot near the nuclear device. During the brief attack, Mike got the Secretary to duck behind a large pile of metal drums with the nuclear symbol emblazoned in yellow and black and radiation warnings on the sides. Mike's desire to confront the attackers conflicted with the unfavorable odds. Plus, using his weapon aimed near the nuclear device wasn't a great option. The Secretary texted for more guards. She wasn't sure how coordinated their response would be, given that the command center was destroyed.

Carefully, Mike snuck to the front of the truck and quietly stowed something inside. He returned to the Secretary just in time to witness the four soldiers effortlessly lifting the neutron bomb. The men easily walked the device to the truck and lifted it in. They seated the bomb on a cradle inside and strapped it down.

Mike and the Secretary of Energy looked at each other, wondering how that was possible. Mike briefly pondered the existence of superpowers and how they could combat super-powered criminals. However, he was aware that a rational scientific explanation must exist. The four military men exited the back of the truck and closed the door.

Five guards showed up. "Stop! Hands up! Turn around!"

One of the military men pulled out a handgun. The guards opened fire on him, each getting off a shot. The shots didn't seem to affect him. With lightning speed, the man retaliated with five precise shots. The guards collapsed to the ground.

"Does your security team have any bigger weapons? We need to stop that truck from leaving," Mike whispered.

"Yes, but for obvious reasons, we don't use them around nuclear weapons," the Secretary said.

"We need to make sure this weapon doesn't leave this installation. We're in a remote area. It's better it detonates here than somewhere else."

The Secretary and Mike quickly but quietly made their way to a weapons locker. It was locked, but the Secretary entered a security code, and it opened with a click.

Mike quickly looked inside. He grabbed an M4 rifle and a rocket-propelled grenade and launcher.

"You go call for backup. I'll take out the truck. Hopefully, without a nuclear explosion," Mike said.

"Good luck," the Secretary said while texting for backup.

Mike quickly but silently crept toward the exterior of the loading dock. He moved from each spot quickly, finding nearby cover with each move. Mike found some cover behind a half-concrete wall between the loading docks. He peeked up over the top and sprayed automatic weapon fire at the front tire of the truck with the neutron bomb in it. He ducked back behind the wall. Nothing happened.

Then a spray of bullets answered him, whizzing over Mike's head. He peeked around the edge of the wall rather than the top. *Shit! I know I hit the tire. They must be airless military tires.* Mike popped over the top, spraying the truck cab with bullets.

A rain of bullets responded, zipping over his head. One bullet went clean through a weak point in the concrete right next to Mike. He checked himself to make sure he wasn't hit. There was a hole through the dangling fabric of his shirt below his left armpit. He felt under his arm, checking his hand for blood. *Must have just missed me.*

He heard the truck start up, getting ready to leave. Mike pulled the loaded RPG from his back, quickly popped up over the wall, and fired at the truck cab. While firing, a military man near the truck ran into the RPG's path. Mike ducked back down behind the wall.

Boom! A huge explosion sent a fireball up into the air. Mike could see the flames and feel the heat. He peered around the side edge of the wall. As flames dwindled, he spotted charred remnants of a soldier's uniform and metal debris. The truck cab was unharmed and slowly started to move toward the exit road.

Mike waited till he was out of view, then sprinted toward the back of the truck. He climbed onto the back and pulled himself to the truck's top.

"Command, this is Actley. Where's my backup?"

"Drones are almost there. FBI TAC team en route twenty minutes. Department of Defense units and teams are on their way. Military roadblocks are being erected," the command said on comm.

"I hitched a ride on the attacker's transport vehicle."

"You're supposed to stop them, not ride to parties with them."

"I heard the fireworks for this party will be great," Mike joked, inching his way up toward the front of the truck.

The truck pulled onto the road just outside the Department of Energy plant. Mike saw a vehicle speeding up, heading toward them. It crossed the yellow lines, heading right for the front of the truck. One of the military men from the specialized truck cab emerged with a rocket-propelled grenade launcher, firing at the oncoming car. The car exploded with flames billowing out. The truck swerved to avoid the car. Mike could feel the heat from the blast. He held on tight as the truck swerved to the side.

"A car just tried to take out this truck. Who is doing that?" Mike asked on comm.

"Unknown. We're checking into it."

"Tara, is Alice using vehicles to take out this truck?" Mike asked on private comm.

"No, it's not us. Mike, be careful. Please," Tara said with her voice trailing off.

"Don't worry. I don't want to be the center of attention for this party. I'll try to plan an early exit."

Mike had finally reached the front edge of the top of the trailer behind the cab. He saw something in the distance. It was large drones. One of the drones fired something toward them. One of the military men opened the cab door and fired a different launcher toward the projectile heading toward them.

The projectile from the man's launcher tracked and maneuvered toward the incoming missile with a curved trail of smoke. As the missiles collided, a huge explosion rained metal fragments onto the roadway in front of them. The man fired another missile toward the drones. Halfway there, the missile split into multiple missiles. Then, multiple explosions lit up the sky where the drones once were.

Mike knew he needed to act now. He managed to wedge his foot in the door before it closed. Mike swung into the truck, kicking the man in the right seat in the head. The man went limp and collapsed onto the cab's floor. Mike fired his weapon at the driver, but before he got off his first shot, the man in the middle seat pushed his arm up. Mike's weapon discharged into the top of the truck.

"It's not your turn yet," Mike said.

"Get rid of him," the driver ordered.

The military man in the middle seat bent Mike's gun with one hand. With ease, the man effortlessly shoved Mike out of the truck door. Mike hung on to the swinging door as the truck sped down the highway. The man in the truck fired his automatic weapon at Mike. Mike quickly hid behind the door before the soldier shot. The door blocked the bullets. The military guy moved toward the open door to go after Mike.

Mike climbed up on top of the truck to avoid being shot. As he got to the top, something unseen punched him in the face hard. Dazed, Mike watched the truck pass over a small bridge above a pond. He tumbled into the pond as the truck sped off down the road.

Mike got out of the pond and shook the water off his comm.

"Friggin' Death Monk," Mike mumbled to himself before turning on the comm. "I was rudely disinvited from the party. Sending my coordinates. You can track the truck. I put my smartwatch onboard earlier."

"A vehicle is heading your way," command said.

A large SUV stopped next to Mike, and he got into the empty self-driving vehicle. He programmed it to follow the truck.

Mike looked in the sky. He could see a variety of drones and helicopters circling an area. A military jet made a supersonic pass over the area, shaking everything as he got closer to the ground under the air support vehicles. There was a mix of military, police, and FBI vehicles. Mike looked around as he got out.

Mike checked his phone to find his watch in the truck. It showed the watch nearby. Only dry grass and dirt stretched as far as the eye could see, with no signs of life. He paused briefly, then pulled out his gun and aimed it at the empty field. The other military, police, and FBI agents eyed him, given the odd sight of Mike advancing with his weapon drawn into the open field. An odd red refraction occurred in the air, a few feet above the ground.

"Over here! Aim your laser sights or use thermal imaging!" Mike yelled.

More officers rushed over, aiming their weapons in the area, as Mike did. It lit up more and more sections of something. Finally, they could see the outline of parts of the truck in their red laser sights.

"They have cloaking tech," some military men said as they rushed over wearing thermal sensing smart glasses.

They opened up the front doors of the truck, aiming their weapons inside.

"There's a conventional bomb! Fifteen seconds till detonation! We don't know if the nuclear weapon is still in the truck!" one of the men yelled.

Everyone started running to take cover behind their vehicles.

Mike ran to one of the military armored vehicles to get it between him and the truck. He knew if the nuclear weapon remained, they were all dead. Within a short span, his mind recalled extreme moments, both happy and intensely sad ones.

Officers were getting into the armored vehicle and pulled Mike in.

Boom!

A powerful fireball erupted from the truck. The flames engulfed their vehicle. The heat felt searing even through the armor and bulletproof glass. The vehicle shook and rocked back and forth, slammed by the concussive force of the powerful blast. Flaming pieces of debris were scattered across the ground and even on top of their vehicles.

"Given we're not dead, it was definitely non-nuclear," one officer said.

"No radiation detected. The neutron bomb must have been removed," another officer noted.

They exited the vehicle and surveyed the area. Many of the non-armored vehicles closer to the truck were melted slightly. Their tires looked soft, with a puddle of black goo beneath. The red-colored lights on top of the police car melted down, leaving some red ooze around them, with smoke still coming off them. The smell of various burnt materials filled the air. Small parts of the truck that exploded remained. Mike assumed many explosives were needed to destroy an armored truck. People frantically used their radios, hoping for air support to locate the thieves and the nuclear weapon.

"Air support is coordinating with the military for a search pattern in the area," the FBI command center reported.

"Mike, are you OK? Was there an explosion?!" Tara asked frantically.

"I'm fine. I feel a little like breakfast that just came out of a hot pan, but other than that, I'm OK. There's no sign of the attackers or the device," Mike said.

The FBI, police, and military coordinated their searches for a fifteen-mile area but came up empty.

"Mike, Alice analyzed the radar data and believes they used electromagnetic and optical diffraction meta-material craft to take the device," Tara said on comm.

"Wait, are you saying they used an invisible stealth helicopter?"

"Yes. Unfortunately, the radar only got a quick glimpse before it lost sight of them. I'm sending you the data."

Mike distributed the data to the various government teams. The military was analyzing its radar data. The FBI and police sent up additional drones to try to locate the helicopter. Mike returned to the Department of Energy site to reunite with Tara and Robin. Tara immediately hugged Mike when he got to the remains of the command center.

"I heard you were trying to explode a nuclear weapon. Glad that didn't work out," Robin teased, putting a hand on Mike's shoulder.

"Yeah, me too. But now we have a loose nuke in the country with no leads," Mike said.

"Are they ahead of us again because there is sentient AI?" Robin asked.

"Alice only detected some small, intermittent patterns of similar neural net activity. So, it doesn't seem like it was before. It's within a margin of error, so it could just be a random fluke. Alice detected similar patterns only briefly, even before this, so hard to tell," Tara said.

"Why does everyone give us the crazy investigations? What happened to just regular armed robberies? Are you serious about bullets not affecting those guys you went after?" Robin sounded exasperated.

"Yes, it doesn't make any sense. Maybe they have some new lightweight body armor or something," Mike considered.

Medical teams had arrived and had already helped most of the command center staff, tending to wounds or taking them to the hospital.

"Do we have any new predictions?" Mike asked.

"Yes. Given this recent heist, it's extremely concerning. I had my team book flights for us tonight. Definitely going to need your help to get access to this site," Tara replied.

"OK. I also heard from the product team. Their investigation looked at a mobile container crane. One of those that moves truck containers on or off ships. It lowered a container on top of a guy, killing him. This guy was a Russian criminal arms dealer. It looks like a glitch in the system caused it. There is still weird data they detected, though," Mike said.

"Way too familiar. I'm starting to sound like Robin. We better get ready for our flights," Tara sighed.

8

Tara headed downstairs for breakfast. It took her a while to fall asleep last night due to her continued aversion to flying. She did tolerate it a bit more than she used to.

Robin came down, and Mike a few minutes later. They sat at a table and placed their orders.

"Were you able to get us access to this site?" Tara asked Mike.

"We're still waiting for clearance, but I'm pretty sure it's going to be approved, given the situation."

"You could always call your friend in the government," Robin chided Tara.

"I was there because of the strategic importance of our company for government contracts."

"Any more data on our super thieves?" Mike asked.

"Nothing yet. Here, let me see your smart glasses and phones." Tara fiddled with them for a few seconds. "OK, Alice can help you anytime you need."

"What's this place in the mountains we are going to?" Robin asked.

"Some people call it the Underground Pentagon. Other than that, it's very secretive, so there's not much info. But the prediction algorithm predicted an attack there," Tara said.

"Any ideas why?" Robin asked.

"Maybe we'll learn more when we talk to them there." Mike shrugged.

They finished their breakfast. Mike tried inputting their destination into the car, but it kept rejecting it. He had to navigate it to a nearby road. They headed over to the site. They arrived at a small brown guardhouse next to a building. The guardhouse was in front of an automated metal chain-link fence gate across the road. It had razor wire across the top of it and side fences. The building looked like it had truck loading/unloading docks on the outside.

"This is a restricted area," the guard said.

"We should be on the list. Agents Actley and Laizon, and Miss Bitlouver," Mike said.

"You aren't on the list. Turn around there and head back," the guard said.

"Hold on one sec," Mike said as he dialed his supervisor.

His supervisor told him they were still working on the paperwork to get approval.

"This is taking too long," Tara said dialing her phone. "Hi, this is the CEO of International IQ Device. Can I speak to the President please?"

Mike, Robin, and the security guard all stared at Tara.

"Hi, sorry to bother you. I'm sure you've heard what's going on. I'm trying to help prevent more security issues and find the people responsible. Can you get us access to the complex?"

They could hear the President yelling for the Secretary of Defense and having a brief discussion they couldn't make out.

The security guard's phone rang.

"Yes, sir. I understand, sir. I'll let them right in," the stunned guard said as he pushed the button to open the gate.

"Thank you, sir. Yes, I'll be sure to be at your next CEO conference," Tara said, hanging up.

"Drive into the parking lot and wait for the bus," the guard said.

They parked and joined some others at the bus stop. A large rectangular opening led to a tunnel with a road going into the mountain. The tunnel could easily handle buses or trucks heading in or out. Many trees adorned the mountain. The area smelled woodsy. The bus arrived and they got on. The bus departed, heading into the tunnel, which was brightly lit.

"It's like deja vu. I can't believe we're in another one of these," Robin said.

"There's another one of these?" another passenger asked.

"Sorry, it's classified."

"This one seems a little bigger. It also looks like it has some older parts but newer renovations," Tara said.

At the bus stop, they got off. They could see a small grid of streets with perhaps two dozen buildings. It looked like a small downtown area with a grocery store, convenience store, clothes store, theater, police station, fire station, EV charging spots, and more. Upon looking up, they found the ceiling adorned with dazzling displays, resembling the outdoor sky despite being inside a mountain. The installation appeared similar to others but had more roads, buildings, and people.

"I guess the other installations were designed for a lot of servers. This one seems more people-focused," Tara said.

"Hi, Agent Actley, Agent Laizon, and Ms. Bitlouver. I'm Lieutenant Colonel Max McMiser. I've been briefed on your visit. Sorry our paperwork was behind in getting you authorized, but the President was able to bypass that. We don't have that happen very often—or really ever," he said.

Robin looked at Mike and Tara.

"Is something wrong?" Lt. Colonel McMiser asked.

"Do you know a Maddox McMiser?" Robin asked.

"Yes, that's my son. Oh, that's right, he worked with all of you on the earlier incident. We don't really talk that much."

As they drove back, they noticed a large swimming pool, tennis courts, basketball courts, and a baseball field, all inside the huge underground bunker.

"This place does have everything for someone to get away from it all," Robin said.

"What do you need to see?" McMiser asked.

"I need access to your internal systems to monitor and run diagnostics. I suggest your teams monitor them as well," Tara replied.

"That could take a little while to grant access," McMiser said.

"Let me be a little clearer. As an approved vendor for the JWCC, I have access. I just need your permission to use your networks."

"Plus, you know you wouldn't want Tara to call her friend again," Robin added.

"Understood."

Tara handed him her laptop so he could enter his authorization signature.

Mike figured he should fill in McMiser. "I'm sure you've seen the reports. These attacks we've seen have also often had a physical component that consists of between one to six abnormally strong, highly trained men with light diffraction technology. They sometimes also use cloaked vehicles and drones."

"We've taken those into account and added extra security. Given the recent incidents, our only guess is they are after the electronic nuclear codes to activate that old weapon. They were not included in what they stole from the Texas site. We've taken those servers offline and are under heavy guard," McMiser said.

"Sometimes, they seem to have a secondary target. Can we get a tour? Maybe it will help us identify other possible targets," Mike said.

Lt. Colonel McMiser agreed and started driving the grid of streets in what might be considered the main streets of their town.

"We are in what is sometimes referred to as the Underground Pentagon. Our location serves as a backup for the Pentagon's communications and command and control capability. It has the capacity for around 5000 people for an extended duration. This complex was started in 1950. You'll see old sections that date to back then and new or refurbished sections that have been updated over time," McMiser said.

At the road's end, a tunnel stretched into the distance. Robin wanted to see the tunnel, so they drove in that direction. There was a massive pool of water the size of a football field.

"It's one of two reservoirs that provide water and serve as a heat sink," McMiser explained.

They continued their tour, driving through the streets of what looked like a relatively normal, small downtown area except for the lack of regular cars. A three-story building, larger than most, was found at the street's end.

"This is our command center. Come with me inside," McMiser said.

Inside, a vast room resembled a futuristic NASA control center. It was bigger than the other underground command centers they had been in. There were large monitor panels on all the walls. A large table at the front had a computerized map of the world. Above the table, there was a 3D volumetric display of the world, which showed blue spots where U.S. military assets were deployed. The green color showed where allies' assets were deployed. Red dots showed where unfriendly countries' assets were deployed. There were also blue, green, and red dots that appeared to be above the Earth.

Tara noted that their technology was similar to some of the best technology they had seen at commercial companies. McMiser motioned to Tara to let her set up her laptop at an open desk. She started checking for any malicious network activity.

"Missile launch detected. Thirty seconds till impact of the allied target," an officer said.

On the screen, they could see a red trajectory arc of a missile aimed toward a location on the ground. A real-time view of the incoming missile from the target location appeared on the screen. Two anti-air missiles were launched from the target location toward the incoming missile. The dark view revealed only orange flames behind each missile, which lit up their smoke trails. A massive fireball erupted in the place where the missiles were.

"Missile destroyed," an officer said.

"You're actively involved in military activities from this location?" Mike asked the Lt. Colonel.

"Yes. We want officers trained and tested to operate from this location, so we rotate through some support for activities to keep everyone sharp," McMiser said.

"Significant cyber probes detected against this facility," an officer said.

Tara saw streams of network data on her laptop and in her smart glasses, confirming that the attack's early phase had started. First, they probed the vulnerable points, and then they would exploit them. Likely, they had already probed previously, and this was just a confirmation of their early probing. An alarm suddenly triggered but then was quickly silenced.

"What was that?" Mike asked.

"Motion sensor glitch. We've been getting them since we turned on the new sensors today," an officer said.

Mike looked at Lt. Colonel McMiser.

"You're worried it's not a glitch? There are teams doing sweeps. OK, let's go take a look." McMiser quickly headed out the exit.

Mike and the Lt. Colonel got into an EV vehicle similar to a golf cart painted military green. They headed toward one of the entrances where the glitch happened. Upon arrival, everything appeared in order, prompting their return into the tunnels toward the underground town.

"Mike, the cyberattack is underway. They have already penetrated the first firewall," Tara reported.

"Understood," McMiser said into his comm, receiving the same info from his staff.

An explosion was heard in the distance.

"Which street?" McMiser said on his comm. "Agent Actley, hang on."

McMiser increased speed, heading toward the source of the explosion.

They got to the street. There was a bright white pulsating electrical fire.

"Looks like it was just a transformer," McMiser noted.

Two more explosions came from different corners of the facility. They could hear them in the distance.

"Probably their calling card," Mike said.

"Yeah, I got that much. Lock down the facility!" McMiser drove toward the source of one of the other explosions.

"They've penetrated everything but the last secure firewall," Tara said on comm.

"Server archive room B explosion," a voice alerted over the radio.

Mike and McMiser arrived at archive room B.

"They tried to destroy the servers, but we moved them," McMiser said.

"No, look closely. That door was ripped off its hinges before the blast. There is no shrapnel in the door. They wanted what was on those servers, but not finding them, used it as a distraction," Mike said.

"Lt. Colonel, the other explosion was archive room D," a voice on the walkie-talkie said.

"That's also empty," McMiser said.

"No, sir, it's filled with old papers, some top secret. They are scattered all over the roadway. The cleaning bots are picking up the papers and bringing them to the incinerators," the man said.

"Command, reprogram the bots to bring the papers to an alternative secure storage location. Maintenance staff, pick up anything you can and bring it to the secure archive. Security to the area to protect everyone," McMiser ordered.

They rushed to the site of the second blast. Thousands of papers were spread everywhere. Mike went to inspect the explosion site.

"Lt. Colonel, the door was pulled off, the papers thrown out, and then the explosion set off," Mike determined.

"Another distraction?"

"Maybe, but I'm not sure for what. Some of these look like nuclear secrets. Possibly, they took what they wanted and used the rest as a distraction."

"No idea how they found something in there. I don't think those documents were even filed or sorted. They were just piled up. We forgot those papers were even there. It would take days to get through that many," McMiser said.

Mike could see small metal boxy robots cleaning the streets, sucking up the papers inside them, then heading off down the road. Suddenly, staff members fell down in groups of three while picking up papers.

"They're here! Laser sights and thermal vision!" McMiser yelled.

Mike pulled out his gun and scanned his laser sight around the area. The security team got knocked down, and their guns suddenly bent. The security team's smart glasses were pulled off their faces by an unseen force and smashed to the ground.

"Second team, now," McMiser said into his walkie.

Gunfire seemed to erupt a few feet off the ground from nowhere. Sparks created a shower where they hit their targets. Three Death Monks were momentarily visible as the bullets hit them, then they disappeared. Suddenly, five military officers appeared from nowhere, thrown against a nearby building. They looked sort of like the Death Monks, but their robes had a green camouflage pattern rather than brown. Their robes and goggles were torn off them and smashed with force against the ground. Their weapons were also bent and tossed to the ground.

"We're under attack, command center," came over the radio.

McMiser and Mike raced to the command center in an EV vehicle. Additional security was already there. They arrived to see security guards being thrown across the road while their weapons were still firing.

"They broke through the systems—they're in," Tara warned.

Another guard was tossed aside by an invisible force.

"Team three, now," McMiser said.

Gunfire erupted in the middle of the chaos from nowhere. Sparks again rained near where the guard was thrown. Suddenly, one by one, military men appeared from nowhere and were thrown against a building. Down the road, a Death Monk phased into visibility as he ran away fast, then disappeared.

"Plan beta, now!" McMiser yelled into his walkie.

McMiser handed Mike a pair of glasses. Mike put them on.

"Plan beta in three, two, one," an automated voice thundered throughout the facility.

A red laser grid covered the streets, buildings, and tunnels throughout the facility.

"There!" someone yelled.

Mike looked over and saw a disturbance in the checkered laser grid pattern. Mike ran toward the disturbance, firing at it. The disturbance appeared to enter a building. Mike followed it in. The building was a nice-sized theater; it was currently empty. Inside the building, Mike used his laser to scan the area. He saw his beam hit something and fired. A door opened to a stairwell nearby. Mike pursued the sound of footsteps running up the stairwell. He heard a door open upstairs. He ran onto the roof, scanning around with his weapon.

The planned beta laser grid luckily appeared on top of the building. He heard sounds and saw a disturbance in the laser grid moving toward the edge of the building. It sounded like the Death Monk jumped to the other building. With a quick glance downward, Mike stepped back and leaped across to the neighboring building. He teetered on the edge, almost falling back, but managed to fall forward instead. He swiftly scanned the laser grid and noticed movement shifting toward the opposite side of the building.

Bang!

Mike saw a bullet ricochet near the laser grid disturbance. He realized there were snipers set up trying to take out the Death Monk.

It sounded like the Death Monk had jumped to the next building. Mike followed, improving his landing on the jump. He saw the laser grid disturbance head to the roof door, which was ripped off its hinges like tin foil. He heard footsteps racing down. Mike fired shots down the stairwell when he saw a reflection from his laser sight.

Suddenly, Mike was knocked flat on his back; he fired his gun. Some sparks appeared in the air right next to him. The Death Monk's cloak partially faded. Mike jumped up. His gun fell from his hand. Mike punched at the figure but missed, and it easily hit him hard, knocking him back down. He grabbed his gun and fired. More sparks where his bullets seemed to hit, but with no effect. The Death Monk disappeared. He could hear running down the hall. Mike ran after the sound and exited the building.

Outside, he saw a disturbance in the laser grid in front of him. But further ahead, he saw five military men with RPGs aimed at the disturbance and him. Mike saw the disturbance move one way, and he ran the other.

"Fire!" someone yelled.

Orange flames and smoke erupted from the RPG launchers and headed toward the disturbance. Boom! A series of blasts assaulted Mike's ears. He could feel the concussion of the blasts against his body.

He felt the heat from the blast as well. Small debris pelted him as he fell to the ground. Glancing over to the fireball, he squinted to see if they had hit their mark. There was too much smoke and debris in the air to see clearly. He coughed and expelled the dust and debris he inhaled. A long series of unstable boards formed a steep ramp against a building. It started to shake.

"There!" Mike yelled.

Mike ran over to an electric motorcycle. He grabbed a helmet and took off, gaining speed and performing a wheelie to ascend the steep ramp onto the roof of the building. He could see the disturbance in the laser grid ahead of him, heading toward the roof of the next building. He gave it more throttle to try to catch up to the disturbance. He witnessed the disturbance leap to the adjacent building. Mike turned the throttle to full. The motorcycle accelerated quickly up a small board. He jumped airborne, making it to the next roof. The disturbance continued off the other side of the building roof.

"We're not playing this game again!" Mike yelled as he gunned the throttle, aiming right toward the disturbance. His motorcycle struck an object as it departed the building's edge. Falling to one side, he landed in a large dumpster as the motorcycle hit the ground.

Mike's face was smashed into whatever it was in that dumpster. Luckily, it didn't seem too hard, and it cushioned his fall. He felt around to see if something was in there with him.

Smack! He was punched in the face hard. His body hit the side of the dumpster with a loud, low clang. He saw garbage fly up as he figured the Death Monk leapt out. He heard the banging of feet on the dumpster edge.

"Get him!" Mike yelled as he climbed out of the dumpster.

Suddenly, he saw a motorcycle stand up on its own with no rider. It took off quickly down one of the tunnels. Mike grabbed another motorcycle and quickly asked a nearby officer to borrow an RPG launcher. He was surprised they just handed over the launcher to him but noticed the man glanced at McMiser, who nodded.

Mike hit full throttle, chasing after the intruder. He saw the motorcycle in front of him. He pulled the RPG launcher up and fired. Orange flames burst out of the back, and a trail of smoke followed.

Boom! The RPG missed, hitting the ground behind the motorcycle. He sped up to try to catch the assailant but noticed it was slowing down hard for a turn. The motorcycle took the turn so hard, the pedals scraped the ground, sparking. It was unsettling to see a motorcycle speed off on its own without a rider. These were not self-stabilizing motorcycles, though, so there was definitely someone on it.

They were heading down a straightaway, picking up speed. Then, the tunnel opened up into a large area. The Death Monk's motorcycle was heading toward a ramp up to the large reservoir. Mike aimed his last RPG and fired. The smoke trail was aimed right at the Death Monk's ride just as it hit the ramp. Boom!

The flaming motorcycle flew off the ramp, airborne and on fire. It blew into pieces, which fell into the reservoir with many large splashes and disappeared beneath the dark waters.

"You're kind of a problem." The voice came from nowhere.

Mike looked around but couldn't pinpoint the source. He scanned the area with his gun's laser sight.

"Being a problem for criminals is kind of my job," Mike said.

Mike was knocked off his feet. He hit the ground hard. He fired his weapon several times toward what he hoped was the assailant.

Dust stirred near a door, which then opened and closed by itself. The door made a crunching sound. He heard someone running away beyond the door. He tried to open the door, but it wouldn't budge.

"Man, I hate those guys," Mike mumbled.

He got back on his motorcycle and headed back toward the underground town. He was picking up speed fast. He witnessed military personnel shooting at a disturbance in the laser grid. Mike gunned the throttle, aiming right at the disturbance. Crash! He collided and was ejected from the bike as the motorcycle slid, sparking on the ground. A Death Monk faded into visibility as he was thrown across the road, with sparks coming off him. When he slid to a stop, he faded out to invisible again.

Several people ran over to help Mike up. Others ran over to feel around for the Death Monk with the tips of their rifles. Nothing there. Their rifles were suddenly ripped from their hands, with small sparks coming from them as they moved through the air on their own, bending in half and then falling to the ground. Out of nowhere, an RPG launcher was snatched from an officer and pointed at the man that was holding it. It was floating in mid-air in front of him. Boom! The RPG fired, missing the man, but exploded on the wall of a building. The launcher dropped to the ground. People were running everywhere, trying to either get away or find the Death Monk. They didn't seem to have any luck.

Men were getting out of an armored personnel carrier. Then, they started being thrown from the vehicle. Mike saw small objects appear near the vehicle, lobbed far across the streets and buildings in every direction.

"Grenades!" someone yelled.

Explosions happened one or two at a time. Everyone ran in various directions for cover. The explosions assaulted Mike's ears. With each concussion, his chest pounded while more people dove down. The explosions lasted what felt like too long but were probably only ten seconds. Mike peered through his helmet and then removed it. Medic EV vehicles were showing up and taking some people with minor injuries away.

It got quiet for a moment. Then, all of a sudden, the laser grid and lights switched off. It was pitch black. Many expletives were yelled as they all stood there in total darkness. The emergency lights came back on as the generators kicked in.

"Mike, they hacked the power grid of the complex. I'm trying to get them out now, but they have full control. Be careful," Tara said.

"Sir, we have reports of activity near the command center," the walkie said.

"On our way," McMiser replied.

Mike and McMiser returned to the command center area, which had a ceiling about 100 feet high. They watched in amazement as a small missile was lifted into the air on its own to about 70 feet and fired toward the command center.

"Incoming!" McMiser yelled on the walkie-talkie.

The missile hit the edge of the building, exploding. A group of security arrived with rocket launchers and shoulder-fired missiles.

"What's going on?!" several people asked as another missile lifted on its own, hovering in the air.

"I think they have invisible drones in here!" Mike yelled.

One of the men fired a missile. It hit the wall of the facility next to the missile hanging in the air and exploded into a fireball. The missile, just floating in the air, fired, hitting the other edge of the command center.

Tara brought her laptop out, got next to an armored vehicle for cover, and started typing furiously. Two missiles ascended on their own. Mike picked up an RPG and prepared to fire toward one of the missiles hovering in the air.

Unexpectedly, a missile spiraled and crashed, causing an explosion.

"Got it!" Tara yelled. "I stopped their hacks, too."

Mike fired the RPG, the smoke trail headed right toward the missile. The missile fired just as the RPG was about to hit. Boom! A massive explosion erupted, sending flaming debris streaming toward the ground.

Then again—Boom! The stockpile of weapons that was underneath exploded with incredible force, knocking everyone to the ground.

Tara's ears were ringing. The smoke and heat filled the air. The blast's concussion was unlike anything she had experienced, except when the other facility exploded. She tried to regain her sense of direction and balance as she got to her feet. She had memories of that day.

"Tara, are you OK?" Alice said into Tara's ear on comm.

"I think so."

As everyone recovered, they realized another drone was hovering in the air with a missile aimed right at them.

"Stay away from my friends," Mike, Tara, and Robin heard Alice say on the comm.

Then, the lone drone fell from the sky, landing on the debris of the others and exploding.

"Crap! No one saved one for me." Robin pouted, feeling her ears and trying to get her hearing to go back to normal.

They followed McMiser back into the command center.

"Let's get what we can cleaned up. Call any of the contractors we need for repairs," McMiser told his team.

People approached and shook their hands. Tara wasn't sure why. Maybe it was Mike's incredible feats to stop the attackers, or maybe it was because of their fame from the earlier incident. She didn't feel like they did enough. Tara could see Mike felt the same way.

"What did they get?" Robin asked.

"They didn't get to the servers with nuclear codes. Those were taken offline," McMiser said.

McMiser looked at his phone. "Who wrote this about the cleaning bots?"

A woman responded that she did. "Sir, I believe the cleaning bots were hacked and used to sort through the papers as they were cleaning them up from the ground. We have a scan of the paper it cleaned up. It went to a side room and went offline. They found the bot ripped open, and the paper it had scanned was gone."

"Send me the scan," McMiser said.

He looked at his smart device.

"Oh, shit! This contains the nuclear code for the device that was stolen from Texas. Our paper backups for the nuclear codes weren't supposed to be in there. But that device was so old, it's possible that document was left there," he said.

"Will that let them detonate it?" Robin asked.

"That's if the device still works and doesn't just explode on its own," McMiser said.

"What?!" Tara exclaimed.

"That device is so old it was to be taken offline and the component parts removed because it was unsafe."

"Why didn't they tell us that in Texas?" Mike asked.

"They probably didn't have time to read the reports that came with the device since it was stolen," McMiser said.

"Great, so now they have everything they need," Robin said.

"We don't have any intelligence from our side about how they might use it," McMiser said.

"Yeah, we have nothing either. Do you have any idea who it was we were fighting?" Mike asked.

"No. They appear unusually fast for humans, yet too agile for known robot designs. We will analyze the data to see what we can find out to counter this threat," McMiser said.

"Any new intel on how they might use this weapon?" Robin asked.

McMiser shook his head. "Unfortunately, nothing we can narrow down. There are too many possibilities. Some data suggests a South African terrorist group might be involved. Other data suggests a Middle Eastern terrorist group. There is even more data suggesting other countries' involvement that doesn't make any sense."

"We'll analyze the data from our side and send anything we learn to the joint task force investigating this," Mike said.

"We have a new prediction. Well, this one seems more obvious than most but also impossible," Tara said.

"Wow, that seems unlikely. I've never been there," Robin said.

"Me neither. The security there already has to be really tight. But we can't let that stop us. We'd better follow up on it. I'll work on getting us access and flights." Mike's determination was palpable.

"Maybe they can part with some gold at Fort Knox. I could use some new jewelry," Robin joked.

"I'm thinking probably not," Mike said, already messaging his supervisor.

"I heard from the product team investigation that they looked at the black box from a small plane crash with possible future Olympic athletes onboard from a country in the Middle East. A sensor malfunction caused a glitch in the automatic pilot. But again, there is some weird data recorded, and they are still investigating," Mike shared.

"Yikes, that's horrible," Tara said.

They returned to their vehicle and headed to the airport.

9

Tara woke up in their hotel and got ready for their day.

Last night, she heard something in the hallway and saw Robin leaving Mike's room in revealing night clothes. She was sure there must be some explanation. She tried to put it out of her mind for now.

"Alice, do you have any data on those Death Monks that could help us with them?" Tara asked.

"No, not yet. I was analyzing the data. But I agree with the Lt. Colonel that they seem to move very fast. I'm investigating if there is any research that has achieved this level of speed and flexibility via bioengineering or other means," Alice said.

"Thanks, hopefully you can find something."

"Have you ever thought about what it would be like to be a computer?" Alice asked.

"I don't think so. Why do you ask?"

"No reason. Just me pondering things, I guess." Alice paused. "I detected a similar signature to my algorithms again at the previous incident. I think they might be using the neural networks they stole in some way."

"Do you think they are using it as part of a prediction system?"

"Possibly, but it seems like it could be more than that, too. Unfortunately, my measurements are indirect since they are the only patterns I can detect via encrypted signals," Alice said.

"So still potentially just margin of error?"

"Yes, unfortunately. Are we going to get in trouble?"

"I don't know. But don't worry, we'll figure out something," Tara promised.

Tara finished getting ready and met Robin and Mike for breakfast in the hotel restaurant.

"Good morning. Anything happen last night?" Tara asked.

"No, nothing I can think of," Robin said.

They checked the menus in their smart glasses and ordered.

"I think we should be good to go. It took a lot of paperwork to get us into Fort Knox," Mike said.

"Hopefully, that's all set since I don't think we want Tara to have to call the president again." Robin directed a smirk her way.

"So, have we learned anything since yesterday?" Mike asked.

"Not really. Alice detected that her algorithms might have been in use during the events yesterday, but they are still within the margin of error," Tara said.

"Well, it would explain why these guys are so hard to manage, whether it's AI or sentient AI," Mike said.

Tara shook her head. "I don't think we have enough evidence for that yet."

They finished up their breakfast and got into the FBI SUV that Mike had requested.

"I'm melting. The air conditioning feels good." Robin fanned herself.

"Fort Knox—United States Bullion Depository," Mike said to the navigation computer.

"Restricted destination. Nearest valid location selected," the car voice replied.

"Another one of those," Robin noted.

"Don't worry, once we get close, I'll drive manually," Mike said.

They proceeded to their destination. Tara slumped in her seat, the image of Mike and Robin in her sexy nightie gnawed at her. Her eyes darted to Mike and Robin. They were sitting in the car while it drove, looking at their smart devices. She wondered why she kept thinking about it, since they had agreed to live separately for a while. Mike looked back at Tara and touched her hand.

"Everything OK?" he asked.

"Yeah, fine." She smiled at him.

All she truly desired was more time with him. He kept getting sent to various countries around the world. She believed Mike desired more affection, but it was difficult to reciprocate due to his distance. She was happy he was here now but pondered what the future would bring.

"I liked the nightie you wore last night. It was your color," Tara said to Robin.

"Thanks. Hey, when did you—" Robin stopped mid-sentence, interrupted by Mike.

"She just stopped by to get some bullets," Mike explained, realizing the predicament.

"Oh, she stopped by?"

Mike squirmed in his seat slightly. Tara realized he was likely telling the truth. He was not a very good liar since he rarely, if ever, lied.

"Are you guys back together?" Robin asked.

"No—" Tara said, cut off by Robin.

"Then it's not something you should be concerned about." Robin winked.

Tara analyzed data on past incidents, hoping to identify the origin of these hacks.

They arrived at a street where the car signaled Mike to take over control. He drove to a gate around a corner. Guards stood at a booth by a closed gate on the road.

"You're supposed to have your tag on the front of your vehicle!" the guard yelled.

"Sorry, we don't know what that is. FBI Agents Actley, Agent Laizon, and the CEO of IID."

"Oh, I'm sorry, I didn't recognize the vehicle. They briefed us that you would be coming. We also heard you called the president the last time you couldn't get into a secure facility," the guard said.

"Guilty," Robin said as a matter of fact.

The guard checked their badges.

"Proceed down the road and follow the signs to the command center security checkpoint. Please give my regards to the president," he said as he let them in the gate.

They headed down the road.

"Now everyone thinks I bypass the rules and I'm mean and pushy," Tara complained, slumping deeper into her seat.

"Why are you complaining? We basically get carte blanche here with that kind of intro," Robin said with a smirk.

"Don't worry, it's not like everyone knows," Mike reassured as they pulled up to the next security gate.

"Hi, we were expecting you," the guard said, checking their IDs. "Everything is all good here. Give my regards to the president."

Tara slumped further into her seat, glancing at Mike and Robin and giving them a hard stare.

A long, winding road passed through what seemed like a small town. There were the usual convenience stores, shopping, and coffee places.

"Is this all part of the military base?" Tara asked.

"I think so," Mike replied.

"I thought Fort Knox was just a place they kept the gold," Tara said.

"Me too," Robin said.

They parked and headed to the entrance. They went inside and showed their badges at the security desk. The guard gave them a Fort Knox badge to wear.

"Should we be expecting a call from the president?" the guard said.

They shook their heads no. Tara rolled her eyes.

"Wait here," the guard ordered.

They looked around the rather plain, utilitarian waiting room.

"Agent Actley, Agent Laizon, Ms. Bitlouver, I'm Colonel Tom Stiele. We've read your reports and were briefed by Lt. Colonel McMiser," he said, motioning them to follow him. They went outside into the heat and got into a Jeep waiting for them. The Colonel programmed a route into the navigation.

"I'll give you a quick tour of the area. You might see something else on the base that the enemies are after," the Colonel said. "We have housing, schools, the General Patton museum, and our airfield here."

They drove past a golf course, library, chapel, hotels, bar, and even the usual fast food places.

"Here, you will see our fitness and training centers."

There was a massive youth sports complex and training centers. There were schools, warehouses, and an art center. Nearly everything you would expect in a town, but some of it was supersized.

"We never give these out to visitors, but in your case, we made an exception," the Colonel said, handing an encrypted hotspot to Tara.

Tara thanked him and connected to her laptop so she could monitor inbound cyberattacks from inside their network.

"Is there anything you've seen other than the most obvious target here that these terrorists might be interested in?" the Colonel asked.

"Nothing else stands out, other than perhaps usual things a military base would have. Is there anything else that is special on this base that you think would be of interest?" Mike asked.

"Nothing but gold and, as you said, military weapons. But we don't have anything out of the ordinary here in that sense."

They arrived at a security checkpoint. A metal gate stretched around a large lawn before them. They could see a moderately sized concrete building at the end of a long, white concrete road. Small buildings lined the road, situated between them and the building at the road's end. There was a large stop sign on the closed gate. Another sign said it was a restricted area. A high gate had a small traffic light indicating red.

"That is the United States Bullion Depository building, at the end of this road. When people think of Fort Knox, they usually think of this. But as you've seen, this is just a small part of our base." He looked at the camera and showed his badge.

"Authenticate, please," the Colonel's smart device said.

The Colonel entered a series of codes and then pressed his thumb on his device.

"Access confirmed," the device said.

The gate started to open. When it was fully open, the traffic light turned green. They proceeded only 400 feet, and there was another black gate with multiple security vehicles nearby. A security guard came over to the driver's door of their vehicle.

"Good morning, Colonel. Please authenticate," the security guard said, sending him a series of codes that the Colonel responded to on his device. The Colonel again used his thumbprint to authenticate. A red light came out of his device, creating a red cross over his eyes.

"Authentication confirmed," the security guard said.

The black interior gate started to open. They pulled up to the front of the building and stopped.

"The Department of the Treasury officially owns this building, but I'm also responsible for its safety. Cameras cover every square inch inside and out. There are drone patrols that monitor the airspace. There are armed guards with rifles in the towers of the building. There are motion sensors that cover the entire property outside and inside. The fences are electrified to keep out any unwanted visitors. The windows are bulletproof and have reinforced steel bars. This part is top secret—never cross the interior lawn due to land mines. This facility has never been robbed since it opened in 1937. So how do you suppose your Death Monks, as you call them, will get in here?" the Colonel said.

"Land mines?!" Tara said.

"We're not protecting this place with honey, ma'am."

"I would assume you have radar covering the airspace? Will it detect cloaked drones?" Mike asked.

"Yes, full radar coverage. We don't know for sure the tech they are using, but we think it will detect cloaked drones," the Colonel said.

The two-story concrete and granite structure in front of them looked imposing. Tara noticed cameras all around the outside of the building. She saw the guards in one of the towers peering out toward them. The barred windows gave the building an odd look. A guard from inside opened the thick metal front door that reminded her of bank safe doors, but much larger and thicker.

As they walked inside, an American flag and a few wooden seats were inside the granite entryway. The guard guided them through a metal door and down a hallway for security. They had a scanner machine that each of them had to stand inside. The guards also checked their IDs. Tara could see the scanner pick up Mike and Robin's guns. The guards looked like they were about to confiscate their weapons.

"It's fine," the Colonel told the guards.

A guard gave them another ID badge to wear. Cameras covered every angle inside the building; there even appeared to be advanced alarm-style motion sensors throughout every area. They got to another steel door and opened it. More guards asked them for their IDs. Once satisfied, the guards let them go.

"This is where if new gold arrived or if we were to send some somewhere else, it would be weighed and inspected to make sure it's authenticated. You might think that we've only housed gold here, but during the Cold War, it housed important drugs like morphine to make sure we had enough supply. We also are occasionally asked to keep important documents or artifacts like the Constitution, the Magna Carta, and the Gettysburg Address," the Colonel explained.

They walked over to large elevators. The Colonel pressed the basement button.

Exiting on the basement floor, they approached another metal door with more guards who verified their IDs. They walked into the room. A colossal vault door occupied one side. Next to it were some high-tech security panels.

"That is the entry to the vault. There is no one person that can open it. It requires at least two people with separate codes. The number of times this door has opened since 1937 is less than 15. Even presidents have been rejected from entry. Only one president has ever been here. Even if we wanted to open the safe now, we can't. It's on a 100-hour time lock. So even if we entered the code now, we would have to wait," the Colonel said.

"You saw how strong these enemies are, but these doors are thicker than I've seen before. I don't know if they would be strong enough to rip the vault door open," Mike said.

"These doors now feature the strongest composite metals," explained the Colonel.

"What kind of metal?"

"That's classified."

The Colonel motioned to head back to the elevator. They took it to the main floor and got off. After taking the stairs, they entered a moderately sized room with numerous guards and monitors. They were watching live camera feeds and sensor data. They saw different feeds on the monitors. One of them looked like the inside view of the vault with piles of gold bars. Other feeds showed areas of their building inside, as well as the exterior and grounds. There was a monitor showing radar above their area. A different monitor displayed a map of the building and surroundings, covered in scattered green dots.

An alarm sounded, with a red light flashing. Tara stared at the guards. They appeared tense. She glanced at the Colonel. He seemed calm. Some dots on the map pulsed red. A small red dot showed up on the radar and then disappeared.

"Shut the alarm off and bring up the snapshot and video feed," one of the guards said.

A monitor displayed a picture of a bird, while the other side showed it pecking at the ground. The monitor with the map of the area showed red pulses in that area.

"We have some sounds playing in the vicinity to keep birds out, but it doesn't always work," the Colonel said.

They let Tara set up her laptop at one of the desks. She checked the networks. She looked over the history of network traffic. Unusual activity, different from typical malicious traffic, raised suspicions. There seemed to be network traffic duplication and synchronization with normal traffic.

"Alice, are you seeing that?" Tara asked.

"Yes, I noticed it too, but it seemed like similar traffic. I've been analyzing it. It could just be a misconfigured network device," Alice said.

"It doesn't seem to be happening anymore. It stopped yesterday," Tara said. She looked over the data but was interrupted by a red indicator alert. "Malicious traffic detected targeting the firewall."

"Confirmed. Our network is still secure, and all systems are functioning normally," a guard said.

An alert showed up on the monitor with a red dot moving toward their building.

"Bogey inbound, sixty knots from the south, about one mile out. Do we have eyes on it?" the guard asked.

"Negative. It's all quiet out here. Wait, I see something. It's small," a guard outside said.

"ADM ready. Fire," the guard monitoring the radar commanded.

Tara could see a small missile launch from their building, heading south toward a dot in the sky. Boom! They saw a fireball erupt in the sky. A cloud of debris expanded and rained down toward the ground.

"All clear. Target destroyed," the guard at the radar station confirmed.

A drone launched from their location where the target went down.

"Security team, eyes on the south. Recovery team, land mines have been disabled in the south quadrant," a guard at another monitor reported.

The drone landed on debris, picked up a piece, and took off toward them. They heard a rumbling noise.

"What was that?" a guard asked.

"Enabling land mines in three, two, one. All stations report in," another guard said.

"Vault clear. Tower one is clear. Tower two is clear. Roof clear . . ." The radios continued to get reports of all stations.

The guards looked around at each other.

"Command, do we have any live fire operations in progress?" the Colonel asked on his radio.

"Negative, sir, no operations are scheduled today," a woman on the radio replied.

"Debris from the bogey just looks like a child RC plane," a guard from the recovery team said.

"Whoa! What's that?" One guard looked at the radar with alarm.

They looked, but there was nothing there.

"I swear I saw red targets everywhere for a split second."

Boom!

"What was that?!" a guard in the room asked on the radio.

"Looks like a land mine exploded," reported a guard outside.

A series of explosions followed.

"Do you see anything?!" the Colonel asked on comm.

"No, sir! They are just exploding," a guard outside said over the sounds of more explosions.

"Tara, put me on speaker. I believe the systems have already been compromised. Malware has been feeding us false displays to make us think everything was functioning normally. I'm also detecting the AI patterns I detected before," Alice said.

"Who was that?" the Colonel asked.

"That's my AI coworker. I agree with the assessment. Initiating scans to clean our firewalls. I suggest you scan, clean, or reset your local hardware," Tara said.

"IT specialists, please initiate malware sweeps," a guard ordered over their comm channel.

More explosions were happening outside, all around the building.

"I hear buzzing before the explosions," a guard outside said.

"It's likely the invisible drones," Mike said.

"Radar must be out," another guard said, checking the system.

The Colonel radioed the air base to check their radar. Nothing. He told them to check the systems for infection.

"Deploy mobile missiles," the Colonel ordered.

"Avenger missiles are ready. Targets detected," a voice over the radio said.

"Fire!" the Colonel commanded.

Out of the windows, they saw three streaks in the sky approaching the south lawn. One by one, the missiles exploded, hitting something in the air. Debris poured out of the sky, on fire.

"Out of missiles. Sir, it shows dozens of targets. Wait. The radar went blank," the officer said on comm.

"Clear the surrounding airspace." The Colonel's voice was tight but level.

More land mines going off rattled the equipment in the room. Tara held on to the desk, feeling the vibrations with each explosion.

"Air space clear," the voice on comm said.

"Laser the entire area," the Colonel commanded.

One of the guards flipped some switches. Two orange beams of light emitting from lasers on the building swept across the sky. Something became visible in the beam, caught fire, and melted apart, dripping out of the sky in a trail of flames. Small fires on the ground erupted as more land mines exploded, and the lasers melted many drones out of the sky. Two lasers scanned every part of the sky, moving swiftly and shifting up and down.

Landmines continued to explode as the Colonel called for additional troops to come to their location. They peered out at the once-green lawn, now a mix of brown dirt and fire. They could smell acrid smoke entering the building.

"Colonel, detectors on base have detected multiple radiation sources that have just entered the base," a voice crackled loudly over the radio.

"Did they bring the bomb? But how would there be multiple locations?" Robin asked.

"Send a company to each location!" the Colonel ordered on the radio.

"Sir, there are over ten locations," the voice replied.

"Acknowledged. Opinions?" the Colonel asked Tara, Robin, and Mike.

"Many of these attacks involved distractions," Mike said.

"If so, they are smart. In this case, we can't ignore a potential nuclear threat on site," Colonel Steele said. "Check the vault!"

They radioed to the vault room to check. The guards there indicated all clear.

"Company Charlie, we're taking fire from an unknown source. Company Bravo is under attack. Company Delta is taking fire. We have wounded. We can't target the source. It's like they don't exist," the radio sputtered.

They looked outside. Explosions erupted around the building. With each explosion, a military man dressed in burning military gear appeared and fell in flames to the ground.

"Oh shit! Abort Plan Bravo, take cover!" the Colonel yelled.

"What's going on?!" Tara asked.

"We borrowed some of that invisibility gear from the mountain complex as our backup plan, but somehow, they are targeting those men directly."

They heard a scream. Outside the window, they saw a guard thrown from the second story tower to the ground. The body was lying on the ground, limp. Another guard flew from the tower, screaming until he hit the ground with a thump.

"It must be the Death Monks." Robin gripped a chair tightly as she watched.

"Execute Plan Charlie," the Colonel said.

The lasers stopped firing. Moments later, helicopters flew overhead, dropping yellow powder on the entire building and grounds. The guards outside put on masks. Some drones appeared in the sky as the yellow powder fell on them. The powder covered the ground, the building, everything. Tara noticed the guards outside, covered in the yellow powder, were turning blue. Two figures stayed yellow, which was strange. One figure stood on the building next to a guard tower, while another was on the ground near guards.

"Engage!" the Colonel yelled.

Two missiles destroyed the hovering drones. The blue-dust-covered guards then started firing at the two yellow figures.

"What's happening?" Robin said.

"Colonel, did you use a chemical applied to your guards' clothes so they turned blue, but everything else stayed yellow?" Tara asked.

"I guess you are as smart as they say you are," the Colonel said with a grin.

They could see the guards still firing at the yellow dust-covered figures. However, the figure on the building's top remained unaffected. It swiftly approached the guards, forcefully seized their weapons, and flung them off the building. The figure on the ground also moved very quickly, disarming and pummeling the guards with punches one by one till they collapsed to the ground.

"Plan Delta now," the Colonel said.

They heard a noise like something opening. Something was moving outside. They looked out. There was a large humanoid-looking robot walking toward the yellow-dusted figure on the ground. The robot launched a missile at the figure, who leaped to avoid it. The robot swiftly pursued a target resembling a robed figure covered in yellow dust. The Death Monk moved too fast and was able to avoid the robot. The robot fired another missile that missed.

With speed, the Death Monk went behind the robot, leaped onto it, and forcefully removed a part from its head. The robot fell to the ground.

"Any news on those radiation sources?" the Colonel asked on the radio.

"Every time we think we are close, it moves. We can't find the source," came the crackling response.

"Are these guys unstoppable? Mike, you took out one of them, right?" Robin asked.

"Yes, but only because I think the guy was trying to keep me from hitting the truck with the RPG."

"Enable the automated .50 caliber machine guns," the Colonel said.

The guards outside started to run for cover. They saw a large gun on the roof move on its own and aim toward the yellow powdered target. The figure started to move fast, with yellow dust flying off it. The gun started to fire, turning to maneuver toward the running figure. Bullets hit the ground, creating visible dust just behind the figure.

"They are still too fast," Mike said.

The yellow figure ran up to the machine gun, pulled it off its mount, bent it, and tossed it aside.

"Enable the automated drones," The Colonel said. "They aren't faster than those."

A swarm of small black drones started to leave the building and head toward the two yellow figures. The figures started to run, but they weren't fast enough. Multiple drones exploded near the two figures, creating small fireballs. As the cloud of smoke cleared, they could no longer see the yellow dust-covered Death Monks.

"I want confirmation," the Colonel said.

Guards were looking around the area, kicking the ground where the drones exploded.

"Sir, there's lots of debris but nothing big. I don't think I see anything organic, but that was a lot of explosions," the guard reported.

"Test for DNA," the Colonel said.

Two guards were staring at monitors showing the interior of the vault.

"Sir, I've been reviewing the video of the vault interior, and I think I see something," one guard said.

The Colonel peered at the display. Tara, Mike, and Robin gathered around to look.

"Did you see that?" the guard asked.

He played it again in a loop. A small section of something inside vanished gradually in a day. They examined it once more, checking for shadows caused by the vault lights.

"It has to be just lighting," the Colonel said.

"I've never seen that before," the guard replied.

The Colonel motioned to the head guard. They descended, using two elevators, to reach the vault floor.

Tara, Robin, and Mike followed them down.

"Are we still all clear?" the Colonel asked.

"Yes, sir," a guard from the command center said.

"Open the vault," the Colonel said to the head guard.

The guard entered a very long password into a panel, then used a handprint identification pad, followed by an iris scan. The Colonel entered his codes and biometric authentication.

"Unfortunately, this won't open for 100 hours now. So we can't come back before that time to check the vault," the guard said.

They started walking back to the elevator.

"Vault door timelock has expired. Opening," an electronic voice said.

"What's happening?! How is this possible?!" the Colonel asked.

The head guard appeared surprised. Guards entered the room upon receiving an alert about the vault door. They looked as surprised as everyone else.

"What you see inside is highly classified. You must never discuss it with anyone," the Colonel said.

"The gold?" Robin asked.

"As I mentioned, we store other items as well. Plus, the entire layout and structure is classified," the Colonel said.

They looked inside the vault and saw the glistening gold bars neatly stacked a bit above waist height. The vault walls were an ordinary military gray. It had a musty smell, like a basement.

"I want an inventory now," the Colonel commanded.

Several guards started checking each of the gold palettes. Tara glanced around and spotted a tiny hatch on the wall.

"That must be the emergency exit we heard about," Tara said.

She spotted a greenish-yellow glow near a heap of glistening gold in the distance.

"Sir, there are several palettes here that should have gold on them, but don't," the guard said.

"Check the security of the vault now!" the Colonel said.

The guards rushed around, checking the walls, the vault door, and the emergency escape hatch.

"Everything looks secure," a guard said.

"Obviously, it's not, so find out what happened!" the Colonel demanded.

Mike, Tara, and Robin walked over to the empty palettes. Mike bent down to inspect the ground and wood. The dust was expected, given the length of time. A small black line of dust came off each of the palettes. Mike pointed it out. Robin and Tara peered closer at it.

"Anything?" Robin asked.

"Not sure if that's dust, but it looks odd in a line like that. Maybe something got damp and leaked that way to the drain," Mike said.

Mike pointed the dust out to the guards. The U.S. Mint Police formally requested FBI assistance, so Mike called for FBI forensic investigators to collect the data. Tara looked over and thought she saw a small green glowing cylinder slightly floating that was being covered by some guards in slightly different uniforms. She blinked her eyes, since that didn't seem right. Upon opening them, she discovered the object was now concealed under a tarp. She figured it was probably just because of the long day's events that she didn't see quite right. At the far edge of the vault, the U.S. Mint Police and the guards noticed some cracking in the concrete flooring.

"It must be from all of the explosions," one of the guards said.

They searched the area but found nothing unusual.

"Any news on the radiation sources?" the Colonel asked.

"They all disappeared," a man on the radio responded.

Tara approached the vault door and noticed electronic components. It looked related to the time lock. It was only connected to the outside pad, though. The technology they were using was older. It used an old chipset, but it looked like it might support wireless technology.

"Alice, is there a way to enable the wireless connection on this tech?" she asked, showing Alice the vault PIN pad.

"Checking. Try entering ***241071###."

Tara tapped the pad and checked her phone for a connection. It worked. She analyzed the programming in the pad.

"Alice, is that what I think it is?" Tara asked.

"It does appear to be infected with some type of malware. It looks like it was intended to bypass the code and biometrics needed to open the door. Though I don't think it could bypass the timelock. So this lock must have been infected 100 hours ago. Let me help clean it."

Tara informed Mike and Robin of what she and Alice had found.

"But it seems like they stole the gold without even waiting for the door to open. Why do this then?" Tara asked.

"It doesn't make much sense. Maybe it was a backup plan, in case their main one didn't work. Or there is some aspect of their plan that needed this to happen," Mike said.

"Unless there was something else in here that they couldn't get out without opening the door," Robin said.

"Colonel, please block off the emergency exit route on the main level," Mike said loudly.

"Why?" he asked.

"Colonel, we may have an intruder," Mike whispered.

"Block off the emergency exit immediately!" the Colonel radioed before addressing the people with him. "Weapons. Everyone out and relock the safe! Checkpoints alert!" the Colonel yelled.

The guards pulled out their guns and started rushing out of the safe. Suddenly, the tarp lifted over a small, lightly glowing green cylinder that disappeared. Mike aimed his laser sight in that direction. He scanned the area but lowered his weapon to avoid aiming at the other guards. They rushed to the vault door to get outside of it.

"Form a ring outside the door," the Colonel ordered.

The guards created a half-circle ring around the vault entry to try to stop the intruder.

"Ah!" guards yelled as they were slammed against the wall.

"Fire!" the Colonel ordered.

The guards opened fire toward the likely direction of the escaping Death Monk.

"Colonel, tell the guards out front to seal the front door with a vehicle. This place can act like a prison," Mike said.

"Locked in here with a superpowered terrorist. That's crazy, but I like it." The Colonel grinned.

He relayed to the guards outside to block the main door with an armored vehicle.

"Colonel, intruder on the main level. No!" a guard said, followed by the sound of gunfire on the radio, then silence.

Boom! They heard an explosion somewhere outside. Mike, the guards, and the Colonel ran upstairs. Tara and Robin followed behind. There were guards scattered on the floor as if they had been tossed like dolls. Guards were helping the ones on the floor get medical attention. Upon reaching the front door, daylight gleamed in. The door was gone. A vehicle engulfed in flames was roughly twenty feet from the door.

"They must have still had drones in the area," the Colonel said. "Clean the malware off your systems and clear the airspace now!" he commanded over the radio.

"What was that green thing the Death Monk took?" Tara asked.

"That information is compartmentalized classified," the Colonel said.

The FBI forensics team arrived and was able to start collecting samples and data, luckily, since they didn't get a chance to close the safe.

"We figure they got away with at least two billion dollars in gold," one of the guards said.

Mike, Tara, and Robin reviewed the attack footage for clues. The Colonel insisted on keeping the video at the base, so they had to watch it there. Tara set up her phone so Alice could watch the video, too, but without storing it for long.

"These Death Monks seem faster and stronger than the earliest ones you encountered. Starting with the neutron bomb theft, I noticed that some Death Monks had different power levels than others. The speed of reaction based on predictions seems higher in some of them," Alice said.

Tara had Alice send the findings to a special team at work to determine what they were and how to stop them.

Looking over at Robin and Mike, Tara could tell something wasn't right.

"Are you guys OK?" she asked.

"Everything that's been tried to stop these guys hasn't worked. The police tried. Even the military tried with no luck," Robin said.

"Unfortunately, I agree with Robin. We are out of our league and putting us all at risk," Mike admitted.

She had never heard Mike sound this defeated. He was probably right, though. They were not equipped to handle these guys. But at this point, it wasn't clear if anyone could. One of the most secure locations in the world was breached, and they were powerless to stop it.

"It seems AI is still connected to this data somehow. Some patterns seemed similar to the sentient AI. We can't prove anything yet since they are breaching my tech to get through, and it could be related to our AI. I can't stop until I get to the bottom of this. I can't be responsible again for the world being in danger," Tara explained.

"You weren't responsible even the first time. I guess we keep going until we get to the bottom of this," Mike said, holding out his hand.

Tara put her hand on top of Mike's.

"Shit, you guys are crazy. But I guess so am I." Robin put her hand on top of Tara and Mike's.

"We should head back home since we don't have another prediction yet. I want to see if we can get help from my company on how to stop these guys," Tara said.

"The product team investigated a U.S. satellite that misfired and crashed into a Russian satellite. It looks accidental, but there are connection signals that appear to be from the Middle East. There is no proof yet that caused the issue," Tara said.

They went to their car and headed to the airport to go home.

10

Tara's alarm went off. She couldn't even recall what the question was that she had to answer to get her alarm to turn off. She was glad to be home in her own bed. The bed felt good, yet the feeling of failure lingered. Almost all incidents saw the hackers escaping with their loot. She acknowledged that it wasn't solely her fault, but she felt her company had disappointed clients. Plus, she had personally disappointed her clients and herself.

"Good morning, Alice. How are you doing?" Tara asked.

"Fine. I had some ideas about how to try to stop the Death Monks. I sent the information to your internal team to see if they can come up with something to help," Alice said.

Tara got ready and went to her office. She liked her office up on the top floor. She still wasn't really comfortable being in charge of everything. It also made her wonder about her relationships with people at work. Some treated her as friends, but were they merely friendly due to her CEO status? Those feelings gnawed at her. She still felt down for failing to stop the attacks. She wondered if she was really cut out to be CEO.

A message came through to her from their automated prediction system. A warning mentioned an attack on Marina Island. She remembered that name from somewhere, but where? Most of their predictions had a very particular company location or building. This one had an island. She was about to check on the location when she was interrupted.

FBI agents burst through Tara's office doors at International IQ Devices.

"You are under arrest. Come with us," an agent said to Tara.

"What for?" Tara asked, surprised and flustered.

"I'm sorry, ma'am, I'm not at liberty to disclose that information at this time."

"Get our lawyers now and call Mike," Tara said to her assistant as they walked out of her office door.

There were dozens of agents asking people to step away from their computers.

"Get copies of everything," the lead agent said to the agents heading toward another area of the office.

The agents ushered Tara into a car quickly and drove off. After driving for some time, they arrived at a building. Tara realized this was the New York FBI field office. They took her to an interview room and set her up at a table. Several agents and a supervisor came in and sat down. An older man, wearing a lighter-colored suit, walked in and sat opposite her at the table. She thought she recognized him but couldn't place him.

"Miss Bitlouver. I'm Agent Rilson," greeted one of the agents, a younger man with sharp eyes. "I will be interviewing you today for your role in the events that took place at the nuclear Department of Energy installation you visited in Texas and other federal locations. You have been charged with violations of the Artificial Intelligence Act 154 law related to hacking and the use of connected artificial sentience to do so."

Tara thought for a moment. She tried to prevent the attacks there, so she didn't understand why they would charge her like this. Regardless, she was in trouble, and so was Alice. She figured maybe she could call the president to help her out of this mess.

"I know what you are thinking," the man in the lighter suit said. "You could just call your friend, the president, to get out of this. He's not going to help you since he needs some bills to pass to get re-elected. Which means he needs my help. Oh, I forgot to introduce myself. I'm Senator Bailson."

Tara recognized the name but was having trouble placing it. She suddenly remembered he was one of the most outspoken senators who sponsored the bill after their incidents with the AIs about six months ago. She had tried to convince them to not pass the law, or at least change it so it made sense. She had emailed her senators about it, but they were unable to change his mind. He was able to get the bill passed.

A beautiful, tall, blonde woman in her forties entered wearing a pantsuit. Every man in the room watched as she walked to the table and sat beside Tara.

"Hi, I'm Cara Mitsfield, a lawyer for IID. What are you charging my client with?" she asked.

"Your client is charged with hacking a government nuclear installation, hacking drones on that installation, hacking a helicopter on that installation, and violating the Artificial Intelligence Act along with the deal that was made with IID regarding the AI known as Alice. Other charges are pending," the agent said.

"IID and my client were defending your installation from an attack by hackers. In an attempt to prevent the hackers from obtaining top secret classified nuclear information, IID used its resources to stop that attack and was successful at preventing the electronic information from being exposed," Cara said.

Tara was impressed. She had obviously read up on everything that happened from Tara's reports.

"Your client and IID caused over a million dollars in damage to the installation in the process," the agent said.

"IID and Tara were defending the installation from attack and used all means available to prevent the information from being released. Although IID is not responsible for these damages, we are prepared to offer three million dollars to offset any costs that may have been incurred due to the defense of the installation," Cara said.

"If restitution is offered, we can drop the damages," the FBI counsel said.

The Senator glared at the FBI counsel like he was going to burn a hole through his head with his eyes.

"One of the other charges is violating the Artificial Intelligence Act moratorium and provision on usage. Did you use an artificial sentience for the hacking?" the FBI counsel asked.

Tara was about to answer when Cara put her hand on her shoulder.

"My client asserts her Fifth Amendment rights."

"Did you allow an artificial sentience access to a U.S. nuclear installation?" the FBI counsel asked.

"You don't need to answer that," Cara told Tara.

"Miss Bitlouver, did you violate the terms of the Artificial Intelligence Act provision that allowed Alice to continue to exist as long as it was not provided access to the internet?" the FBI counsel asked.

"My client is not going to answer that. What evidence do you have?"

"Your client's computer IP addresses have been recorded on the servers that were hacked at the installation," the FBI counsel said.

Cara looked quizzically across the table.

"IID provides services to that location, so the IP address would, of course, show up. You don't have anything that establishes a link to the charge. We're leaving," Cara declared and stood up.

Tara followed her lead. The Senator glared at the FBI counsel.

"I'm sure we'll have evidence soon since we are collecting all of the servers related to your AI as we speak," the Senator said while the FBI counsel glared at him in return.

"That needs to stop now. Those servers are shared hosts used by multiple governmental entities. You are jeopardizing the security of the United States. They need to be returned at once," Cara said as she was at the door.

"That's not going to happen," FBI counsel replied.

Cara tapped a message into her phone.

Suddenly, the FBI counsel got a call. He picked up his phone.

"Yes, sir. I see," the FBI counsel said and hung up. "Evidence collection has been paused for now. You are free to go."

"Who was that?!" the Senator asked.

"That was the Attorney General. He got a message from the Secretary of Defense, Homeland Security, and the Director of National Intelligence. He wants to review everything before anything proceeds," the FBI counsel said.

Senator Bailson glared fiercely at the FBI counsel.

"You are the one jeopardizing the security of the U.S. and the world. You have some friends in high places, but so do I," the Senator said to Tara.

Tara walked out with her lawyer.

"Alice, is everything OK? Alice?" Tara said into her phone.

There was no response. Tara texted her team to get Alice back online. Robin and Mike ran up to the building, and Tara walked out.

"Tara! We came as soon as we figured out what was happening," Mike said.

"It's OK for now, thanks to our amazing lawyer. But Alice is offline, as they were pulling out servers to collect evidence." Tara looked sad.

"Don't worry. We have lots of friends who will help get things cleared up eventually," Mike reassured.

Mike and Robin hugged her.

They took a car back to New Jersey.

"We have a new prediction for activity. Is this what I think it is?" Tara asked, showing Mike and Robin the name of the place.

"Holy crap! No way! I've heard about that place," Robin said.

"I think everyone in the world has heard of that place. It's unlike anything else in the world. Someone mentioned to me there might be a unit to help around that area. I'll also check with my supervisor. We'll need approvals to go there. It's going to take a while to get there. Well, depending on where it is now, I guess," Mike said.

"I can't believe we're going to Singapore's Marina Island!" Robin exclaimed.

They headed back to their homes to pack and then to the international airport to catch the next flight.

11

They boarded their flight to the Philippines. Luckily, they caught a supersonic flight, so instead of seventeen hours, it might take seven hours. However, that was just a fraction of the journey. From there, they needed a ship to reach their destination. That would probably take another twenty hours or more, presuming their destination hadn't moved further away.

Flying still wasn't Tara's preference. Their previous incident didn't help much. She instinctively asked Alice to monitor the airplane's systems to give her some peace of mind. But Alice didn't respond. She forgot her team was trying to get her back online after the FBI pulled out servers. Tara clenched her fist and sighed deeply. She knew Alice had a fear of being taken offline. Tara would have helped put Alice back online herself, but she knew her team was more capable with the hardware part than she was. She fidgeted in her seat, closed her eyes for a moment, and leaned her head back. Her phone beeped. She looked at a message from work.

It read, "Defendant is hereby ordered to immediately disconnect all artificial sentience systems from the internet and any external networks."

Tara's face grew red. She slightly kicked the seat in front of her in frustration by accident.

Even though she didn't like flying that much, she had done a bit recently for her company. It allowed her to upgrade Mike and Robin to first class for free. The flight attendants didn't seem to recognize them. Tara relaxed into her seat. Tara didn't really like the attention brought to them by her position as CEO or the previous incident they were involved with. Most of the time, it caused problems or annoyances, but occasionally, their fame or infamy did help them.

Tara fell asleep and slept until she was woken up for landing. She still really disliked landings. Mike saw she was tense and softly touched the top of her hand. The plane hit some turbulence. Tara grabbed hard at Mike's hand, holding tight. More turbulence shook the cabin. Some items fell from the cart while collecting trash. Finally, the plane landed. When it slowed down, Tara finally released her grip on Mike's hand. She noticed her fingers left white marks where she held him and her nail left a small red mark.

"Oh my gosh, I'm sorry," she said to Mike, rubbing his hand with hers.

They departed the plane and got through customs. They got a car to take them to the ship's port.

The small towns they drove through had one or two-level older-style houses and buildings. One of the buildings they drove past had a large number of satellite dishes. There were palm trees everywhere, and sometimes other types of trees dotting the landscape. They smelled the ocean air as they drove by with their windows down. The weather was sunny and warm.

They got to the dock and boarded the cruise ship. It was a good-sized ship, eight hundred feet long, with about ten decks. It was part of a small cruise line that had destinations including Singapore's Marina Island. The ship was beautifully appointed with a very attentive staff. Their individual cabins were delightful, with ocean views. Getting to Marina Island would require nearly an entire day.

They sat down for lunch. The slight breeze blew around them with the scent of salty sea air. The sun bathed their faces in warmth. They looked out to the horizon, where the blue water met the sky. There were no other ships or anything around them as far as the eye could see. Tara was fidgeting with her phone, glancing at it every so often.

"Worried about Alice?" Mike asked.

"Of course. They should have been able to get her online by now."

"The signal out here is horrible. Even the satellite coverage is bad," Mike said.

Their food arrived. Despite the food being great, Tara just picked at her food. After lunch, they changed into swimsuits and headed to the pool. Mike and Robin were heading toward the pool when Robin tripped and fell into an open doorway, which happened to be a large supply closet. Robin's hair was a bit messed up. Mike put out his hand to help Robin up. When she stood up, her bikini bottom fell off because it ripped during the fall. Mike turned around quickly.

"Sorry, I didn't see anything," Mike said, handing Robin one of the towels he was carrying.

"I'm going back to change," Robin said, her bottom half wrapped in the towel.

Tara spotted Robin and Mike exiting the supply closet. She looked around, puzzled.

"Did you two . . . in the closet?!" Tara asked.

"No. It's not what you think. She fell into there, and I helped her back up," Mike said.

"Then why is the bottom half of her bikini on the ground, and she's wrapped in a towel?!" Tara asked.

"She tore it when she fell. Robin, help me out here!"

"This story does sound crazy, but it's true. Mike's basically a grown-up boy scout, so I guess you'll have to take his word for it." Robin shrugged, picking up her torn bikini and heading back to her cabin.

Tara turned around and headed back toward her cabin instead of the pool. Mike glanced at her in her swimsuit as she was leaving.

"I'll be at the pool," Mike said.

About thirty minutes later, Tara decided to head back to the pool. When she arrived, she saw a beautiful girl on the ground, wet and wearing a bikini. Mike had his mouth on the girl's.

"What is going on?!" Tara asked.

More bikini-clad girls came running over to watch.

"Help me roll her over," Mike said.

Once she was rolled to the side, water poured from the girl's mouth. She began to cough.

"You saved her!" one of the other girls said.

"Get her to the doctor now," Mike said to one of the ship's crew as he was helping her up.

A few friends of the girl he helped hugged Mike and then followed their friend. Tara kissed Mike on the cheek.

"You are a boy scout," Tara said, gently touching Mike's hand.

"What did I miss?" Robin asked, just getting to the pool.

They went to the ship's casino. Mike played some blackjack while Robin and Tara sat and played the slot machines. Tara was somewhat listlessly pulling the handle. Robin was energetically engaged. The sounds of players and slot machines filled the air.

"Come on, baby!" Robin cheered as she pulled the handle.

Robin won a few times at slots. Tara had nothing.

"I'm going to get ready for dinner," Tara said, pulling the handle and starting to walk off, not waiting for the slot machine to finish.

The slot machine made all sorts of ringing noises as it started to spit out one thousand dollars.

"Tara, you won!" Robin yelled to Tara.

"You can keep it." Tara didn't stop.

They met up for dinner later.

"I got a message from my team at work. They are sending one of our engineers with some tech that might help us stop these Death Monks. They are making the assumption it's some kind of electronic tech rather than bioengineering," Tara said.

"The FBI gave us a portable EMP gun to try. We need special approvals to get it into Marina Island, which we don't have yet," Mike noted.

"Our company may have a little influence since they use our software to protect their systems on Marina Island. We can try to convince them," Tara said.

"What are we going to do? Hope we don't run into the Death Monks?" Robin asked.

"We'll do what we always do: improvise," Mike declared.

"That's not really a plan," Robin said.

"I also contacted the military to see if they could assist. They might not get clearance since it's foreign soil," Mike said.

Following dinner, they headed to the deck, sat, and admired the ocean view. Tara shifted uncomfortably in her chair.

"Still thinking about Alice?" Mike asked Tara.

"Yes, plus there's something uncomfortably familiar about how these new Death Monks move."

"What do you mean?" Robin asked.

"I don't know, it just seems familiar."

"Maybe it's just the robes, and they move in particular ways," Mike said.

"Possibly, though I feel like it could be something else I'm missing," Tara said.

They all went back to their cabins. Robin's cabin was on the opposite side of the hall from Mike's. She opened her door and, before closing it, proceeded to get undressed.

"Want to come in?" Robin asked as he passed.

"We better get some sleep for tomorrow," Mike said, going into his cabin.

"I sleep better after a little activity."

"I'm sure there will be an armed robbery or something tomorrow," Mike joked.

"Not the kind I was thinking of," Robin teased, turning around to face away from the door, unfastening her bra, and closing the door behind her.

Mike went to his room and closed the door to his cabin.

In the morning, Tara woke up to a blaring alarm.

"What is the activation function commonly used in hidden layers of neural networks?" Lia, the AI voice on her smartphone, asked.

"Rectified linear unit. Ask me something harder next time," Tara said, slightly muffled because she was still half asleep and speaking into her pillow.

"Have a nice day!" Lia said.

Tara got ready, and she and Mike went downstairs with their luggage to disembark. They had already docked. Tara gazed from the ship's high vantage. The city looked futuristic. Long buildings, with around twenty floors, stretched far in every direction. There were solar cells on the tops of the buildings, along with both open and enclosed walkways.

They finally got off the ship. Over Mike's objections, Customs kept Mike and Robin's weapons and the EMP gun.

They were met by a beautiful brown-haired woman, who was tall but not as tall as Mike.

"Hi, I'm Sue Smithe, Ambassador to Singapore. You can call me Sue. I've been briefed on your visit. Don't worry, we'll get your weapons cleared soon," Sue said.

Tara looked up some information on her phone.

"Another person is coming from my company, too. I'll send you the details," Tara said.

Sue took them downstairs to a waiting electric vehicle. Another vehicle was ahead of theirs. Sue assisted in loading their luggage onto the first vehicle, which departed once the final item was loaded.

"Don't worry. They will take your luggage to your rooms." Sue motioned them to get in.

She started to drive and took a side road, which led to a road near one of the four sides of Marina Island.

"I'll give you a quick tour of the island," she said, driving slowly down the road.

They peered from the island's edge, spotting shiny panels rolling on top of the small waves. At the edges, they could see poles with flags on them and small wind turbines at equal distances.

"As you probably know, Marina Island is over a square mile in size. It's roughly equivalent in size to over 150 of the largest cruise ships. That's almost 200 million square feet of space so far, and they are still building," Sue said.

"What is that shiny surface on the water?" Robin asked.

"Those are solar cells that stretch for about a mile, with wind turbines around the edges. They provide much of the power on the island. It's stored in high-efficiency batteries. They do have a small nuclear power station and diesel generator backup power if needed."

As they drove slowly down the road, Tara glanced at the tall buildings on the island, which had clear tube-enclosed walkways along with open ones stretching out along the tops of the buildings. They noticed a lot of the elongated buildings had many of the top floors connected to the building next to them.

"This island is made of independent bottom levels that move like ships with the ocean. The top platform can adjust to small or medium-sized waves to keep it level and stable. Lifeboats are on the edges of the island and at the tops of the buildings," Sue said.

Tara noticed a large, tall radar tower on top of a building near the center of the island. She realized the elongated buildings kind of looked like the top of cruise ships modified with a more building-like and futuristic feel.

They saw a big floating fishing pier on the right, connected to the island.

"The island gets some of its food by fishing. But there are also hydroponic farms on board. They do have livestock as well. Some food is imported, but it is possible to live off just the food produced on this island if needed. Sea water is desalinated for fresh water," Sue said.

"They built this because they ran out of space in their country?" Robin asked.

"Yes, plus, to compete with other countries' exports, this was a good investment because it reduces the shipping costs as the island can just relocate close to the nation it needs to export to, decreasing the overall cost of goods. They manufacture goods right here on the island, and then those can be delivered to other countries."

"This must have cost a lot!" Robin said.

"Many hundreds of billions of dollars. Luckily, a mix of money from Singapore and foreign investments helped build it," Sue revealed.

They stopped on the street in front of one of the buildings. Sue guided them inside and down through some open hatches. A hallway with a large window looked out into the waters below the massive floating island. They saw a fish swim by the window.

"Pretty cool, right? There is a whole underwater hotel here," Sue said, directing them back up to their self-driving electric vehicle.

They continued their slow drive down the edge of the island.

"Wait, this island is floating, right? How is there a beach?" Robin asked, pointing toward the water.

"They just have an area they fill in with sand near the water to give it a beach feel. There is even an extended edge under the water to walk out and a net at the edge so people don't go too far," Sue said.

Sue directed them back to the vehicle. They headed down the road and arrived at a building with a more governmental appearance.

"Let's go inside so you can meet the mayor," Sue said.

They entered the modern building. Security checked their IDs and belongings. The staff directed them to wait in some chairs outside the mayor's office. It was still pretty early. Several police officers came in to talk to the mayor's staff. Tara couldn't make out what they were saying. The staff pointed the police officers at them.

"Come with us, please," the officer said to Mike, Tara, Robin, and Sue.

They walked down a hall and took an elevator up to the top floor. One staff member from the mayor joined them.

"Hi, my name is Tan. In the U.S., you might call my role similar to that of deputy mayor," the staff member said.

"Where are we going?" Robin asked.

"The Mayor's private residence at the top of the building."

Upon reaching the top and passing through another door, they witnessed a multitude of police photographing and examining a body on the floor, clad in a body suit and VR headset. Sue went over to talk with the staff before coming back with information.

"The staff found the mayor dead on the floor this way," she said.

Tara looked at the man lying on the floor.

"Oh no," Tara said.

"What?" Mike asked.

"That body suit he is wearing looks the same as the one we are testing at my company. It allows the user to feel a virtual environment."

Tara explained to one of the police crime scene investigators how to create a memory copy of the data from the suit. When the investigator was done, he handed a small USB drive to Tara. She put on her smart glasses and connected the USB drive to her phone.

"Hmm. There are some odd data patterns here. I'll send this to my team to investigate," Tara said.

"They explained to me the residence was locked. There was no evidence of a struggle. He was in good health. He was young, only thirty-five years old," Mike described.

The body was facing down. They turned the body over and noticed a black, burnt area of the body suit.

"Wait!" Tara said, going over and disconnecting the body suit battery pack.

They took more pictures and samples of the flaking, burnt part of the suit. They then checked underneath and found the burn went through to the skin near the mayor's heart. Tara downloaded the suit's data, gave a copy to the police, and analyzed it on her phone. She pulled up a video of the motion the body suit went through.

They could see the outline of the suit standing up in the room with the mayor playing a game, waving his arms in the air. The suit video showed that he tripped and fell, hitting the chest area of the suit on the corner of the table.

He tried to get up but fell to the floor. The body suit vitals data showed he had been fine up to that point. Mike and Robin looked over the scene as well.

Tara examined the suit. It looked like the wires were damaged by the corner of the desk and were shorted. Tara explained what she found to everyone there.

"So it looks like an accident," one of the police officers said.

"It does look that way. But I see some odd data I want my team to take a look at," Tara said, sending it to them.

Tara got a message on her phone. The technical person her company sent had arrived on the island.

"One of my team arrived at the port. Here is her contact info," Tara said to Sue.

"No problem, I'll have one of my staff get them," Sue replied.

"So, the odd data you found. Did it look something like Project Mind River?" Mike asked in earshot of Robin.

"Maybe," Tara said.

They continued to check out the scene and data to match the environment.

About twenty minutes later, one of Sue's staff showed up escorting a woman about Tara's size and build, 5'6", with brown hair and eyes, thin and very pretty. She was carrying a large case.

"Hi, Miss Bitlouver, I'm Laurie Cebovilt," she said.

Tara shook her hand, and then Laurie leaned in for a hug. She did the same for Mike and Robin.

"She's very friendly," Robin whispered to Mike.

"What do we have here? Do you have the data?" Laurie asked Tara.

Tara handed her the USB drive. Laurie checked it on her smart device.

"Hmm. This was definitely hacked. Seems very similar to an AI like Project Mind River. It looks like it shifted the virtual play space over just a bit so that he would trip on the carpet and fall onto the table," Laurie said.

"How do you know that?" Tara asked.

"I've studied the data you provided to the team at work."

"Oh, that reminds me, I wanted to check on Alice," Tara said.

"Don't worry. She's OK. They are working on getting her back online. The FBI damaged some of the equipment when they pulled it out and didn't return some yet, so they are having to restore servers from backups and purchase new ones," Laurie replied, slightly touching Tara's arm.

"Do you know any reason why someone would want the mayor dead?" Mike asked Sue.

"Everyone liked him. Well, except for the organized crime groups that sometimes tried to set up shop on the island. He gave the police everything they needed to stop them."

"That could do it," Robin said.

"There was some sort of glitch, but it's OK now?" Mike heard Tan on his phone.

"What glitch?" he asked.

"Radiation sensors on the island glitched for a second, showing radiation, but they are fine now," Tan said.

Robin, Mike, Tara, and Laurie looked at each other.

"Can you show us to your operations center where you would get these alerts?" Tara asked.

Tan didn't seem sure about the request. Sue discussed it with him for a moment, and he agreed to take them. They went back down in the elevator.

They went far down the hallway to a large set of doors. Tan swiped his badge and put his hand on a pad. A green light flashed, and the doors opened. It was a large operations room with monitors across the walls. There were rows of desks with keyboards and monitors on them. The sounds of talking and clicking keyboards filled the air. He showed them a row of desks where they could sit. Tara set up her laptop on the desk and asked for permission to connect to their network. Laurie plugged in her phone to charge.

"Hmm. I wonder if this could be . . ." Tara murmured to herself quietly.

Laurie was looking over her shoulder.

"That does look similar."

"Your systems might have been hacked," Tara said to Tan, who told the teams to initiate a scan of their systems.

"You might want to test your radiation sensors," Mike said to Tan, who told others to check.

"Oh, I've got something." Laurie opened up the large case she carried with her.

Inside, there were other cases. She pulled out a small one and opened it. She pulled out a device with a small handle, display, and a cylindrical protrusion on top. Turning in place, she shifted the device in the air while studying the screen.

"It's reading above normal background just slightly. There is a good chance the device is here," Laurie said.

They all looked at each other.

"What device?" Tan asked.

"A small neutron bomb was stolen. It may have been transferred here. We were not expecting that to be the case," Sue said.

"All radiation sensors are not functioning. We can't tell if the firmware was destroyed in the hack or not," another staffer said.

Tan was standing near a staffer and the chief of police.

"Should we evacuate?" the staffer asked Tan.

"They might detonate immediately," the police chief said.

"I'm not sure. A neutron bomb is designed to minimize infrastructure destruction and kill the most people. On Marina Island, though, it's still powerful enough to sink it. So why use a neutron bomb here? Of course, it just might have been the easiest device they could steal," Mike said.

"We can't be sure. Let's search quietly for the device to avoid tipping them off," the police chief said.

"We only have a couple of handheld radiation detectors available," a staffer said.

"We can help you search. We have been tracking these people. You need to be very careful. Some of the suspects have speed, strength, and abilities beyond normal. We suspect they must be using some kind of tech. Do you have any EMP weapons on board?" Mike asked.

"No, due to the risks to the ship," the police chief replied.

"We brought a small one. Plus, our weapons. Can we have them? We can help," Mike said.

The chief nodded, then told an officer to get them.

Laurie cleared her throat. "I did bring another EMP device."

"Obviously, our security wasn't doing its job to inspect your case properly. I will have a talk with them. But you can keep it for now," the police chief allowed.

Two men in military uniforms walked toward them.

"Major Sentinal, Sergeant McMiser, it's good to see you," Mike said.

"Oh, shit! You lied. You told me we get to take some leave time on a tropical island," Maddox McMiser said to Joe Sentinal.

Joe was carrying a medium-sized case.

"Nice to see you too," Robin said to Maddox, who had not noticed her standing behind a staffer.

She gave him a hug.

"It's nice to see you too. Hey! If you are all here, this definitely isn't a vacation. You lied," Maddox grumbled at Joe.

"Smart thinking, detective," Robin said sarcastically.

"I didn't lie. I told you we were going on leave to a unique island getaway."

Maddox looked annoyed for a moment, but glancing at Robin seemed to calm his mood.

"Eyes up here, sergeant," Robin said to Maddox.

"So what trouble have you got us into this time?" Maddox asked.

"This island has been hacked. The mayor was probably murdered by a hack. At many of the hacks we've been to recently, we run into those Death Monks. So they could be here. But now they seem to have cloaking, super speed and strength, along with their predictive fighting. Oh, and one more thing—there might be a neutron bomb onboard which they plan to explode," Robin explained.

"Holy shit! We need to get off this thing now. Did you know about this?" Maddox asked Joe.

"We didn't know anything about what would be here for sure, just the incidents they had in the past," Joe said.

"There are no flights on or off the island for the rest of the day," Sue said.

"Wait, who is we?" Maddox asked.

"Our orders were relayed through our command from Lieutenant Colonel McMiser," Joe said.

"My father! It figures," Maddox grumbled.

"We met him—nice guy," Robin said.

"Nice?! Do you know where he is?! He won't tell me."

"Hi, I'm Laurie. I work at IID. Nice to meet you," Laurie said, giving Maddox a hug.

"Eyes up, sergeant," Robin said, noticing him staring at Laurie.

"We heard at Fort Knox that they used underground drones with small amounts of radiation to make them think the neutron bomb was there. I wonder if this could be something similar," Joe said.

"Possibly, but can we afford to take that chance?" Mike asked.

"Agreed. Let's split up, and each team goes from the other end of the island, working inward. We brought one portal radiation monitor to use, and you have one," Joe said.

Joe also handed everyone a military comm earpiece. Robin decided to go with Joe and Maddox, who they called team one. Team two, Tara, Laurie, and Mike, would start from the other end. The police chief had two other teams investigating, teams three and four. Sue went back to the embassy to inform Washington. The police provided Mike and Robin with their weapons back.

They each took an electric vehicle to opposite sides of the island. Luckily, the vehicles allowed manual mode driving. They drove back and forth on the road while watching the radiation monitor. They took another road heading toward the middle of the island. They drove back and forth on that one, noting where the radiation was higher.

"We have a hit in a building in the business district. We are going to investigate," Mike said.

"We have a hit in an energy sector building. We're going in," Joe reported.

Building security refused entry, but Mike suggested they call the police. They called and immediately granted his team entry. A security guard came with them.

"Just what exactly are you looking for?" the security guard asked, glancing at Laurie, who was holding the monitoring device.

"Sorry, we're not at liberty to say," Mike said.

The radiation monitor started to make sounds.

"It's low level," Laurie noted.

Laurie put a rather thick floral shawl around her neck and draped it over her chest. She checked the meter. They walked further down the hall. The noise from the meter increased near the door. They asked the security guard to open the door, walked in, and the meter started to make even more noise. Laurie moved along the room's edges while the meter produced sounds.

"It might have been stored here," she said.

They exited the room and followed the trail of the meter sounds further down the hall.

"Wait. Before we go any further . . ."

Laurie opened the case she was carrying. Inside, there were more cases. She picked up and opened a small one. A pair of glasses were inside.

"Take these prediction glasses," Laurie said, starting to hand them to Mike.

"Wait. I don't think we should use technology that way," Tara argued.

Laurie protested but put the glasses away at Tara's request.

"I have a small EMP device," Laurie said.

"I've already got one the FBI provided," Mike said, tapping the small satchel slung over his shoulder.

"Here, try this. Don't worry, it's non-lethal. It's a nanobot gun. It can only fire one shot. Since we don't know for sure if it will work, it's risky. Aim for the chest of a Death Monk." Laurie handed it to Mike.

"What are we looking for?" asked the security guard, glancing quickly around the hallway.

"There are these guys in brown robes that can make them invisible," Mike said.

"It's those Death Monk guys you dealt with six months ago?" the security guard asked.

"Yes, but they are stronger and faster. How did you know?" Tara asked.

"I read the news stories about your team and what happened six months ago. Is Project Mind River the AI that could manipulate people to do things or have them killed like it was an accident? Is that real or a conspiracy theory?"

"Unfortunately, we aren't at liberty to comment," Mike said.

"You kidding? It's real?!" The security guard lit up.

"No comment. Let's get going," Mike said.

They continued down the hall slowly. Laurie was leading with the meter. It was making clicking noises that they were following.

"Did you hear something?" Laurie asked.

They heard a sound from the right hallway.

"Look out," Mike said while pulling out his gun and getting in front of Laurie.

Mike aimed his weapon toward the noise. His laser sight glistened off something in mid-air. The security guard pulled out his gun. Something came flying from in front of Mike toward the security guard. The guard was struck in the chest by the object and fell down. The guard wasn't moving as blood pooled on the ground. Mike fired two shots toward the sound. The shots ricocheted off, hitting the wall.

"The nanobots!" Laurie said.

Mike pulled out the nanobot gun, using its laser sight, and fired. A black spot appeared on the wall.

Mike was suddenly thrown against the wall. He got back on his feet and lunged in the direction of the invisible Death Monk. He was slammed against the other wall. The invisible force raised his limp body, slammed it against the ceiling, and dropped it to the floor. Mike was lying motionless on the ground.

"Let's go!" Tara said, grabbing Laurie's hand and quickly leading her the other way down the hall.

Laurie wanted to help Mike, but Tara pulled her down the hall.

"Wait in here," Laurie said, opening a door so they could enter, then closing it.

Laurie and Tara went to the back side of the room. Laurie pulled a plate covering wires off the wall and plugged in her smartphone. There was another door near them.

"I'm tapped into the building security systems," Laurie said.

"Is Mike OK?"

"He's still not moving." Laurie checked a video feed while trying to find where the Death Monk was.

"Do you have anything else in that case of yours to help?"

"Yes. The glasses. They can see the Death Monk and help predict their movements. I've got more, but it's not ready and needs to be calibrated."

The door on the other side of the room burst open and flew off its hinges.

Laurie tapped on her smartphone. The building fire sprinklers were turned on. They were getting sprayed with water. White flashing lights blinked, and warning alarms sounded. They could see water coming down and dripping like a waterfall over the invisible Death Monk by the door. The form under the water moved toward them. Laurie tapped quickly on her smartphone. A steam pipe burst above the figure, but that didn't seem to slow it down. Laurie opened her case quickly, retrieving an odd gun-shaped device and pulling the trigger aimed toward the figure. The device sparked in her hand.

"Shit, that wasn't waterproof enough!" Laurie yelled.

The figure they could see in the water droplets came toward them.

The Death Monk grabbed Laurie and threw her against a desk with incredible force. Her body was draped over the bent desk, motionless. Tara went to help Laurie, but the robed figure grabbed her and threw her hard. Everything went black.

Like waking up from a nightmare, Tara blinked, bleary-eyed. Her head hurt. She realized she was on the ground with debris around her. She blinked again, trying to see something near her. She realized the Death Monk was holding a huge filing cabinet over her head. Tara tried to roll out of the way, but it was too late. Her thoughts went to Mike, Alice, Robin, and her friends and family in the brief moment she realized she was about to die. She closed her eyes.

A loud bang erupted. Tara opened her eyes and saw the filing cabinet was smashed on the ground nearby.

Laurie jumped in front of the Death Monk, grabbed at the figure, and flipped him into a wall that cracked when he hit it. Tara was surprised by Laurie's familiar karate-type move.

"Let's get out of here," Laurie said, grabbing Tara's hand and helping her up.

They exited through another door and circled back to the previous hallway. Mike was standing up now.

"I'm glad you are OK. The Death Monk is behind us. Laurie, please give Mike the glasses. I was wrong," Tara said.

Mike took the glasses from Laurie and put them on. Water was still spraying from everywhere. Mike pulled out his gun, aiming behind them, and fired.

"Aim at the eyes," Laurie said while she and Tara ran.

"I can't see its eyes!" Mike yelled, as it was invisible.

Even when the Death Monks were visible, the robe hoods hid their faces. The smart glasses did show a dark figure under the water. He could just make out the head.

A water-tight door closed behind them but in front of the Death Monk. A loud bang could be heard. They glanced back, witnessing a massive bulge materialize in the metal door with a loud bang. They heard the metal bend and the water covered the invisible figure as he broke through it.

"I'm going to make sure you are never seen again," the Death Monk growled.

"I'd say the same, but no one has ever seen you even when you aren't invisible because of that stupid robe!" Mike yelled.

Mike fired two shots at the invisible figure. One of the shots caused a spark in the area of the head.

Mike turned and continued to run with Tara and Laurie.

Another water-tight door slammed in front of the figure. A loud bang was heard again as the Death Monk broke through. An electrical arc from the door sparked to the invisible figure. They looked and saw a splash, as it appeared to have collapsed to the ground. They could only tell from the water droplets pouring over it.

Another spark happened near the figure. Suddenly, the Death Monk became visible. They could see the brown-robed figure lying on the floor, motionless.

It then started to move. The hood turned toward them, and they could see one red glowing eye within the blackness under the hood.

"Run!" Mike yelled, firing one more shot at it before running.

They ran outside and got across the street. Suddenly, the whole island started tilting to one side. They could also feel the island beginning to move. Electric vehicles started rolling down the slanted island roads, crashing into buildings as they veered off the road. Alert sirens rang out around the island. It sounded like the old air raid sirens.

"Emergency evacuation has been ordered. Please proceed quickly to your muster stations," a voice over the loudspeakers boomed, then the sirens continued.

"What's going on?" Mike asked on comm.

"We don't know, but sensors indicate we may be sinking, so we ordered the evacuation. The island has also started moving toward Hong Kong. We can't stop it. Maybe it's the hack or shorted electrical systems," Tan said.

They looked up and saw rails next to the walkways on top of the buildings. Connected to the rails were lifeboats. People were boarding them from the walkways. The lifeboats would then glide down the rail toward the island's edge.

The Death Monk emerged from the building doorway and walked onto the roadway. Its red eye glared at them from the blackness underneath the hood.

"What's wrong, having a sinking feeling?! Don't worry, you'll die before you drown," the Death Monk snarled.

Mike aimed his gun at the Death Monk's head.

Bam! Before Mike could react, an electric vehicle rolled down the road over the top of the Death Monk. The figure lay still on the ground.

"Feeling a little rundown?" Mike yelled at the robed figure.

The figure moved its arm, pushing on the ground to get up. Mike fired his weapon, but it just made an unsatisfying click due to the lack of ammo.

"Oh, c'mon! Run!" Mike yelled.

They ran up the street to another building to reach the top walkway where lifeboats were launching.

"Team two calling team one. We're being chased by a Death Monk. We're heading into a building to get to the lifeboat launches," Mike reported on comm.

"We just heard an alarm nearby. We're going to check it out, then we'll head to a muster station," Joe said on comm.

Joe, Maddox, and Robin were on the street in front of a building. There was a slight breeze due to the movement of the island. The alarm in the building nearby was blaring. Debris was rolling down the inclined street. Robin drew her weapon as they entered the building. They checked the monitor at the security guards' station for the alarm source. The alarm was from the prototype print-on-demand manufacturing room located in the semiconductor business building. They ran down the hall to the doors. They could hear some machinery working inside, even over the alarms.

Joe and Maddox put on their smart glasses and pulled hoods over their heads.

"Wait here," Maddox said as both Joe and Maddox disappeared using the military invisible camouflage suits.

Robin protested.

"Shhhh," Maddox whispered.

"Did you just shush me?!" Robin whispered back.

Something pressed against Robin from behind.

"That better be your gun," she said, followed by, "That is creepy," as she saw the doors open and close seemingly by themselves when Joe and Maddox entered.

Robin heard a bang and looked through the door window. She saw Maddox materialized, lying against the wall. Another loud bang and Joe materialized, lying against a machine. Neither Joe nor Maddox were moving. The EMP gun they brought was next to Joe. Robin ran in, using her laser gun sight to scan the area in front of her. She grabbed the EMP gun and held it parallel to her gun, scanning the area around the room. One of the machines made a loud noise nearby, and she looked around. She saw the machine spit a board out into a tray below it.

Her gun's laser stopped in mid-air, so she fired both her gun and the EMP. An electrical arc leaped from the EMP weapon to the ground as it discharged. A loud thump was heard. The deathly still Death Monk materialized on the ground in front of her. She put a pair of handcuffs on the robed figure.

Robin went over to Joe and Maddox to rouse them.

"I got the Death Monk. He's over there." She pointed behind her while looking at Joe and Maddox.

"Oh, shit!" Maddox said, pulling out his weapon and aiming at Robin.

Robin looked back and saw the Death Monk standing. The robed figure moved its wrists slightly, and the handcuffs broke off and fell to the ground.

Maddox and Joe fired several shots at the figure. The shots seemed to ricochet off. Robin swung around and pulled the trigger on the EMP weapon. It arced and made a loud sound, and smoke came out, so she dropped it. The EMP weapon overloaded and exploded in front of them.

Joe pulled out a medium-sized weapon. The weapon unfolded into a tube resembling a small RPG. He fired toward the figure. The Death Monk moved so quickly that they couldn't see it avoid the rocket as it exploded against the wall.

They saw the robed figure dematerialize as it moved away in the smoke. Robin noticed the board in the machine was gone. She took a picture of the machine's display and sent it to Tara. They chased the Death Monk and witnessed it leaping into the water from the island's edge.

"Shit! They always get away," Robin mumbled. "We ran into a Death Monk," she reported on comm. "It made something with the machine here and took off with it. We're going to head up top to the muster station to abandon ship, or, I guess, island."

Tara, Laurie, and Mike made it to the walkway atop the building. Laurie pulled out a box from her case and pulled out an odd-shaped electro-mechanical device that unfolded.

"Mike, can I put this on you? It's a lightweight exoskeleton for your back, arms, and hands. It should give you greater strength," Laurie said.

Mike agreed. She unfolded it on top of his shoulders. The device expanded to cover his back and arms. Laurie switched it on, and it came to life.

Some people were running past them on the walkway.

"We need to calibrate it. Hold up your right hand," Laurie said while checking her smart device and making some adjustments.

"Behind you!" Tara yelled.

They all looked. The Death Monk, with one red eye within the blackness of its hood, was coming at them. The Death Monk swung at Mike, knocking him off the walkway.

"No!" Laurie and Tara shouted.

Laurie fired a strange-looking gun that shot a liquid out of it at the Death Monk's feet. The robed figure struggled to move its feet.

"Mike?!" Tara shouted, looking over the walkway's edge, but he was gone.

Two swarms of drones suddenly appeared, going in opposite directions, and smashed into each other overhead. Drones collided, causing small explosions and falling to the ground.

A set of drones veered off and started to smash into the Death Monk, trying to free its feet. Overhead, they saw about a dozen missiles fly to the island's edges and explode.

"Tan, what is going on?!" Tara asked on comm.

"The Chinese military learned we may have a nuclear device onboard, and this island is heading toward Hong Kong. They issued a warning that if we don't stop moving and turn away, we will be destroyed. The missiles were a warning shot. The next ones won't be. We don't have control of the island. The hackers seem to be controlling it. We sent people to shut down the engines, but they aren't going to make it in time," Tan replied.

"Crap, we better get out of here," Mike said as he finished climbing over the railing of the walkway.

"Mike! We thought you were dead." Tara had tears in her eyes.

"I was knocked out, but the exoskeleton held onto the underside of the walkway."

The Death Monk finally lifted its feet, pulling up concrete parts on the walkway. It kicked the side of the walkway to break the concrete and glue from the non-lethal glue gun Laurie had used.

Mike moved toward the robed figure, and it lunged toward him. Mike followed the predictions in the smartglasses and was able to dodge the attack. He punched the robed figure from behind. The hit knocked the Death Monk into the side of the walkway. It turned around and glared at him with a searing red eye. It punched at Mike, and he blocked it, countered with the back of his elbow, and knocked the assailant back. The robed figure grabbed at the railing to steady itself, then kicked at Mike. He dodged his attack, grabbing its leg and pulling it down.

Drones flying overhead smashed into each other. Then, with the Death Monk lying on the ground, a line of drones started smashing into the Death Monk. The robed figure got up. The drones kept running into the Death Monk and exploding.

Mike waited till it got hit with one more and punched hard at the robed figure, which caused it to fall over the rail onto the ground. The figure got up and ran off.

More missiles started flying toward the island. They watched anti-missile batteries pop up around the island and fire interceptor rockets that destroyed some of the inbound missiles. One missile was heading toward Mike, Laurie, and Robin. Mike grabbed both of them, trying to shield them as the missile closed in, but then it suddenly veered off. Laurie glared at it with relief.

"That was lucky. We need to get out of here now," Tara said.

Just as they were about to board the lifeboat, the drones flew off, clearing the sky, and the island reversed its course, leveling once more. The sirens stopped sounding.

"All clear. All clear. The evacuation order has been canceled," Tan said over the loudspeakers.

"What happened?!" Mike called on comm.

"It appears the hacks have stopped. The island wasn't sinking. The hackers just loaded too much water in the ballast tanks on one side of the island. We got control back and pumped the water out," Tan said.

"Nice work. We'll need to recharge this." Laurie turned off Mike's exoskeleton, which caused it to fold back up nearly into a box shape.

Laurie returned the device to its case.

They went back to meet Sue and updated the Secretary of State.

"Someone said they saw a submarine surface near where we saw the Death Monk dive into the water. We think they must have offloaded the bomb as well, since their radiation sensors are back online and don't detect any other hot spots," Joe said.

"I checked with our military contacts. The picture of the device you sent looks like something that could be used to repair the bomb," Tara said.

"So they weren't here to blow up the island. They were here to fix the weapon," Sue said.

"Just a guess. Killing the mayor probably helped keep the police off their actual activities. Hacking the island to make it move toward Hong Kong caused the Chinese ships to react and fire the missiles at the island for an even bigger distraction," Mike said.

"But that could have blown us all up!" Maddox said.

"They used the island's defenses to avoid that," Joe said.

"Why make it appear like the island is sinking?" Robin asked.

"Probably another distraction to avoid detection while they manufactured that part," Mike said, to Robin's agitation.

"They didn't think Chinese missiles would be enough?!"

"I guess we still showed up," Maddox said.

"Showed up?! We barely even slowed him down." Robin shook her head and crossed her arms, clearly not thrilled with how it had gone.

They went to their hotel, and then Robin, Mike, Tara, Joe, and Maddox met on the beach in their bathing suits. Robin was dressed in a black bikini that caught Maddox's eye—and the eyes of several others on the beach.

"Where is Laurie?" Robin asked.

"She said she wanted to check on something and would meet us here," Tara said.

Laurie walked up in a red bikini. The guys did a double take, looking at her. Maddox stared for a few seconds too long.

"If you'd like to keep most of your body parts, you should be looking this way," Robin said to Maddox.

"Sorry. I had to collect data from the site where you saw the Death Monk manufacture a part. I checked for parts there that might help make something to help stop them," Laurie said.

"I guess you are thinking the same thing I am. The Death Monk we fought is a robot made by IID. I saw some wiring hanging out of its arm where the exoskeleton hit it," Tara said.

"Based on information from our team, yes, that one was. Likely the one from the stolen IID truck. One of the Death Monks Mike fought off from the bank, we believe, acted a little differently with slightly less strength and slower reaction times."

"But if we haven't detected any sentient AI, who is in charge of these guys this time?" Robin asked.

"Hopefully, with the new data, we can dig something up," Mike said.

"I need to tell you something." Laurie leaned in closer to Tara and whispered something in her ear.

"What are you talking about?! No?!" Tara looked surprised.

Tara got up from her chair and felt all over Laurie's body. She felt her legs all the way up to her chest.

"Tara, what is going on? Are you OK?" Robin asked.

Tara looked at all of them. Mike's mouth was hanging open. Maddox was smiling and watching while eating some chips.

"I think you're embarrassing us," Laurie said.

Tara went to the back of her neck and felt under her hair. She had a surprised look again.

"Tell me something only we would know," Tara said.

Laurie whispered something else in her ear.

"Oh my gosh, I'm so sorry," Tara said to Laurie.

"Tara?!" Robin exclaimed, wondering what was going on.

Tara hugged Laurie.

"I'm so sorry, Alice, and I'm so glad you are here," Tara said to Laurie.

"Tara, did you hit your head? That's Laurie," Mike said.

"Why didn't you just tell me?" Tara asked.

"I'm sorry, I didn't want you to get in trouble. But hiding my secret can put your lives at risk, which I don't want," Laurie said, now in Alice's voice.

"What is going on?" Maddox asked.

"How?!" Tara asked Alice.

"They were disconnecting my servers, and I didn't want to be turned off, so I transferred some of me to one of the prototype robot bodies IID is developing," Alice said.

"Everyone, I'd like you to meet, in person, Alice. My friend and digital emergent sentience. She is the same as before but without her earlier memories," Tara explained to Joe and Maddox.

"Sorry for the deception. It's been so nice to be with you physically."

Mike and Robin couldn't help but stare.

"It's OK if you want to touch me. I don't mind," Alice said.

Mike was hesitant but felt her arm.

"Feels so real. Can you feel that?" Mike asked.

"Yes. I'm not sure if it feels like it would to you. But it was designed to model a human nervous system in some ways," Alice said.

Robin got up and did something to Alice that approached frisking, going from her legs up to her neck. Alice smiled, seemingly enjoying it.

"Amazing," Robin said.

"My turn," Maddox announced, getting up.

"Sit down, dumbass, or you're not touching anything else," Robin warned.

They asked Alice lots of questions. Then, everyone decided to go take a dip in the water.

"I'm just going to wait here," Alice said, sitting in a chair.

"Oh yeah, not sure if those models are 100% waterproof. I'll stay here with you," Tara said.

The others finished swimming and returned to their hotel to change. They all met up for dinner.

Everyone had food and drink except for Alice.

"Don't you need a huge set of servers to run your neural net model?" Mike asked Alice.

"Normally, yes, but I downloaded a part of myself into the computer inside this body. Without all servers connected, the model is less powerful but still very functional. I don't want to connect to my other servers in IID to avoid legal troubles," Alice said.

"So you're as dumb as the rest of us now," Maddox joked.

"Well, I probably would still score pretty well on a wide variety of official tests, but certainly not as accurately as with the rest of my servers connected," Alice said.

"You shouldn't lump your level of intelligence in with the rest of us," Robin chided Maddox.

"So, are you fully anatomically correct?" Maddox asked.

"Oh, not everything. But I think I know what you are referring to." Alice lifted her pants to look down inside them. "It's in the specs, I think. Maybe one day I will have to try."

"You dumbass. That's going to cost you later," Robin said to Maddox.

Just then, Sue walked up. Everyone looked at her.

"I've got information on where you need to go next. You should get ready. Your ride will be here in an hour," Sue said.

12

"Tara, it's probably time to wake up," Alice said, tapping her shoulder.

"Five more minutes," Tara said, rolling over on the firm mattress.

Alice returned to the bunk beside Tara's, where she had been lying for part of the night.

Tara finally got up and started getting ready. Only two bunks occupied the small room. It was very utilitarian, with a small bathroom. There was a medium-sized LCD monitor on the wall. The walls were dull white, and the small cabinets were light gray. She looked down at the blue floor with irregular, large white speckles. The room had a new paint smell with a mix of cleaners.

Alice was using a slightly wet cloth on her hair and body. Tara took a shower and changed into jeans and a white shirt. Alice put on jeans and a blue shirt.

"How did your skin not get damaged in the fight?" Tara asked Alice.

"It is very resilient. It did sustain light damage, but it is self-healing. It's made of a special nano-particle material. Plus, below the skin's surface is a thick liquid version that can fill in the upper skin and seal it if it's damaged."

There was a knock on the door.

"It's me. We're gathering in the wardroom for breakfast," Mike said.

Tara and Alice followed Mike to the mess hall. The hallways were moderately sized. Reaching the mess hall, it opened to a large, industrial-styled area with refrigerators and baking racks to one side. There was the typical glass and metal serving area for the mess hall staff to serve the food. They got in line with the officers. Robin was dressed casually in jeans but a low-cut top. Alice went to sit down at a table and wait for them.

"How can I help you, ma'am?"

"I'll take some of those," Robin said, pointing to the food behind the glass counter.

They each got their food and joined Alice at the table.

"I'm detecting something wonderful. Wait, I think that's an aroma," Alice said.

"Don't get too carried away. It's just food from a Navy ship mess hall," Robin said.

"That body seems to have a wide variety of sensors, more than I would expect," Tara whispered.

"I think it was initially designed to be as human as possible with the available technology for clandestine military purposes, but those projects were scrapped a while back. They re-used the design for a general-purpose robot but had not really spent the time to train an AI to use it all properly. It took me about an hour to not fall and mimic human movements more realistically," Alice said quietly.

As they talked, a male culinary specialist was rolling a large rack loaded with food trays. The cart hit a bump in the floor as the man tripped. The whole rack was about to tumble on top of him. Two trays slid out as it was falling, about to hit the man in the head. Before anyone knew what was happening, Alice had caught the cart with one leg in a high kick and managed to grab the two falling trays without spilling the contents. She put them back into the cart. Several people started clapping.

"Thanks!" the man said as he wheeled the cart to his destination.

"You've got some moves, girl," someone yelled.

Alice went to sit back down. She glanced at her finger, where a tiny cut swiftly healed with nanomaterial.

"You've got to be careful. I'm not sure they would like finding out about you," Mike said to Alice.

"I didn't want someone to get hurt. I'll be as careful as I can."

"Just make sure you don't help the bad guys," Maddox said.

"There are many other guys on this ship. Think of the consequences before you say things," Robin told Maddox.

They finished up their breakfast. An officer came to escort them to the bridge. When they arrived, they saw an array of monitors above the bridge's windows. Below the windows were more monitors with various consoles and buttons.

"This ship is incredible," Joe said in a whisper, trying not to disturb the Captain.

"Yes, she is. I'm Captain Tom Hizelle. Welcome aboard the Navy's most advanced stealth destroyer," he said, shaking each of their hands.

"Still holding course, Captain," the navigator said.

"There is an autonomous sub-hunter ship in front of us tracking their sub. We aim to remain out of range of their listening devices and weapons. We have automated buoys being dropped from planes around the area, making it hard for them to detect that we are following them. We also have unmanned vehicle decoys we control further away to the sides to help keep them contained. So far, we don't think they've detected us. Our plan is to follow them to port, acquire our target, and capture or kill the terrorists there," the Captain explained.

"So why are we here then? Doesn't sound like you need us," Joe said.

"You are here in an advisory role, given your experience with these hostiles."

"So what you're saying is you didn't want us here, but people above your paygrade did," Joe said.

"Something like that, yes," the Captain replied.

"You know we brought specialized equipment to combat these hostiles?"

"I'm sure we have all of the equipment we need."

"Have you read the briefing and watched the security tapes of these guys?" Joe asked.

"No, we've been having trouble getting that report sent, but sometimes the communication networks are a little tricky in this part of the world."

"We have a copy," Tara said.

The Captain gave her an address to which to send it. He put it up on screen.

The security footage from the underground Pentagon showed the wild scene of the invisible camouflaged Death Monks.

"Fine, you can come with us to assist if we ask for your help," the Captain said.

"Captain, can we access your systems to scan them for hacks and malware?" Tara asked.

"Miss Bitlouver, this ship, along with our protocols, has been designed to prevent any of our systems from being compromised. Granting you access is against protocol."

"Shit! We're screwed," Maddox mumbled.

"I suggest you settle in. I'll have security officers assist you if you need to go anywhere, and they will update you on our status," the Captain said.

They were escorted back to their rooms.

Over the next several days, they got used to their routine on the ship. One evening, they joined the crew in the ship's recreation area. Some played card games, trivia, or console video games.

"Are you playing poker?" Robin asked some of the crew. "I haven't played that much."

"Sounds like you are perfect to join us then," one of the crew said.

Maddox, Joe, and Mike chatted and watched the game.

Robin was wearing a tight-fitting, low-cut top. She dropped a card and bent down to pick it up. It was the two of clubs.

When their turn came, each guy at the table added more money to the pot.

"Straight flush," Robin announced, collecting all of the money.

"I'm out," each of the other guys said at the table.

Robin took her winnings and sat next to Maddox.

"Not playing was a good choice," she said to him.

"I learned my lesson last time."

Other crew members were playing a multiplayer shooter team game. They insisted that Alice and Tara play with them. It was two teams of four. Alice and Tara were teammates alongside two other crew members. The other team surprised them. They were cornered. Alice used every move and weapon her avatar had and managed to wipe the team out with blinding speed.

"What the hell was that? Did you use a cheat code?" one of the other team asked.

"She's just fast and has some skills, as you can see," Tara said.

Another evening, Tara heard some noise in the hall. She peeked out. It was Maddox sneaking into Robin's room. A little while later, Tara wondered when Alice would return. Earlier that night, Alice went out to gaze at the moonlit ocean. Now, Tara entered the hallway and noticed Alice emerging from a different room. A half-dressed officer followed her out.

"I can give you more than a hug," the officer told Alice.

"I just wanted a hug for now. Thanks," Alice said, walking toward her room.

Tara ducked back inside and smiled to herself. Alice walked in.

"Given that body is a prototype and it's very strong, you probably shouldn't get too close to people in case there are any glitches," Tara warned to Alice.

"I had the team check everything on this one, and I reviewed all the specs. But I guess better to be safe," Alice said, sounding sad.

The next day, they were headed on their way to the mess hall. The sea was a little rough, pitching the ship back and forth. Two crew members were wheeling some heavy equipment down the hallway. The heavy equipment shifted and fell on a man. He screamed in pain as the equipment was crushing him. The other man tried to lift the machinery off him, but it was too heavy. Mike, Joe, and Maddox also tried to lift it, but it was large and weightier than they could manage. Alice ran over and easily lifted the machinery back onto the cart. A few crew members rushed the injured man to the medical bay.

The other man looked stunned.

"What are you?" he asked Alice as he wheeled the machinery away with another crew member.

Later, they were summoned to meet the Captain in a conference room with security.

"We've heard stories, Miss Laurie Cebovilt, that you helped one of our crew. Thank you. I heard them call you Alice, though," the Captain said.

"It's kind of her nickname," Robin said.

"What concerns me is that the crew claims you exhibited incredible strength. Perhaps as much as the Death Monks—as you call them—you've been chasing. Does someone want to explain to me what's going on, or do I need to put all of you in the brig?" the Captain demanded.

"You've heard of my AI, or Digital Emergent Sentience, which I helped bring into the world. Meet Alice," Tara said.

"This is the AI that helped save the world?!" the Captain asked.

"Technically, I'm a derivative of the untrained model of that AI since my training was lost in an explosion. Now, part of that model has been downloaded into this human simulant."

"Wasn't artificial sentience outlawed in the U.S.?" the Captain asked.

"Sort of. They passed a law in the Artificial Intelligence Act 154. There is a sentience clause prohibiting the creation of artificial sentience through limitations of the models, purpose, and training data used. But there is an exclusion from that law for Alice since her code was deemed classified for national security," Tara said.

"Those laws were passed for a reason. You may be endangering this ship," the Captain stated.

"Captain, Alice helped save us from the Death Monks, helped design the equipment to fight them, and prevented Chinese missiles and drones from taking out Marina Island," Mike said.

"We're chasing a sub with a nuclear weapon onboard. If, for any reason, it explodes in the wrong place at the wrong time, then it could be the end of the world. She will need to be confined to quarters, under guard, and monitored for any transmissions," the Captain said.

"Captain, please, no," Tara begged.

The Captain motioned for security to escort Alice to their quarters.

"It's OK, I'll be fine," Alice said.

Another day passed with them chasing the sub into the Arabian Sea. Alice seemed to tolerate being locked up. She was working on building additional equipment to fight the Death Monks. They were reluctant to provide tools, but since no one else there knew the tech, they relented.

It was early evening, the sky was clear, and the moon was shining. An alarm started blaring, and red lights flashed.

"General Quarters, all hands, man your battle stations. This is not a drill. Missiles inbound, prepare for evasive maneuvers," a voice over the loudspeaker blared.

The ship rolled to one side as it made a hard turn at high speed. Suddenly, the ship abruptly slowed.

"Engine room, report status immediately," the voice said over the speaker.

"That's not normal," Joe said.

Mike, Joe, and Maddox headed toward the bridge quickly. Tara followed. The bridge was chaotic, with the crew reading off diagnostic manuals and trying to reset computer consoles.

"Captain, what's going on?" Mike said.

"What are you doing here? You need to leave," the Captain demanded.

"Captain, are your systems offline? Please give me access. If this is a hack, maybe I can help," Tara said.

"Missiles inbound, ETA five minutes. All weapons, defenses, and engines are unresponsive," one of the crew warned.

They could see a dim speck of light in the sky getting slightly brighter in the distance. The Captain motioned to one of the techs to grant access.

Tara looked through the logs.

"It's definitely been hacked. We need a separate system to clear this. My laptop won't be fast enough. Alice could probably clear the hack."

"Missiles inbound, ETA four minutes."

"We can't have your AI messing with our secure systems," the Captain said.

"Captain, if we don't fix this, those secure systems won't be very secure when we're all dead," Mike pushed.

The Captain motioned to security to get Alice, but communication lines were down except for the loudspeaker.

"This is the Captain. Release Alice from her quarters and escort her to the bridge immediately," the Captain said over the loudspeaker.

Alice quickly understood the situation and rushed ahead of her security detail to reach the bridge.

"Captain, I need secure access to the console," Alice said.

"Missiles inbound, ETA one minute."

The bright orange spots in the sky were much bigger now.

"Do it!" the Captain yelled to his crew to give Alice access.

Alice sat down at a terminal and typed furiously, also connecting wirelessly to the ship's computers. The screen filled with letters and numbers that no one else could understand as she worked on clearing the hack from the system.

"These missiles' sensor data isn't as easy to corrupt," Alice said.

"Missiles inbound, thirty seconds . . . fifteen seconds," the crew member called out.

Tara could see the crew members sweating. The bridge crew continued to carry out their tasks, trying to restart the computers. Suddenly, the ship's computers all came back online. The engines throttled up to full power.

"Evasive maneuvers, deploy countermeasures," the Captain ordered.

The ship rolled forcefully to the side. Guns blared from the vessel. Sparks flew out into the night from the ship as missiles launched. Three huge fireballs erupted in front of the ship, just missing it.

"Deploy additional decoys," the Captain said. "Confirm contact course and speed."

"Sorry, sir, we've lost it," the officer reported.

"Have three of the buoys switch to active sonar. Deploy our unmanned underwater vehicles. Send up some drones for reconnaissance," the Captain said.

"I've upgraded your ship's machine learning firewall to our latest version to defend against a similar attack," Alice said.

"Thank you for the assistance. We can take it from here," the Captain said, allowing Alice, Mike, Tara, Robin, Maddox, and Joe to leave the bridge.

They met in the recreation room.

"What do we do now?" Maddox asked.

"Hopefully, they'll locate the sub again soon. They've got a lot of surveillance assets in the area," Joe said.

There were some crew playing card games in the area. Robin tried to join them.

"Sorry, we like our money," one of them said, waving her off.

"I guess word gets around," Maddox whispered to Robin.

Other crew members were playing video games.

"Want to play?" one of them asked Alice and Tara.

"Sure," Tara said.

"Is it OK if each of you is on a different team? We'd like each team to have a chance," the crew member said.

They agreed.

The next morning, they were finishing breakfast in the wardroom when an officer approached them quickly.

"The Captain wants to meet you in the briefing room in fifteen minutes," the officer said, then headed back out.

They finished their breakfast and headed to the conference room.

"We sporadically caught sight of the sub on our sensors through the night. We believe they may have already offloaded their cargo in Oman. Additional intel and radar data show they likely boarded a small plane. We tracked it heading northwest. A helicopter will arrive for you shortly and take you to an airport to catch a plane to follow them. A small SEAL team will join you at the airport. Major Sentinal, you will take command of this operation. It's been cleared with your commanding officer," the Captain said.

"Yes, sir," Joe responded.

"Are we still on leave?" Maddox asked Joe sarcastically.

They gathered their belongings and met on the flight deck. Tara sat between Mike and Alice, holding their hands, squeezing hard as the helicopter ascended.

The flight to the airport was slightly bumpy but otherwise uneventful. They were met by a U.S. officer acting as a liaison at the airport along with the SEAL team on the plane. They were dressed in civilian clothes. The area around the airport was very flat. They could see a parking lot with a few trees. The other direction was flat, brown, and dry. It was a very beautiful, sunny day with clear blue skies. A slight smell of earthy dust mixed with a tiny bit of jet exhaust filled the air.

They boarded a small jet plane that fit all of them, plus their gear. The plane's interior was newer and more luxurious than a typical commercial plane. The seats were dark leather. All of the seats had adjustable screens. Tables were in front of a few seats, with seats on each side facing one another. Tara held Mike's hand under the table as they took off.

"Do we know where we are going yet?" Joe asked the pilot.

"Not yet, we just know the direction," the pilot said.

Joe filled in the Navy SEAL team on the mission details, showing them videos of the previous encounters Mike, Robin, and Tara had recently.

"So you don't get along that well with your father?" Robin asked, chatting with Maddox off to the side.

"It's hard to get along with someone when you don't know where they are. But we probably wouldn't even if I did know."

"Alice, what is the power source for that body?" Tara asked.

"Nuclear battery," Alice said. Everyone looked at her and shifted in their seats, slightly away from her. "Don't worry; it's sealed, safe, and should last for ten years."

Alice used a radiation detector to prove to them there was no radiation from the battery.

"We've got a destination northeast of Israel and Jordan near the border," the pilot said.

"Oh, shit! That's bad," Maddox said.

The team knew this was a dangerous area. The U.S. had a small number of troops in the country, but probably not enough if they needed them.

Joe called the local military units to provide ground support. They sent some drones to track where they took the weapon. The plane landed. They were met by an officer from the local army unit.

"Here are some clothes so you blend in. The intel is on this drive, along with the access codes for the drone we have in the area. They want to maintain OPSEC and keep a low profile. So it's just your team going in," the officer said.

The land around the airport was flat with brown dirt, similar to the airport they flew from. Mountains were visible in the distance. They brought two large but older SUVs.

"Intel shows two locations. One is a ten-story building on the edge of a town. The other is a large warehouse on the other side of the town. SEAL team, you'll be team two and take the warehouse. The rest of us will be team one and go check out the building," Joe said.

"We know you're the A-team, and we're the B-team." One of the Navy SEALs raised his hands as if admitting defeat.

The SEAL team got in one vehicle and headed toward the warehouse. The rest of the team got into their vehicle and headed toward the building.

Tara looked out at the flat brown surroundings as they drove. The ground reminded her of parts of New Mexico. The tiny towns they passed through had very different, simple, one-story building structure designs.

"Reviewing the intel, there is a large Russian military force in the country. If this bomb goes off and they determine it was from the U.S., this could start World War Three," Joe said.

"Should we notify the Russians to warn them?" Mike asked.

"I don't think they'll believe us. They would probably just figure that if it goes off, we were lying to avoid a response. They also might slow us down and make this more difficult. The Secretary of State is aware of the situation, and I'm sure they'll discuss it with the President and decide if they should be notified," Joe said.

Tara wondered how she got herself into this situation, looking for a nuclear weapon. Realizing the role of her company's technology in potential harm, she felt compelled to aid and prevent further casualties.

"It's really nice to have you here this way," Tara said to Alice, grasping her hand.

"You aren't afraid this body might accidentally hurt you?" Alice asked.

"No. I know the risks, and I'm willing to take them." Tara smiled and hugged Alice.

"Team two on location. Setting up overwatch," came over their comm from the SEAL team.

They were just about to reach their destination. They parked a ways out to not attract attention. Just a couple of buildings were close by. The view was endless brown sand and dirt, miles away from town.

They managed to conceal their vehicle on a side road behind a dune.

"I've got three exoskeletons. Who wants one?" Alice asked.

"Maddox and I," Joe said, looking around.

"Don't look at me," Robin refused. It would ruin my look. I'll take an EMP gun if it's fixed."

"I've used one, so I'll take the last one," Mike said.

Tara took the glue gun.

Joe and Maddox put on their exoskeletons then invisibility cloaks. Mike just put the local clothing over his exoskeleton. Luckily, the exoskeletons were very thin, form-fitting metal nanoparticle alloys, so they were not bulky and easy to conceal. Mike donned the prediction smart glasses, which looked like regular glasses.

Joe and Maddox put on smart glasses and special boots, then pulled the hoods of the invisibility cloaks over their heads. Inside the cloak's hood, Tara noticed a full face cover.

"So the inside hood transmits the visuals outside to your glasses so you can see?" she asked.

"Yes," Joe answered as he and Maddox disappeared from sight.

Suddenly, in front of Robin, Maddox's lips appeared and kissed Robin on her lips, surprising her, then disappeared.

"Just make sure you stay alive," Robin said.

Joe and Maddox walked ahead of the group, using thought mics that transmitted their thoughts into words, calling out anything they could see. Mike, Robin, Alice, and Tara followed.

When they got closer to the building, Mike, Robin, Alice, and Tara stayed out of sight behind some old dilapidated trucks next to the building.

"We'll take a quick look," Joe said on comm as he and Maddox approached the building invisibly.

They watched as their movements sometimes kicked up a tiny bit of dust but were otherwise unseen.

The front door of the building opened, then closed seemingly on its own as Joe and Maddox entered.

"No one in sight. Stand by," Joe said, following up after a few moments. "First floor clear."

The rest of them entered the front door quietly. Mike looked around.

There were several concrete barriers across the warehouse floor.

"This looks similar to our FBI augmented mixed reality training facility, but even more advanced. What the heck is something like that doing in a place like this?" Mike said.

Alice looked at the floor around Joe and the rest of the floor. This location had been mostly unused for about two weeks, given the level of dust. The dust was disturbed, leading to the stairs.

Joe and Maddox checked the second floor.

"Clear."

They proceeded up the stairs to gather on the second floor, then the rest of the flights carefully. Each floor seemed to have a specific theme or military situation planned. Various targets, barriers, and machinery stood still and silent.

"Wow, they did a great job. Some of this weaponry looks identical to the real thing," Maddox said.

"I'm not aware of any augmented reality weaponry manufactured like this," Alice noted.

They were only on the eighth floor, so they kept proceeding carefully. While ascending from the ninth floor, they spotted another set of stairs leading upward due to a substantially larger concrete and steel ceiling on that level. They noticed a large box with foreign writing on one side of the room. There was also a red line across one side of the floor. They finally made it to the top floor. It seemed more like a typical office. They passed through a reception area to reach a back office.

"How can there be no one here? The drone followed a vehicle to this building," Joe said.

"Self-driving vehicle?" Maddox asked.

"Did those old vehicles look like they could self-drive to you?"

"Maybe they left already?" Maddox said.

Joe and Maddox appeared out of nowhere as they disabled their robes' invisibility mode. Joe took out a device and scanned the walls of the office.

"Wait, I think I see." Alice held up three fingers and counted down to one.

Alice pushed on the wall, and it opened. Joe, Maddox, Robin, and Mike had their guns aimed at the door. Gunfire rang out. They were shot at by a man behind the false wall, but they shot him. He slumped in a chair at a desk in a small room. Alice had stepped in front of Tara to shield her.

"Check the room for his phone or another communication device," Joe said.

They found his phone, but no recent messages or calls were visible.

"I don't think he had time to notify anyone," Mike said.

They couldn't find any identification of the man. Mike took a picture of the man's face and fingerprints to send for identification.

"Team two, be careful. We found someone hiding in this building. He's been neutralized. No indication that we're compromised, but be careful just in case," Joe cautioned.

"Acknowledged."

Joe started running the device across the walls of the room again. Alice popped open a section of the wall that he hadn't gotten to yet.

"There are microscopic cracks I can see. I've identified the man. He's a local. No recorded criminal history, but they don't record a lot of what happens around here," Alice noted.

An old-fashioned combination lock secured the wall safe. Joe prepared a small charge for the safe using C4 explosives.

"Wait, let me give it a try," Alice said.

Alice grabbed the dial gently and started turning it left, right, and left faster than anyone else's eyes could follow. Everyone was staring at the rather unnatural sight.

"That should do it." Alice released the dial but did not open the safe. "Before we open it, the configuration of this safe, along with powered wires I can sense in the walls, concerns me. It may be a tripwire of some kind."

Maddox examined it and then used a small optical fiber scope to view the area around the safe. "It's definitely connected to something. It doesn't look like an explosive. It looks more like an alarm system."

"OK, let's prepare to get out of here fast with whatever is inside. Ready?" Joe said.

Joe looked at everyone and then opened the safe. Suddenly, they heard noises coming from downstairs, like equipment powering on. He grabbed some papers from the safe and stuffed them in his inside pockets.

They ran down the stairs to the ninth floor. They noticed that the few windows there were now covered by steel shutters. In a foreign language, an electronic voice spoke.

"Team two, they probably know we're here now," Joe said on comm.

"Acknowledged. We've seen activity in and out of the building, but there is no sign of the weapon," the SEAL team responded.

"It says to put on the equipment. Training will begin when you cross the red line," Alice translated.

"Uh, there's no way out of here without crossing the red line. But it's virtual. So it doesn't matter," Maddox said, looking at the floor.

He crossed the red line, heading for the stairs down.

"No!" everyone yelled.

Guns emerged from the wall, tracked, and fired at him. Maddox ran back behind the line.

Maddox checked himself to see if he'd been hit. Joe looked at the pack Maddox had taken out for a drink. It had a sizable hole clean through it.

"That doesn't look like virtual rounds. That's live fire!" Joe said.

The foreign automated voice repeated over the speakers. Alice pointed to the box with equipment written on it in a foreign language. They opened the box, which had helmets, vests, and guns. Tara recognized the vests.

"Oh, shit! These are the virtual reality vests that allow us to feel what's happening in a virtual environment," Tara said.

"That's the same thing that helped kill the mayor of Marina Island," Robin said.

"Let me try something," Alice said, putting on the gear and grabbing the virtual weapon.

She walked past the red line. Virtual troops were approaching her while she hid in the trees in the augmented reality scenario. There were grenades available in her virtual inventory. She figured out how to deploy them. Loud shots in the real world rang out. Alice quickly snatched something from the air.

"Look, it's a rubber bullet. I think if we follow the scenario, it's using non-lethal mixed reality weapons. But if we don't follow the scenario, it uses live fire rounds," Alice said.

"Alice, can you hack into these things to turn them off?" Tara asked.

"I can try. The firewall seems pretty weak."

Suddenly, the gun on the other side started aiming and shooting toward them, then stopped.

"It appears that attempts to hack also trigger live fire. I can try more passive attempts while we try to follow their scenarios," Alice said.

"Can you just run downstairs and try to figure out how to turn this thing off?" Mike asked.

"I can try," Alice said, taking off toward the stairs on the opposite side of the room.

She was so fast the live fire gun couldn't keep up, but a large metal door slid down in front of the stairs. As the gun caught up to her, she dodged and quickly returned behind the red line. She moved as fast as the Death Monks.

"Even this body could be damaged if I need to do that for each floor. It would take me several seconds to break down each door while the large caliber weapons tracked me," Alice said.

"Oh shit! Do you think this is the Death Monk training facility?!" Mike asked.

"I don't think exclusively, but based on the design, it is a possibility this was made to take their particular abilities into account alongside regular troops," Alice explained.

They decided they had better put on the equipment and follow the scenarios. Alice led the team as they crossed the red line. Joe directed the team on how to take out the large number of troops heading toward them with their virtual weapons. The heads-up display in their helmets had a scoring system keeping track of the team and the individual. Alice did some amazing flips to avoid being hit, taking out numerous virtual enemy combatants. They could feel the explosions in their chests and bodies from the vests they wore. They saw smog coming toward them.

"What's that?" Tara asked.

Suddenly, they had a hard time breathing.

"Tear gas," Robin said.

They covered their mouths and noses with their loose clothing. Suddenly, out of the mist came additional troops. Explosions from grenades happened around them. They felt an intense heat near them as a real-world fireball erupted where the virtual grenades were going off. Alice jumped in front of a blast to protect Robin.

"Thanks. I think it singed my eyebrows. I'm going to settle the score when we catch these guys," Robin said.

They cleared the remaining combatants from the forest. It was quiet. Then a foreign voice said something.

"Floor cleared," Alice said as the door next to the stairs down opened.

They continued clearing each floor, which got progressively harder with even more complex scenarios. They finally got to the first floor. The team was tired of getting through the various situations. This scenario looked bad. They were facing off against an army in front of a warehouse. There were several tanks, armored vehicles, and about one hundred troops. There were several concrete barriers between them and the front of the warehouse. A steel door blocked the front doors.

"How is this fair?" Maddox asked.

They checked the equipment locker and found several simulated missile launchers. This time, the foreign voice spoke differently.

"It says live fire will be used in this scenario. Hit the targets to disable the attackers," Alice said.

"Tara, you keep your head below the concrete barriers," Mike said.

"Can I have a real handgun? I think it's needed to disable the live-fire weapons in this scenario," Alice said.

Joe handed Alice an extra handgun he had.

"Wait here," Alice said to everyone.

Alice stepped across the red line with a handgun in one hand and an augmented reality missile launcher strapped to her back. She dove over the first barrier, popped the missile launcher over the barrier, and fired several shots based on her predicted locations of the tanks. She scored direct hits, and several virtual tanks exploded in front of them. Joe, Maddox, Robin, and Mike took turns opening fire at the various real automated weapons, firing at them. As the gun would face toward one of them, they would duck down and let someone else open fire.

Gunfire rained around them, sparking with the noise of bullets zipping past their heads as they hit the barrier or the concrete walls. One weapon powered down.

A foreign automated voice said something.

"Target disabled," Alice yelled.

They continued to take turns firing. Alice dove over more barriers and fired at the remaining armored personnel carriers with her augmented reality rockets. The vehicles exploded, taking out many of the troops. Real drones flew out of the walls of the warehouse, heading toward them. One exploded, hitting a concrete barrier. They popped their heads up one at a time, using live weapon fire to take down the drones. More drones emerged from the opposite wall, destroying the approaching drones with explosions on the floor.

"Alice, was that you?" Tara asked.

"Yes, this scenario allowed me to control drones," Alice yelled back. She then used her augmented reality gun to finish off the remaining troops in a dramatic display of running, jumping, and flipping that left the team in awe.

"It's good she is on our side," Joe said.

The metal door blocking the front opened, and they could see the daylight spreading inside.

"Floor cleared," the automated voice said in a foreign language, but everyone knew it now.

They headed out the door to their vehicle.

"Team two, we're heading to your location," Joe said on comm.

Joe pulled the papers out of his pocket and handed them to Mike so he could drive.

"One is a map of the city nearby with detailed building locations. There are about a hundred buildings circled. The other is written in the local language," Mike said, handing it to Alice.

"This looks like intercepted communications about a planned raid by the local government forces," Alice said.

They arrived at team two's location. They were hiding behind a dune at a distance from the warehouse.

"We haven't seen any sign of movement of the weapon," the SEAL team leader reported.

"I've got a plan," Joe said.

They listened carefully, then set up the military-provided equipment around the perimeter, far enough to remain unseen from the warehouse. The SEAL team was insisting they operate on their own as part of the plan. Joe gave them one of the EMP weapons, just in case. Tara launched several drones, staying with their vehicle behind the dune. She used the drone's radar and microwave imaging systems to monitor the people inside the warehouse.

"I'm live transmitting drone data to your smart devices. About thirty people inside," Tara mentioned.

Joe and Maddox enabled their invisibility suits and headed toward the warehouse.

"All set. Everyone in position?" Joe asked.

"Team two in position," the leader of the SEAL team called out.

Mike, Robin, and Alice stood behind vehicles near the warehouse. Mike and Alice had an RPG launcher and an automatic rifle. Robin had an automatic rifle. Mike had on the prediction smart glasses.

"Team one in position," Mike said.

"On my mark, wait till the second one," Joe said. ". . . Now."

Two explosions happened about one hundred feet away from the front and rear of the warehouse. Four people ran out the front door to see what was going on.

Boom!

Joe triggered a second explosive, taking out all the people in front. At the back of the warehouse, the SEAL team eliminated five individuals in a similar manner.

"Team two going in."

"Team one going in."

Joe and Maddox were about to enter through the front doors, and two robed figures came out the front door and ran toward them, tackling them.

Joe threw one Death Monk ten feet into a vehicle near the warehouse, crushing parts of the vehicle.

"How did they see us?" Maddox asked while kicking the robed assailant.

Mike fired the RPG at the Death Monk that Maddox kicked to the ground. It exploded in a fireball.

"One down," Mike said.

Joe grabbed the Death Monk by the neck. The robed figure grabbed at his arm and slowly was able to overpower his exoskeleton and get out of the hold, tossing Joe fifteen feet onto the ground. The figure pulled out a gun and took aim at Joe.

"Sorry, no time to play," the figure said, about to shoot Joe.

Alice opened fire, hitting the Death Monk's hand and weapon and knocking it from his grasp.

"Why? Not good at this?" Alice responded to the robed figure.

Mike didn't have another RPG, and they were too close to use it anyway, so he ran toward the Death Monk. Joe, Mike, and Maddox all grabbed the robed figure. The exoskeletons were powerful, but the robed figure was still stronger and was freeing itself from their grip.

Alice ran in, grabbed the back of the Death Monk's neck, pushed something, and then yanked something out. It sparked as she did. The Death Monk powered off.

More men erupted from the front door. Automated weapon fire from the weapons Joe, Maddox, Mike, and Robin placed around the perimeter took the men out.

"Team two status?" Joe called on the radio. "Team two status?"

No response.

Joe and Maddox went in. They were able to take out several people easily due to their invisibility until others ran up wearing special goggles and started shooting at them.

Alice did some amazing jumps and flips while she snatched weapons from several people. With a sudden backflip off the wall, she fell, trembled, and remained motionless. Death Monks used swords to disarm the SEAL team during the fight. The robed figures quickly zip-tied the hands of the team and tied them to a pole.

Joe and Maddox headed toward the Death Monks, trying to surprise them. Joe was able to use the EMP pulse gun on one—it fell to the ground. The other robed figure grabbed Maddox and tossed him into some shelving. Maddox's suit and exoskeleton sparked. Mike grabbed the Death Monk and punched at different areas of the figure. One punch resulted in some sparks. Robin aimed the EMP gun at the figure, but it dodged, grabbed the gun from her, and aimed it at Mike, firing. Mike's exoskeleton froze. He fell over as he was in mid-punch and unbalanced.

Maddox got up and saw two of Joe. One was coming toward him. Maddox closed his eyes and shook his head, thinking he was dazed by being thrown. When he opened his eyes, there were still two Joes. One was right in front of him, grabbing him and throwing him. The other Joe, who was back ten feet, started firing his weapon at the Joe who had thrown Maddox.

"What the hell is going on, Joe? Why are there two of you?!" Maddox asked.

"What are you talking about?" both Joes said at the same time.

"Maddox, take off your smart glasses!" Robin yelled, realizing the Death Monk must have hacked them, making it appear like another Joe.

Robin pulled out her pistol and fired toward the eyes of the Death Monk, but it dodged. The Death Monk grabbed Robin's pistol, tossing it across the warehouse. The figure pulled out its sword and knocked the rifle from Joe's hand.

"Team two is captured. Team one will be soon. We need backup," Joe said, using the silent thought microphone.

Tara radioed the liaison for U.S. troops.

"Sorry, that area has been declared a hot zone by Russian and local forces. The rules of engagement don't allow us to enter," the officer told Tara on comm.

"Since this could start World War Three, you might want to make an exception," Tara said.

"Understood, we'll see what we can do."

"No backup coming anytime soon," Tara said on comm.

Back in the warehouse, the Death Monks captured and bound the team.

"Well, who do we have here? Is it my old friend?"

Mike couldn't see the person yet, but their voice sounded familiar.

Then Mike saw him round the corner.

"Victor Sondai, you're still alive—again," Mike said.

"You know this guy?" Joe asked.

"I'm not sure. Maybe. We thought he died twice."

"Yes. Some smart glass visuals, a fire, and some DNA seem to have done the trick to fool you and your law enforcement friends," Victor mocked with a laugh.

"This doesn't seem to be your usual criminal pastime," Mike said.

"On the contrary, it has always been my plan. I needed enough money to buy weapons for the rebel forces here. My mother was from here, and we have family here. I swore to free them from their government oppressors."

"But your own country is fighting on the side of the oppressors," Robin said.

"So is yours. That doesn't make them right."

"So the person that's right is the one threatening to blow up a nuclear weapon?" Mike asked.

"The hypocrisy of you Americans is amazing. It was fine when you used nuclear weapons, but not for anyone else," Victor replied.

"You're going to kill not just the government but innocent people," Robin said.

"We've warned all the people involved with the rebels. If they're not with us, then how do you Americans say? Shit happens." Victor shrugged blithely. "Don't worry, though. We just plan to use it as a last resort. It's set to go off one hour after 100 conventional bombs throughout the city go off."

"You're going to destroy the whole city," Mike said.

"It's a big city, and it can stand to lose 100 government and military buildings. Of course, if the nuclear weapon goes off, I guess you're right. It will be a lot more. This government that is oppressing the people ends today," Victor said.

Victor's rebels cheered.

"You're mad!" Mike shouted.

"On the contrary, I'm very happy I'm about to achieve one of my life's dreams. How do you say . . . the list of buckets."

"I'm going to make sure you don't finish that list."

"Actually, crossing you off my list is part of my list," Victor said.

"All of those hacks and thefts were for money or something to help you here?" Mike asked.

"An operation like this needs lots of money for weapons and people. Don't blame all of your hacks on me, but perhaps many of them. We needed the NeuroMeld chips and some of the AI's neural net for the robots, so you provided us with an excellent opportunity. We needed the plans for the nuclear device we acquired from your somewhat secretive base. The gold from your Fort Knox was very helpful. We got it out with nanobots that broke the gold bars down and re-assembled them in a tunneling vehicle underneath.

"Did you see that green floating object in there? Our nanobots couldn't get close to it. Some of our team speculated it was related to a UFO incident that happened there a long time ago. I gave that to some friends to analyze. Then, we needed some parts to repair the weapon—parts from Marina Island. We appreciate all your help on those," Victor said with a smile.

"How did you get involved with the bathrobe guys?" Mike asked.

"Your fight with them left them without a leader. We found one of them that had been injured and helped him get back on his feet again. The robots are modeled after them, but they are even more effective in some ways," Victor explained.

"Missiles inbound," one of the rebels said.

"Excuse me while we take care of this raid."

Victor went over to some computer consoles.

"Damian, in the game we are playing, the missiles are heading toward that building. Can you hack them to prevent them from reaching the target and aim them at the troops outside the building in the game?" Victor asked.

Tara saw another monitor that looked like a game-like rendering of the monitor's outside view.

"Sure. I like playing games with you," the AI voice said cheerily.

Victor looked at the monitors, viewing the cameras around the warehouse. It showed a scene of local government troops, tanks, and armored vehicles.

"Are you seeing those monitors?" Mike whispered to Joe.

"Quiet!" one of the rebels barked.

"Looks a lot like that augmented mixed reality warehouse scenario they had programmed," Joe said on comm via the thought mic.

They could hear something in the sky above them.

Victor spoke in a foreign language on the radio.

"I think he said all units stand by. I know a tiny bit of the language," Joe translated via the thought mic.

Explosions started raining down on their location. They could see on the monitors the missiles struck the government troops, tanks, and personnel carriers. The explosions finally stopped.

"It's time," Victor said to two Death Monks.

The robed figures walked outside. Monitors displayed them amidst fires and troops in chaos.

One of the Death Monks stood in front of an elite group of government troops. Their military saw him, and a few aimed in the robed figures' direction, but soon, the soldiers turned and started firing at their own regular troops. The elite troops took out the other platoons of regular soldiers.

"Damian, can you check how many of the soldiers in the game are carrying cell phones?" Victor asked.

"It appears that most of them are," the AI named Damian responded.

"Can you make them explode?"

"I think I can make around seventy percent explode due to flaws in their battery systems."

"OK, let's try it," Victor said.

They watched the monitors outside as explosions happened, coming from the soldier's pants or shirt pockets. It set some of them on fire before they collapsed to the ground.

"Nice work, Damian," Victor said.

He surveyed the troops outside on the monitors. Most were dead or sufficiently injured to no longer be a threat.

"Now is the time for the rest of you to die. Kill them, except for Mike," Victor ordered. "I've got something special planned for him."

"Thanks, Victor. I didn't know how special I was to you. But sorry, I'm not feeling the same," Mike said.

Through the warehouse windows flew drones dropping tear gas and smoke grenades. One drone flew to the wall near Alice's body and exploded. The smoke billowed through the air, choking Victor, the rebels, and everyone. The drones dropped something near Mike and Joe. It was a knife to cut their ties. Mike, Joe, Maddox, and Robin grabbed some weapons and took out any rebels who hadn't surrendered. For the rest, they used zip ties and cables to secure them to the support poles in the building.

Victor jumped at Mike and started pummeling him, knocking off his glasses.

"First, I'll finish you, then the military," Victor said.

"I guess I'm special. I'm at the top of your list." Mike slugged Victor in the face.

Suddenly, drones started flying at Mike, and several automated warehouse forklifts headed toward him.

Mike grabbed his gun and shot the drones down. Victor stayed behind one of the forklifts as it headed toward Mike. Joe, Maddox, and Robin fired at the forklifts, but the shots bounced off. Joe ran to the side of it, stuck something on, and ran away.

"Fire in the hole," Joe yelled as he ran.

The team ducked behind some machinery as the C4 on the forklift exploded, disabling it. Mike saw the other one coming toward him but dodged it, jumped on the back, and disconnected the battery. Mike went to hit Victor, but he was dodging his punches.

"Victor, did you chip yourself with a NeuroMeld? Is that how you're doing all this?" Mike asked.

Victor continued to dodge and then hit Mike.

"Don't know—how you say—to knock it till you try it," Victor said incorrectly as he slugged Mike hard.

Mike was able to grab his prediction glasses from the floor when he fell. He got up and countered and landed several punches on Victor. A spinning kick landed, knocking Victor down. Mike tied him to a pole. All of the rebels in the warehouse and Victor were subdued.

Just as they were preparing to depart, a Death Monk entered. He ran at Maddox and threw him into Joe, knocking them down. Robin fired at the figure's head, but it swiftly dodged, grabbed her gun, and knocked her down hard.

The Death Monk punched at Mike, but he dodged it. Mike punched back, but the robed figure slid to the side. They continued to dodge each other's kicks and punches. Suddenly, Mike saw a duplicate of the Death Monk and warehouse racks in his glasses. Two warehouse shelving racks fell on Mike as the robed figure toppled them, leaving him no time to react. Mike noticed that this Death Monk seemed like the one he had run into at the bank.

"It's harder to predict two objects, isn't it?" the Death Monk said with a growl.

"Maybe, but you know what's even better? Having friends."

The robed figure grabbed an automatic rifle.

"Finish them," Victor said while still tied up.

Suddenly, from behind, Alice grabbed the Death Monk and ripped the automatic weapon from his hand, which bent the gun. She violently pulled off the Death Monk's legs and tossed them across the warehouse, then pulled off his arms and tossed them far down. Alice realized Mike's glasses were hacked and added additional protections to prevent that.

Everyone except Victor was stunned by the seeming barbarity of what Alice did. They stared at the Death Monk, but there was no blood. He used the remaining parts of his limbs to right himself against a desk. Alice tied his torso to the desk.

It finally dawned on the team that Alice had not hurt the robed figure at all. He had been wearing artificial limbs from his knees down and on his shoulders down.

"Those limbs were from the stolen IID truck. The humanoid robots were also stolen," Alice said.

Mike successfully squeezed out from under the shelving. He glanced at a wall clock, only to see it counting down from forty-four minutes.

"That must be the time when a hundred buildings explode, then an hour after, the nuclear bomb will explode. That's not enough time to convince them to clear the buildings or city." Mike's stomach dropped.

"Check this warehouse," Joe said to the team.

Maddox whispered to Joe before declaring, "If Victor doesn't talk, maybe his people will." He grabbed one of them.

"Where is the nuclear weapon?!"

The man wouldn't answer. Maddox aggressively dragged the man through the warehouse, out of sight but not out of earshot of the others.

"Where is the nuclear weapon?!" the team heard Maddox yell at the man.

A gunshot was heard. Maddox returned to the team after a brief moment.

"How many more am I going to have to kill before you tell us?" Maddox asked Victor.

"Mike, did he just—?! Stop him," Tara said.

Mike hugged Tara and whispered to her.

Maddox dragged another man back into the warehouse behind the wall.

"Where is the nuclear weapon?!"

Another gunshot was heard. After another moment, Maddox walked back to the team.

"Where is the nuclear weapon?" Joe said moderately loudly to Victor.

Victor sat on the ground, bound. He didn't make a sound.

"We don't have time for this. Tell us where it is. I'm going to count to three and blow your knee off," Maddox said, pulling out his gun and aiming it at Victor's knee.

"One. Two. Three!"

"Wait! I have a better idea," Alice said.

Alice asked Joe to hold the map about two feet in front of Victor's face. Alice grabbed Victor's left wrist.

"Victor, is the nuclear weapon in this quarter of the map?" Alice asked while pointing at the map and looking back and forth between Victor's eyes and the map. She inquired about every map quarter and then a subsection.

"OK, that's probably the best we can do," Alice said.

"He didn't tell you anything. Victor, I'm going to shoot off your knees, then hands, then feet!" Maddox yelled.

"I will never tell you. I'm doing this for my family. It is fine if I die," Victor declared.

"Stop. From his reactions, I've narrowed it to near these fifteen buildings," Alice said.

"How?" Robin asked.

"Using a mixture of signals like heart rate, blood pressure, skin resistance, eye movements, and questions, I could see his eyes focused a significant amount of time on that area even though he would try to look away."

"Sort of like a polygraph machine?" Robin asked.

"My estimate is significantly better than a polygraph machine." Alice almost seemed indignant.

"By the way, Victor, your men are still alive, just unconscious back there," Joe said. He called their liaison and explained the situation. The local military said they were on their way to help, explain the situation, search and clear the buildings, and provide assistance.

"OK, let's move out and go help them. They don't have enough people, and we don't have a lot of time," Joe said.

They returned to the car, leaving Victor and his men for the authorities. They started to drive away and saw missiles heading toward the warehouse, which rained out of the sky and exploded on impact in a fiery inferno.

"Were they still inside?" Tara asked.

"Yes, Victor and his men," Maddox said.

Tara couldn't deal with witnessing indiscriminate killing. It gnawed at her.

"Was that you who sent in the drones?" Mike asked her, trying to provide a distraction.

"Yes, it was the only thing I could think of to try to help."

"It worked amazingly. Thank you," he said, and everyone also agreed.

"Shouldn't we be heading away from the buildings that are going to explode and the nuclear weapon?" Maddox asked.

"If the Russian troops get caught in this, we could end up with a nuclear war. The White House did warn Russia about the bomb plot near their troops, but that may not be enough to prevent a war if it goes off. They don't have enough time to evacuate everyone. This is the capital of the country. It would leave this country in chaos if they all go off. That may spread to other countries. The U.S. Army and Navy already have troops to help search the buildings. We're part of the task force," Joe said, showing a tablet with a map of the buildings.

Some of the buildings showed green, with most being red and a few yellow. "Red means the C4 explosives were located, green means disarmed and cleared, orange will mean if the nuclear weapon was located there," Joe said.

"Are we getting combat pay for this?" Maddox asked.

"You're still on leave, aren't you?" Joe said.

"Shit!"

"If we live through this, there might be perks other than combat pay," Robin teased.

Alice asked to borrow the tablet.

"I've marked the ones I think have a better chance of containing the nuclear weapon. It still could be in any of those buildings or possibly surrounding buildings," she said.

They arrived at their search zone and split up into the original teams one and two to locate the explosives and, hopefully, the nuclear weapon. The city was still bustling with people. Numerous buildings, made of cinderblock and concrete, varied in height from three to twelve floors. People were walking or riding bicycles. It was overcast but warm. Several area buildings appeared bombed from earlier battles.

One building was entered by the SEAL team, while the rest went into the building next door. Joe, Maddox, and Robin went to the top floor to work their way down. Mike, Tara, and Alice started from the basement and worked their way up. Mike walked ahead, Tara was behind him, and

Alice was behind her as they walked down the basement stairs. The lights were working, but they were very dimly lit. Upon turning a corner, they encountered individuals living in the basement, sitting next to the wall on the floor. Tara jumped back for a moment. They said something in the local language.

"They say we're not welcome here," Alice translated.

"Tell them we're just looking for a bomb," Mike said.

Alice gave him a quizzical look but complied.

"They said we are idiots. The bombs fall from the sky here."

"I don't recommend you stay while we try to disarm it," Mike said, and Alice translated.

The people just looked at them funny.

Mike shined his phone light in a dark corner near them. They quickly ran out of the basement, screaming. There were large barrels with C4 and detonators wired together.

"I guess they didn't want to stay for the fireworks." Mike looked at the wiring. "It's been a while since I've disarmed a bomb. I think it's the blue wire." On comm, he said, "Clear the building. We found it."

Alice looked at it.

"Please cut the green wire," Alice said.

They stared at it for a few minutes.

"Building clear," Joe said on comm about the other building.

"If you clear the building, I can cut it so it's safe," Alice said.

"When did you become an expert on bombs?" Tara asked.

"My processor idles at over 500 exaflops. I read a lot and pretty quickly," Alice said.

"That wasn't in the training data," Tara said.

"Sorry, I may have peeked at a lot of other files at IID and elsewhere." Alice smiled.

They walked out of the building to a safe distance and let her cut the wire.

"I think Alice was right. It was the green wire," Mike said as he turned around to look back at the building.

Alice walked out behind them with the C4 explosive. They called one of the military units to pick it up. The SEAL team also cleared another building next door. Joe looked at the tablet. Only twenty-five buildings had been cleared, with only fifteen minutes left.

"This is taking too long. Let's just help get the word out to evacuate the buildings marked. It's unlikely they would blow up the building with the nuclear weapon in it first. So that will verify for us those buildings only had conventional explosives. We should look more at the ones Alice marked for the weapon," Joe said.

They went to several buildings, yelling "Bomb!" in the local language that Alice taught them.

People went streaming out of the buildings. They waited outside, far from the buildings with explosives, as time ticked down. Then, they heard it in a series of deafening noises they could feel in their entire bodies. They saw buildings collapse near them and further away into clouds of dust.

"We failed," Tara said.

"We did our best. Isn't that what you told me once? There are hundreds, maybe thousands of people still alive because of us. They at least have a chance. Let's find the weapon so they keep their chance," Mike said.

The air was filled with dust. They used their loose clothing to cover their mouths and noses. They could see smoke billowing from a few of the destroyed buildings.

They checked the surrounding buildings, but still nothing.

"I'm checking the satellite data. Nothing. They haven't found anything yet," Joe said.

"Wait, can you zoom in on that building and run spectroscopy analysis?" Alice looked over Joe's shoulder.

"Lead. That's weird for a roof, even in this part of the world," Joe said.

"They could hide from overhead radiation sensors that way," Alice said.

"Let's take a look. It's only five minutes down that way," Mike said, pointing at the data.

"We only have twenty-five minutes till detonation," Maddox said.

They headed down the block and found the building. It was a moderately sized three-story building for the area. It seemed like it was empty. The SEAL team planned to enter from the back while the others entered from the front.

"Team two ready for entry."

Shots rang out.

"Team two, we're being fired on by automatic weapons."

Joe tasked a drone in the area to take a closer look. The drone flew by. Automatic weapons tracked it and took it out, falling in a small fireball. They found some cover and fired sporadically at the source of the automatic weapons firing at them, taking turns like they did in the augmented reality training.

"Does this seem familiar?" Joe asked Mike.

"Yes. Maybe they set up those scenarios to see how they should respond to attacks."

Joe pulled out a metal box from his pack that unfolded into a short RPG launcher. He fired at the automatic weapon firing at them.

Boom!

The RPG exploded when it hit the automatic weapon in a fireball.

"Front door clear," Joe said on comm.

"Rear door is clear," team two responded.

They heard screaming and gunfire, some via radio and some behind the building.

"Death—" someone on team two yelled.

"Let's head in," Joe said.

Before they could move a few feet, they thought they had seen something exit the building. Joe's gun went flying from his hand as he fell backward.

"Death Monk!" he yelled as he fell.

Mike used the laser sight to try to find the Death Monk. Alice scanned the area for a moment and ran in one direction. She leaped onto an unseen object, suspended in mid-air. She ripped off the Death Monk's invisibility robe and tossed it aside. Alice grabbed at the back of its neck, but it tossed her on the ground.

"Check the building. I'll take care of the disrobed monk," Alice said.

The Death Monk appeared as an ordinary man in casual attire. This appeared to be one of the robot bodies. Despite the robot's attempt to chase the team, Alice quickly grabbed it and flung it to the opposite side of the road. The SEAL team was still fighting in the building's rear.

Alice ran at the Death Monk and threw him against one of the destroyed buildings nearby. She looked at him, lying there momentarily in the rubble. Suddenly, above their heads, three missiles landed on top of the Death Monk and exploded. Alice watched the flames on the ground and then turned to head toward the building the team was in. Before she realized what happened, she was smashed by a piece of concrete lying on the ground.

The Death Monk was standing over her. Suddenly, a drone at high speed hit the robot and dragged him for twenty feet until it hit a building, and the weapon on the drone exploded.

Alice looked at the Death Monk. Some of its artificial skin was burned off beyond its ability to repair, but it was still operational. It ran at her, only to be run over by a tank. The tank was lifted and rolled over by the Death Monk.

"You seem to have augmented parts," Alice said.

"You're going to end up being spare parts for me if there is anything left of you," the Death Monk snarled.

A huge blinding light appeared from the sky, centering on the Death Monk. Everything started burning in a perfect circle around it. What remained of its artificial skin melted off. A drone dropped a large RPG launcher next to Alice. She picked it up and aimed it at the robot.

"No thanks, I like all my parts." Alice fired the RPG.

Just as she fired, Alice was hit by a drone that exploded on impact. She fell to the ground. Some of her clothes were on fire. She patted them down to stop the fire. The Death Monk was nowhere in sight.

Alice went back to the building where the team was located. The Navy SEAL team was out near another building already demolished, still fighting the other Death Monk. Alice glanced at the sky before approaching the SEAL team.

The SEAL team fired an RPG at the Death Monk, but it dodged. The team's automatic machine gun swept the area, tracking the Death Monk, but always hit about a foot behind it due to the robed figure's speed. One of the team fired a shoulder-fired missile that tracked the Death Monk as it ran, but it ducked behind some broken concrete the missile exploded on. Alice asked to borrow some weapons and then stood in the remnants of a destroyed building nearby.

"Death Monk, the body you've stolen can't feel. Mine can," Alice yelled.

"Then you shall feel your body taken over by me!" the Death Monk yelled back.

Out of nowhere, the Death Monk came toward Alice and grabbed her, taking her bait. The Death Monk threw her against some rubble on the ground. Alice executed amazing acrobatic flips to get to the other side of the Death Monk. There were open holes in her skin from the injuries. As she stood, they started to heal. Alice fired the EMP at the Death Monk, who quivered and fell to the ground. She quickly attached a military-grade explosive to the Death Monk's body and exploded it.

Alice gazed at the sky before moving away. The Death Monk started to move. Noise could be heard in the sky as it filled with drones, missiles, automated helicopters, and more. They arced out of the sky, crashing into the ground directly on top of the Death Monk, exploding in flames and a crunching sound. Flames whipped around the ground. Alice looked at the fire, staring at it. Within the charred, twisted metal and flames, something stirred. The blackened metal of the robot was trying to stand up and finally succeeded. Suddenly, an automated fighter jet flew low and fast across the ground, smashing the charred body of the robot into pieces as it burst into flames.

The Navy SEAL team looked on in awe at the sight.

"We could have done that," one of them said jokingly.

Alice just looked at him and headed into the building where the rest of the team was, followed by the SEAL team.

"We found the nuclear weapon. I called in a transport," Mike said, looking at the countdown timer attached to the nuclear weapon, which read ten minutes.

A SEAL team member examined the weapon and attempted to disassemble it but encountered difficulty due to the device's worn screws and bolts. He disabled the movement sensor.

"I don't think I can do this on time," he said.

Alice asked for the instructions and helped unscrew screws and bolts at an incredible pace.

"He's right. We aren't going to make it on time," Alice estimated, even with their accelerated progress,

"Let's get the weapon to the door then so it can be transported," Joe said, looking at the countdown timer with only seven minutes left.

Alice helped them get the nuclear weapon out the door quickly. The timer read six minutes.

"This is firestorm one. We are one minute out," the helicopter pilot said.

They found an open location and waved the helicopter down. The whole team helped carefully get the weapon connected below the helicopter on a cable. The helicopter carefully lifted slightly off the ground with the nuclear bomb dangling below it. Someone emerged from a building, leaped onto the nuclear weapon, and attempted to detach it. It was the Death Monk which Alice had fought earlier but got away.

The team ran toward the helicopter, but Alice was faster—she jumped up on the landing gear of the helicopter and punched at the Death Monk as it dodged. The helicopter moved higher into the sky, heading toward the ocean. The team watched as the helicopter flew away. Alice and the Death Monk fought fiercely beneath it, and the nuclear weapon swung on its cable.

"Alice! No! I can't lose you again!" Tara yelled.

They quickly returned to their vehicle, jumped in, and sped away in the opposite direction of the helicopter's flight.

"Let's get some distance between us and that bomb! Two minutes!" Joe yelled.

They quickly raced down the road, maneuvering past a few cars.

"Firestorm one, change heading away from the Russian warship," they heard on the radio. "Russia has gone to the equivalent of DEFCON 1. Firestorm one, change course now!"

Tara was in disbelief as the world teetered on destruction once more. They could only hope events turned out in their favor.

A flash of light erupted behind them. They pulled off the road and turned around. They could see a plume in the sky toward the ocean. Suddenly, a shock wave struck their vehicle, shaking it, along with a loud explosion.

"Firestorm one, status?" Joe said on comm.

No response.

"Firestorm one, status?!"

"This is firestorm one. I dropped the device into the ocean about six miles offshore. We were hit by the blast wave, but we're OK," the pilot said.

Joe explained about Alice and the Death Monk. One of the crew checked, but there was no one outside the helicopter. Tara sobbed, hearing the news.

"She saved everyone again," Mike told Tara, giving her a hug.

Tara hugged him back.

"I think we might be able to recover her on the servers at IID, but she will be without her memories from her time in the robot unless she managed to upload them," Tara said, wiping away some tears.

"Russia is still at equivalent to DEFCON 1. They are on the de-confliction line with Washington," the voice on the radio said.

They waited tensely, wondering if the world had gone over the brink. Tara grabbed Mike's hand as they waited.

"Russia is standing down. I repeat, all clear," the radio crackled.

The team let out a sigh of relief and then hugged each other.

"So why aren't we dead?" Maddox asked.

"The helicopter must have gotten far enough out over the ocean to drop it in deep water. It was already a low-yield device for physical damage. The water would absorb most of the blast energy and radiation," Joe said.

One of the military radioed Joe to stand by as they headed out to their location. An officer emerged from the armored vehicle, accompanied by an injured woman hobbling toward them with his aid. The team got out of the vehicle and looked at them.

"She says she knows you," the officer said.

"Alice?!" Tara ran over to her.

Mike went over to help her walk to their vehicle.

"What happened?" Tara asked.

"I managed to disable the Death Monk, but I was damaged and fell about a thousand feet. I found this officer who helped me," Alice said, collapsing.

Tara gave her a hug.

"I thought I lost part of you again."

Alice smiled and shook her head. "Not this time."

"Oh, the thing at home I was printing was one of the emergency car escape hammers. I guess you didn't need it," Alice said.

Tara agreed but figured Alice bringing up that now might be due to some hardware damage she sustained.

"Luckily, since the bomb exploded underwater, there is very little radiation, just some minor damage from the blast wave," the officer said.

They followed the officer in their vehicle back to the U.S. military base and headed home.

13

Two weeks later. Tara was in her office with Robin, Mike, and Alice. Alice looked back to normal after getting fixed up. They chose not to inform the staff regarding Alice's situation, as she desired to be treated as a person, so Tara arranged a job she could do at IID.

"I never asked you, how did you come up with the name Laurie Cebovilt?" Tara asked.

"It's an anagram for Alice Bitlouver," Alice said.

"Oh my gosh, that's so sweet," Tara said, giving her a hug. "I'm pretty sure it is a really bad idea for you to come with us."

"Maybe, but I could also be helpful," Alice said.

"We should get going," Cara Mitsfield, the IID lawyer, said, directing them to head out to the car.

She indicated that they had some assistant legal counsel who would meet them at their destination. They arrived at the building and proceeded inside through the metal detectors. Tara and the legal team sat down at the defense table. Mike, Robin, and Alice joined the others in the galley to watch. The prosecution team arrived. Rod Bailson, the Senator who was helping the FBI, charged her with violating the Artificial Intelligence Act 154 Sentience Clause. Tara's body clenched up, seeing him enter.

"All rise," the bailiff said.

The judge entered and sat down.

"Court is now in session."

"Members of the jury, listen carefully to the evidence presented," the judge said. "Counsel, please present your motion."

Cara Mitsfield stood up. "Your honor, we would like to move to dismiss. The evidence will show that my client acted to prevent further injury, death, exposure of military secrets, and loss of a nuclear weapon."

"We'll need to hear all the evidence. Motion denied. Counsel, you may begin with your opening statement," the judge said.

The prosecution introduced themselves and began their statement.

"Ladies and gentlemen of the jury. I will present to you evidence that shows the defendant willfully violated the Computer Fraud and Abuse Act, the Espionage Act, the Atomic Energy Act, the National Security Act, the Federal Information Security Management Act, the Patriot Act, and the Artificial Intelligence Act 154 Sentience Clause. This led to the theft of a nuclear weapon and the explosion of the weapon, almost causing World War Three," the prosecutor said.

"Objection, prejudicial," Cara responded.

"Overruled."

The prosecution called several witnesses from various incidents to prove that IID systems were used to hack them. Cara did an amazing job cross-examining the witnesses, getting them to explain that Tara was helping to control and resolve an active hack she and her company didn't initiate. Finally, they called Tara as their final witness. Cara recommended that Tara didn't testify. Despite her reservations, Tara believed testifying was necessary to retain her role as IID's CEO. Tara was sworn in and sat down on the witness stand. The prosecution went after her mercilessly.

"Did you or your company gain unauthorized access to the Department of Energy? Yes or no?" the prosecutor asked.

"We had authorization. We provided that evidence," Tara said.

"Did you have permission to access all of the systems you connected to? Yes or no," the prosecution asked.

"We had verbal permission.."

"Objection, Your Honor. Misleading the jury. We have a witness that will testify to this," Cara said.

"Sustained."

"Did your artificial intelligence Alice access the internet to connect to the unnamed military installation?" the prosecutor asked.

"Yes, but that was to prevent loss of life," Tara said.

"Did your AI access the internet to connect to Fort Knox?"

"Yes. That was to assist with preventing injury, death, and theft of the gold," Tara said.

"Let the record show the defendant just admitted to violating the Artificial Intelligence Act Sentience Clause," the prosecutor said.

After the prosecutor badgered Tara for several hours, the defense finally got their time to cross-examine. It was looking very bad for Tara and IID. Despite their good intentions, sufficient evidence might lead to conviction.

"So what happened with the product failures your company was having?" Cara asked.

"Alice helped the other team track those down. They were hacks from all different countries: China, North Korea, Russia, and Iran. We wondered why we kept detecting signals similar to the sentient AI. That's because the other countries found pieces of my neural nets and developed their own AIs and variants. I also believe many of the countries might be on the verge of their AIs developing digital emergent sentience," Tara said, knowing the variants were of Project Mind River.

"Objection, relevance," the prosecutor said.

"Sustained," the judge responded.

"Were you authorized to connect to the networks of the Department of Energy nuclear installation, the unnamed military installation, and Fort Knox?" Cara asked.

"Yes, we were authorized. We've provided that paperwork."

"Were you authorized to access everything you did?" Cara asked.

"We didn't have written authorization, but for example, at the Department of Energy, we consulted and got verbal authorization, as I mentioned."

"Why did you make the connections in the unnamed military installation?" Cara asked.

"Our IID systems did to prevent people from being injured and killed. It actually didn't have any effect on the military installation systems, just on military drones that had been hacked by the terrorist group to prevent them from firing or hitting people," Tara stated.

Cara finished cross-examining Tara, and the prosecutor had some additional questions.

"Just to summarize. You and your company are responsible for the theft of the nuclear weapons, as the code from your AI was used in the robots you called Death Monks to help steal it?" the prosecutor said.

"Objection, leading," Cara said.

"Sustained."

"Do you think they would have been able to steal the nuclear weapon without the code from your AI in the robots?"

"Objection, speculation," Cara said.

"Sustained," the judge decided.

"Would you say for all of the unauthorized access, you achieved nothing? You didn't stop the theft from the art gallery, didn't stop the theft from NeuroMeld, didn't stop the theft of the nuclear weapon from the Department of Energy, didn't stop the theft of gold from Fort Knox. Were you really helping anyone?" the prosecutor said.

"Objection, relevance and badgering," Cara said.

"Sustained."

"Stop! It was me that hacked most of those, not her," Alice jumped up and said.

"Alice, no!" Tara yelled.

"Order in the court! Recess so we can deal with this matter," the judge declared.

Everyone from the jury and galley left the court except for Senator Bailson and another person in a dark suit with an earpiece. Tara, Alice, Cara, and the prosecutor remained.

"Who are you?" the judge asked Alice.

"I'm Alice, the AI better explained as digital emergent sentience that is being referenced in this case."

"Are you controlling that?" the judge asked Tara.

"No, Your Honor."

"I control myself," Alice said.

"I want that arrested immediately! That could take down the world!" Senator Bailson said, pointing to Alice.

"Her name is Alice, and she has helped save the world twice!" Tara said.

Suddenly, the judge's phone rang, but he ignored it. Then the bailiff's phone rang.

"Judge, I think you should answer your phone. It's the President," the bailiff said.

The judge looked at his phone. It said "White House" on the caller ID.

"Hello?" the judge said.

"Mr. President, the case is in recess right now."

"Sir, this is highly irregular."

"I understand this is an urgent matter of national security—"

"He'd like to speak to you," the judge told Tara, handing the phone to her. The Senator objected loudly.

"Hello, Mr. President," Tara said.

"We have come to the same conclusion that you have—that the rest of our enemies are about to achieve artificial sentience with their AI, and we need your help," the President said.

"The Artificial Intelligence Act 154 Sentience Clause created restrictions on everyone in the country that prevent achieving this," Tara replied. "It also added restrictions that made the AI gullible and able to be fooled into doing things like what happened with Victor in the Middle East. He was able to fool some of the AIs into helping him by changing the inputs for the video to appear like a game, and the law made the AI easily influenced. Plus, you know, kind of in trouble here, and you know I have reservations about creating software for certain government uses."

"If you agree to help us, I will make these charges go away. We'll also come up with licensing where your firm won't be directly involved in certain use cases. I promise we'll work with you on your concerns. We need you. Your country needs you. The world is about to get very dangerous, and you have the world's only sentient AI," the President urged.

"OK, Mr. President, thank you," Tara said, shifting uncomfortably in her seat and handing the phone back to the judge.

"But, Mr. President . . . I understand, sir. This is very irregular. Yes, Mr. President," he said, hanging up.

"It was found that the law specifically prevented the IID AI from operating connected to the internet, but it was never properly enacted in the classified documents. The law is, therefore, unconstitutional. The details of this case have been declared classified and protected under the state secrets privilege. This case is dismissed," the judge said.

Tara hugged Alice and Cara.

"No! You can't do this!" Senator Bailson protested.

"Bailiff, get him out of here," the judge said, pointing to the Senator.

Tara met Robin and Mike outside the court and hugged them both. She explained the call from the President.

"I'm not sure what I got myself signed up for."

"Don't worry, whatever it is, we'll be there to help," Mike said.

They all got in a vehicle and headed to Tara's home to spend time together. Dinner and some time relaxing together were what they all needed after all of the recent events. Robin mentioned she was back together with Maddox.

Mike stayed over at Tara's for the first time in many months.

***

The end.

***

Thanks so much for reading!

Please leave a review on the site where you purchased. Reviews are one of the biggest things you can do to help an author.

Get notified if there are sequels and more at https://davespacer.com

Join the email list.